# KILL
# IRISH

MAYI NGWALA

# KILL IRISH

GENET PRESS
Published by Genet Press, Ltd. Liability Co.
USA
Copyright © 2018 Mayi M. Ngwala
All rights reserved

Scripture taken from the New King James Version®.
Copyright © 1982 by Thomas Nelson, Inc. Used by permission. All rights reserved.

Visit us on the World Wide Web: www.genetpress.com

Cataloging-in-publication data is on file with the Library of Congress

ISBN: 978-0-9846663-2-4 (Hardback)
ISBN: 978-0-9846663-3-1 (Paperback)
ISBN: 978-0-9846663-4-8 (eBook)
Fiction.
Printed in the United States of America
MARCH 2018
First Edition

Book cover designs by Carolina Fiandri (Hardback) and Andrea Orlic (Paperback)
Book interior layout by Jerry Dorris and Carolina Fiandri
Author photograph by Nathan Amedee

PUBLISHER'S NOTE
This book is a work of fiction. Names, characters, places, and incidents either are the product of the author's imagination or are used fictitiously, and any resemblance to actual persons, living or dead, business establishments, events, or locales is entirely coincidental.

*For Xavier and Xander. My cherished sprogs.*
*Stretch your wings and realize your hearts' desires.*

*Being Irish is infectious.*
*For this reason, this work of fiction is dedicated to all Irish blood*
*and my brethren, the grand People of Ireland,*
*whom I've come to love and appreciate.*

*"We all have a bit of Irish in us... And today I'm Irish."*

# Author's Note

Though there are actual settings presented in this novel, this work of art is purely fictional and should not be construed or used as a source for factual accounts. Case in point, instances whereby places were non-existent such as "the hamlet," the fictional small fisherman area, they were created and added to allow readers to experience superior entertainment enjoyment. Likewise, Gardaí are not armed, and I made them to be armed. Hence, it is no fantasy that truth and fiction have been merged in concord to create this captivating tale.

An Garda Síochána, Ireland's National Police Service in Ireland is a respectful and vital establishment that works laboriously day in and day out to protect and serve communities throughout the magnificent Republic of Ireland. Its officers are dedicated and bright individuals committed to the cause they serve, which continues to be the protection of their citizens. Any characterization in this novel is no reflection at all and in its entirety to the wonderful and dedicated working body of Garda men and women who serve to improve the overall quality of life of their nation and to protect a country they cherish and love, the Republic of Ireland.

The Merrion Hotel Dublin is one of Ireland's finest and highly regarded hotels, staffed with the most excellent and most qualified workers.

Likewise, the Dublin City Coroner's Court is an expeditious and efficient establishment. All references to these fine institutions are purely fictional.

Once again, any attempt at pursuing facts from this work of art will prove to be a fruitless effort as truth and fiction exist in concord within the narrative.

This is wholly for entertainment purpose.

Mate,

Bend your frame of mind, as you are entering the soul of the most fascinating chap you will ever know: 'Irish.'

*Dia spede!*—Cain Angus Seamróg

"And God will wipe away every tear from their eyes; there shall be no more death, nor sorrow, nor crying. There shall be no more pain, for the former things have passed away."

**Revelation 21:4**

"Emergency Service."

"Ambulance... I need an ambulance."

"Please hold while I transfer your call to the emergency medical dispatcher."

I left the cellular line unattended. I knew the call would be traced and *help* would arrive in time while I attended to my dying son, as he lay on the mat, his still frame turning flaccid while I revived him; madly calling out on him to:

"Breathe," I pleaded desperately, "... Aidan, breathe... No, no, no... Stay with me. Aidan, stay with me. Please, don't go ... No, don't go. Breathe. Breathe... "

And then in a fleeting second, when I wondered if Aidan was still with us, I heard death angels draw nearer, within reach of Aidan, to haul his soul back to heaven.

It was the day I'd forever remember as the day I lost faith in God.

And it became clear that my wife Hannah and my father Jack had killed my son. He was certainly dead, as when he landed on the cerulean mat, his spine snapped cleanly—a fatal cervical fracture.

Till this day I wonder if, given the choice, I'd settle for him to be a quadriplegic.

I don't know. Yet I knew I would not set eyes on his face again, nor would I ruffle his fine flaxen hair, letting it slip through my pale fingers.

I was numb as dead.

I was absent: lost in the shadows of a man who will never come to forgive himself for not saving his chiseller's life.

I will forever mourn his departure till the day I die.

# 1

Atop Ireland's highest overhangs, the Cliffs of Moher, a dark and grand wind swayed shamrocks where colonies of Northern Gannets came to rest.

The birds observed lightning descend upon the earth like gods descending on golden chariots of flame, striking the soil then vanishing in front of mud-covered, bloodied bare-chested bearded men, with titanic biceps and calves the size of Irish draft-horse breeds, clad in Irish kilts and knee-high wool socks on ankle boots. They hunt me, *Irish*, formally Cain Angus Seamróg, buzz cut, bearded and chisel-jawed, in the first part of my forties yet solidly built, ripped with the physique of a Celtic god, fitter than I was in my twenties, with a muddied elliptical object clutched in my hands against my chest, running in space.

Flashes of lightning struck while I skipped sideways, dodging the gods' penance. My bulging emerald green veins pumped adrenaline, and my unhinged mind loved every bit of the rush that brought me escape from the morbid reality of daily life, playing the game that only Irish gods dared to play in the realm of their holy arenas.

I dashed across the mud-spattered field daring the gods' weapon, lightning, and competing with my mortal mates. Call them tightheads, looseheads, flankers, hookers, or call them what you will; I don't care, as they sought the ball in my hand or my death.

"Kill Irish," they yelled. "Kill that slippery bastard!"

I swerved, I dodged. I knew where they would strike. I escaped collisions unerringly.

Men chasing behind clashed and crashed far and wide, like a colony of fallen *Orthetrum coerulescens*. Pardon the Latin name, as I'd been enthralled with binomial nomenclature as a child, and it stuck.

They bone-crush-tackled each other with no mercy, like a mob of brawling Vikings, like they had a death wish. Heads thumped. Bodies smashed together. Bones shattered. The match was a downright massacre, such pain in their faces. They were so muddy only their eyes showed.

*Dead Mate* rugby was the name of the sport. No Six Nations shite—a real fucking death sport. We lost two mates a few years back. Their deaths were the reason we played, to honor their memories.

With the more visible rugby ball tucked under my arm, I swerved once more, winging my way to the line, when from the left came soaring Goliath, a huge chap, knocking me off balance, inches from a cliff. A rupture echoed. A loud scream followed. The adrenaline spiked, jolting in my organs. The thrill was my drug. Not the cannabis kind. Something different. Nevertheless a drug, I was certain of it. It was addictive, and I could not live without this fix once in a while. It was my necessary evil. It was how I escaped the memories of my dead son.

Say what you will. I don't give a shite. You will never come to love your son as I did.

Maybe, just maybe, that was the reason for his death. A test of faith? I don't know. I didn't have faith in God anymore.

I stared down at the foot of the cliff, part of me wanting to jump, the better half fighting. But it was a strong current that pulled me, assuring me it was safe and sound to cross to the other world. "Make the dive. And you'll see your son again." I loved my son dearly, but I had to pull it together.

Our mud-spattered rugby mates promptly gathered around Goliath who lay on top of me, their lips all soundless, glaring down at us. They were used to this. We had done this a thousand times before. My arm emerged, puncturing through space, ball in my palm. The men clapped and clinched each other.

I suffered not a single injury. I was born with a rare gift, almost a superhuman ability. Except I was no Superman. Bear with me. You will come to understand.

I rolled Goliath to the side as if he were a hefty sack of *praities*. The men stared once more. I stood and positioned myself as I always did, same bearing, same arm. I grabbed Goliath's arm. I stared down deep into the soul of his eyes. He bore a bushy ruthless Viking beard. I treasured that. It was a threatening feature, something that struck fear into a foe, nothing the French could understand with their clean-shaven features.

I nodded. Goliath nodded in agreement. The men watched impatiently. They waited. This was what they waited for.

# 2

Goliath was huge. Six-foot-five, three hundred and sixteen pounds, with broad troglodyte shoulders and nothing but lean body mass. A bloody killing machine. With a bulk resembling the *Hulk*, he was a menacing personage. But not to me. I was unique, and everyone knew it.

Some thought we were playing the Devil's game, a compulsion to inflict pain upon ourselves. Nevertheless, that was never the intent. We enjoyed a good match—it was just that simple. Though the extremes may seem a bit farfetched—the ruthlessness, treacherous tackling, dodgy shoving, kicking, pitiless fists, knockouts—it was all part of the game.

We lived and breathed the essence of a brutal street rugby. *Raw. That's the sport, mate. We are men. Let's play like real men.*

I looked once more at Goliath before I swiftly wrenched his dislocated shoulder back into place. I did the same to his right ankle. There was a loud pop. Goliath bawled in agony, but, after a brief moment, he broke into a smile, through his missing teeth. It was always like this. It was the rule of the game. Except, and truthfully, there were no rules.

"That's a good lad," I said.

I grabbed his cheeks, squeezed. It was a gesture of brotherhood, honor, recognition of the cherished feeling for a game well played.

"But today, ya lose again," I said.

I kissed his forehead and gazed at the other teammates. Call it a ritual, call it what you want.

"May your bones heal ye," I chanted blithely.

"May your wives feed ye," the gang followed.

The best chant came last; "In six full moons, let us break bones again."

The gang of rugged, bloodied rugby contestants cheered boisterously. Broken legs, ribs, dislocated thumbs and lost teeth, but contentment, match over. In six months, we'd reunite and try hard to martyr ourselves at the Devil's game again. That was the beauty of playing with true mates. They understood the repercussions that death was a possibility in the game we played.

I had only a bruise or two, no broken bones. Some mates were on crutches, plenty were walking while leaning on their mates' shoulders.

The celebration carried on. The team embraced, lifting up my pride and joy, Cody Seamróg, now seven years old, knee braces, pale and frail, and raised him high as both the winning and losing squad celebrated a grand match while singing the old Irish folk song: *A brave and jolly yeoman long, Lived on the River Foyle, When work was throng, a simple song, Beguil'd his daily toil...*

Heavy rain continued, as if the Irish gods demanded an encore, as the storm hadn't subsided and came crashing down hard and heavy on the crushed and mucky shamrock. But we had given the gods a grand game and I for one wanted time with my little boy, as his days were numbered, and the time I spent with him the rest of the lads knew would be my most precious days.

We put on wool sweaters to keep our blood warm. Then we embraced once more ahead of assembling our belongings, and departing teammates planted kisses on Cody's forehead, hidden behind his fringe. I thanked them in silence knowing full well if I spoke I'd break down. The love they showed my son was for no other reason than to show love to a boy who was slowly dying.

# 3

Windshield wipers battled rain that nearly obliterated the view ahead on our three-hour drive back to the south coast shore of Ireland.

My eighty-three Toyota pickup's engine knocked along the paved road. I wanted a newer car, but money was scarce.

*Focus, Irish.* I thought. *Cody's dying.*

Cody eyed me, that proud stare a son gives his father.

"The match was brilliant, mate," Cody said.

"Mate?" I replied.

"Daddy," Cody said with a broad smile.

*More like it.*

"You know what I think? One day you'll be grand. Mastering the sport better than your aul man," I said.

Cody had been around us adults for ages. He had no friends I could remember, let alone a pet. The boy was lonely and too lonely to admit it. I guessed the other lads wanted someone tougher, one they could bully. Cody was just too bloody frail: the knee braces, the shortness of breath, the funny walk. Even the lads could see that was no fun to bear, hence they abandoned him; "Better leave limp-legs on his own." Though his legs weren't the real issue, that was the problem. "He wasn't made to be alive," one once said. That drilled a hole in my chest.

A specky four-eyes in the infirmary said to me that the reason for Aidan's loss was that I was a slipshod father—a real spit in my face. I very nearly buried the lad alive, except that would have done nothing to bring back my son, and his mommy was Cody's school principal. I'd never get away with it. Believe me; I thought many times to get back at the chubby gimp. That cruel deliberation ended when my truck's engine knocked yet again.

"I love you, son," I said to Cody.

"I know, Daddy," he replied. "You've always loved me."

I lobbed a soft jab at Cody's chin. He grinned. I hated seeing Cody in those restraining knee braces. I felt responsible for his impairment, somehow. Hannah and I were as fit as Irish wolfhounds. Why the bloody physical baggage? If it was the last thing I did, I had to get him off those bleedin braces.

"Eighty kilometers to our next stop," I said. Cody knew the distance. He frowned.

"You're going the wrong way, Daddy."

"I know. That's the point. Isn't it? You can't be surprised if you know where we're going," I said.

"Surprises are nice."

"I concur."

"I concur second," Cody said, laughing.

I laughed too. He was a special kid, and the love I felt for him was pretty special too. However, the love I felt for Cody was like none other.

"Feel all right today?"

"Sure, Daddy. I've been slow-walking for a minute at a time to calm my cardiomyopathy... It's part of my F.I.T.T. plan," Cody said with an awkward grin on his face.

"*Fitt*?" I asked.

"Sure, Daddy. Saw it on the telly," Cody answered.

"All right. I've got to ask—" I started to say, but the snotty-bock boyo cut me off.

"Frequency, Intensity, Time and Type... acronym's F.I.T.T. Helps stimulate the heart," Cody said.

I frowned at him, "Okay. But you must go easy with it."

I gazed back at the road ahead. Cody stared at the weathered and soiled rugby ball in his hand, bored.

"Granddaddy's daddy, Ólchobhar, used to play with that same ball. Did you know that? He was grand—"

"Rugby is for lasses," Cody said.

"Lasses?" I said. I wasn't clear where this conversation was headed.

"Yes. Lasses."

"You're a bit harsh on the lads, don't you think?"

"I didn't say fat-bellied English wankers," he said.

That caught me utterly unawares.

"Hey, watch it," I warned.

I lobbed a playful cuff at Cody's head. Cody fell silent.

"I know that face. What's on your mind?" I said.

"I want to be a professional mixed martial artist. Like you and Aidan," Cody replied.

"You don't want that," I said.

"I'm not going to die like Aidan, Daddy," Cody said.

Instinctively, I pulled over to the side of the dirt road and cut the engine. I breathed out softly, my heart heavy, Aidan's loss still fresh and raw.

# 4

When the car stopped, our chat lapsed into silence. The rainfall had subsided.

*I'm not going to die like Aidan, Daddy.*

The words may have had some truth to them, yet felt so misplaced. So wrong.

Why had Cody reminded me of something that ached so much? Aidan was dead. I was still mourning and in denial that my son was gone, gone forever. My little boyo buried six feet under. I attempted evicting that bold image out of my mind, but my mind had me locked on that visual, six feet under in a bleedin box. I felt violated. Someone had claimed my son's life impulsively. Someone had to be held responsible.

I was a fella of deep faith, although things changed rapidly after Aidan's death. Aidan was just a boy. He was just a kid. *How dare you take him from me?* I wanted to vent, so I did, although I was careful not to insult the All-Knowing, afraid of further curses.

*How can life be so cruel for those who live righteously?*

The thought resurfaced. My father and Hannah had killed Aidan. This was accepted wisdom. Someone surely had to take the blame. Someone in the physical world, in the flesh, whom I could see and touch, had to endure my resentment.

"I'm sorry," Cody said, calmly.

"It's all right. We all loved him. But we must honor his memory, okay?" I replied.

Cody nodded. That looked sincere, and Cody meant well, always. It was just that Aidan's death was still a fresh and deep wound. He died a year or so ago. When I stared down at Cody's knee braces, my anxiety returned. *What about Cody, Irish? What will you do for him?*

At that very moment, I wished I could go against my conscience and rob the wealthy to help my dying son. It was wicked that for a second I thought about *killing* to save my son from his handicap. Enough to make him a healthy child. To witness him grow old, to live and roam freely without prejudice in an unkind world. When I thought of the consequences, and being incarcerated, away from Cody, I quickly dismissed the idea. *What then? Money was scant.*

I stroked my son's hair, throwing off his cowlick, and kissed it. Cody understood I had tried everything to make things right. He had the mind of a maven. He appreciated the gesture of my love for him. So long as I was consistent, he knew he was loved.

"The surprise I've got for ya, you're going to love it, mate," I said.

"Do ya?" Cody asked.

"Sure thin', mate," I replied. "I can't wait to see your face."

"You're all right, Daddy," Cody said with a winning smile that brightened my day. Children have a lot more faith than we do. Cody was so much who I was as a child, full of faith. Once in a while, I got inspired. Not lately. I'd been really down. I'd lost all sense of inspiration. I was tapped out. But to my boy, I had to play daddy. I had to show no sign of weakness.

We were back on the road. The old beat-up truck's engine knocked once more as we drove away.

# 5

Opposite the small harbor on the south coast shore of Ireland, a small fishing area known as "the hamlet," far-off from Cork City's Blackrock, was a large signpost bearing bright lime-green words, "Cormac Petco."

Fishing boats, tied to piers, lined the old dock. Fishing rods were common fishing props on the backs of mucky trucks. A parking space was open—solely reserved for pet punters, small enough for my pickup to slide in without a fuss. When I shut off the engine and cranked the door open, the smell of fresh seafood plagued my nostrils. I loved the stench. It brought memories of my grandfather, Amhlaoibh Seamróg, who had taken me on many fishing expeditions. Those were great memories, ones I hung on to when I felt at my lowest.

When Cody spotted the Cormac Petco sign, he vaulted, though with great difficulty, into my arms. He understood the meaning—at least the reason we were here. I worried a little when I sneaked a quick look at the spare cash in my wallet. Hannah will hang me for this.

*Fuck*, I thought.

We went inside.

The place was a run-down shed where they stored fish. Cormac turned the ugly into the decent, a pet store with enough bright colors that could blind a fella. Yet the smell of animal waste was pretty bad. I'd say Cody was brave. He didn't mind—too thrilled to care. He was the "kid in a candy store" as he moved painfully about from one aisle to another. I asked him to calm down, but he was deaf ears.

At the counter, I chewed the rag with Cormac, the proprietor. He grew up north of the hamlet, a bearded Irishman in his early forties. He had four boys and a wife heavy with their fifth babe, another boy. I didn't envy him. Though he ran a pet shop, the chap had a thing for dressing like a fisherman: yellow water-resistant overalls over a ragged T-shirt. He told me that a few years back, he took out a loan to renovate the premises. The problem was that the hamlet was so tiny his only visitors (who were all from the hamlet), never bought a thing. He made so little cash that he had to travel out once in a while to hawk four-legged friends around the country just to break even.

Cody was having too much fun inspecting puppies. He moved to the next, limping with each step. His knee braces squeaking.

"How's his heart?" Cormac asked.

"He's going to need a new one. We're thinking about putting up the house," I answered.

"Fuck," Cormac said.

"Hey, it's nothin'. We'll manage," I said.

Cormac settled awkwardly, knowing well I was broke. I had lost a load of money in a failed real estate venture a few months back. Hannah had warned me, but I hadn't listened. I wanted Aidan off my bloody mind. I needed something else to do. I took a loan out and invested in some property near our new house, something I had no business getting into.

I watched Cody who pointed to a kennel excitedly.

"This one, Daddy," Cody said.

I gave him a thumbs-up. My eyes locked on the little rascal in the cage.

"How much for that one?" I enquired.

"Jaysus, Irish. Ask him to pick another," Cormac whispered.

"Why?" I replied.

"You need the money—"

"How much?" I insisted.

"It isn't wise. I can't let you do this," Cormac hissed, letting out a heavy sigh when he saw my eyes. He knew I wasn't backing down. It's for my son for heaven's sake. It was going to be like playing roulette. We would each game a turn and always end up in the original place where we started. I wanted the dog for Cody, and I blocked out the thought of the money.

"That's a soft-coated wheaten terrier. Very athletic. Good bone structure," Cormac said, aiming to derail me.

"How much?" I said.

"Seven hundred euros," he replied regretfully.

I looked at Cody, badly wanting him to agree that the pup was not worth it. But Cody had already claimed it. It licked his fingers as he giggled.

"I'll take it," I said, counting out all the money I had. "Two hundred and fifteen. I now owe you a big favor."

Cormac dropped his gaze and shook his head. He had lost the battle.

# 6

Seven hundred euros was no small amount for a puppy. Cormac realized that. The whole town knew I was in a financial trap. It was no secret. I had been Dublin's kickboxing and martial arts champion, twice over, but all my riches were lost to investment schemes gone belly up.

Following Aidan's death, I withdrew from the public. I swore never to set foot in a martial arts club again. I forfeited the match scheduled the day after Aidan's death, the World Championship title, a title I had trained for all my life and one that would bring me a small fortune. I'd call my own shots. Most importantly I'd make certain Cody had the best doctors working on his condition. Hannah, Aidan, Cody, my aul man and I would be happy and together. A real fucking family. Tough luck. I was broke. And Cormac felt compassionate.

"You've done me many favors over the years. Make it even. Two hundred. And I'll throw in the leash for free. It's a bit shabby. Throw it in the washer; it'll be grand," Cormac said.

"You're a good man, Cormac," I replied.

Cormac waved me off. I had helped him a few months back with a small job, fixing his truck's busted water pump. I'd do it any day no charge. Cormac was a good man. Guess he felt obliged to return the favor. Two hundred euros seemed like a fair trade. A bargain, one friend to another, only I was now two hundred euros poorer. Although the smile Cody beamed when he spotted me tender the cash to Cormac was one I'd put my neck out to see again, a smile I hadn't seen since Aidan's death. Surely he'd smiled before. But this was no ordinary grin. This was a smile heaven sent, from the depths of his soul. That gave me reason enough to deem my deed honorable, not in vain.

Though my action was costly, it was all worth it.

On the way home, the terrier licked Cody's face the whole way. The two were a match made in heaven. At least Cody could forget about his condition.

*Would I do it all over again to witness that glorious smile? You bet your ass!*

Our home, settled on a green pasture, overlooked the Celtic Sea, part of the small hamlet. A rare jewel, one imaginable in fairy tales. Only this was no tale. This was as tangible and as grand as the breath that Cody exhales from his lungs.

The abode was made of stone. Greenwood struts held up the roof. Massive oak beams supported its foundation. A porthole in the top brought in Ireland's best sunlight. A dream home for fantasy lovers— Hannah had been a bit of an aficionado of castles in the sky.

Shamrock grew among the flowerbeds, the mild weather perfect for it to thrive.

My pickup truck wasn't discreet. The engine always announced our arrival. We drove up the driveway, Hannah watching. Our eyes met but not for long, as she focused on Cody. Hannah, the charming red-haired woman with a ponytail I had married in my twenties, was still a knockout. Long in the past, she had planned to propose marriage to me one leap year on February 29. But I had surprised her, before she could do it, by getting on one knee, and delivering the words, "Hannah McKenna. Would you marry me?" to which, she answered a loud-mouthed, "Yes."

My secondary school sweetheart. She had been a true beor. Even now while crossing into our early forties, she was still lovely.

Make no mistake, she was an older woman, but her physique was in no way that of a lady in her forties going through early menopause. Simply put, she was gorgeous.

Perhaps she knew this, perhaps she chose to overlook it, but I was still much in love with her. Yet when in her presence I could not find the words to express how I felt. We were so distant, so far apart. And it all stemmed from Aidan's death. To me, she was the cause of my son's loss. She had killed my boy.

Hannah worked on the expanding vegetable garden where radishes, spinach, tomatoes, zucchini, onions, peas, cabbage, and cauliflower thrived. She loved the simple life. Back in Dublin, Hannah had worked in produce at *Tesco* on Baggot Street, a job she had enjoyed for over a decade till Cody's birth, when she was forced to stay home to care for him. I became the breadwinner. Then Aidan's death abruptly sank us deeper into a familial depression, an event so drastic we left Dublin to escape the dark memories and begin a new life in the hamlet.

A loud bark grabbed Hannah's attention. My truck hadn't come to a full stop when Cody hopped out, unsteady gait, with his pet, Séamus. I had warned Cody a dozen times about that stunt, but he was always deaf ears.

I shifted the gear to park, covered the back of the pickup with a vinyl top and followed Cody.

"Look, Mommy. Daddy got me a puppy," Cody said.

"Slow down, Cody," I said.

Hannah, surprised, hunkered down.

"Come on, puppy," she called out.

Séamus jumped into Hannah's arms. She ruffled its fur and kissed it a thousand times and more. For a moment I wished she'd kiss me with such affection. Time will tell. Our wounds were deep. We had lost a son. It still hurt like hell.

Cody breathed heavily. Hannah looked at him, worried.

"I'm okay. I've got me *auld segotia* now," Cody said.

"What's his name?" Hannah asked.

"Séamus," Cody answered.

"A proper Irish name. Strong and beautiful," Hannah replied with a prolonged wet kiss on Cody's temple. Cody kissed his mommy back on her rosy cheek. They embraced the three of them—Hannah, Cody, and Séamus. It seemed Séamus had taken my place, but I didn't mind. I watched, wanting to join in to make it *the happy family of four*. My heart told me otherwise when I thought of Aidan.

# 7

Cody loved Hannah like most boys worship their mothers. I envied the bond they shared. My ma passed away when I was five. I have faint memories of her, though what I do remember I hold dear to my heart. Over the years, I thought about her on many occasions.

I wondered how we would be: if I'd be as close to her as Cody was to Hannah; if she'd still call me *lean bán*—babe. Somehow, I knew I wouldn't have minded. She died too early. Never a chance to know her. That seemed to happen to those I loved. I wondered if Aidan and Ma had found each other in heaven: if she had welcomed her grandson into her home and cared for him. The thought crossed my mind once but never returned—I'd wish I was there with them to be certain they were okay. I figured they must be, hence I never asked again.

Cody stared back at me standing there—the lonely father.

"Daddy's the greatest," he proclaimed and hugged me tightly in his arms. "Mommy. The Irish gods—"

"What about them, potato head?" Hannah said.

"They played again today. It was a grand game as if the gods watched from the heavens. I saw Aidan. I saw him smile. Always enjoyed a smashing game. I miss him, Mommy. I miss me brother. Come on, Séamus. Time for a bath," Cody said as he darted away with Séamus and disappeared into the house.

At this touching revelation, Hannah had turned away from me and faced the budding vegetable plot, tears welling in her eyes and her hand pressed softly against her jaw. I was tempted to comfort her, but then I thought again. She was, after all, the reason for Aidan's death.

Then I thought of Séamus. Was he quickly replacing me? Was Cody happier with his new pet? *A soft-coated wheaten terrier. Very athletic. Good bone structure.* A pet that cost our household two hundred euros. Then again, perhaps it was for the good. Séamus could bring us back together. Dogs are known for that. I was relieved a bit. An appropriate investment. I was convinced of that until Hannah glanced at me.

"Hey," Hannah said.

"Hey," I replied softly.

As silly as it sounds, it was a bit of an awkward moment. You're burning inside, and the words don't come out. I wanted to say more than an inane *Hey*. We had been married for twenty years, for heaven's sake. *Disregard the mindless approach*, I thought. I wanted to tell Hannah how much I missed her. She was still so lovely. Except the thought of Aidan always snuck back in my mind. I tried to push it back. I tried clearing my brain. Each time the visual came back stronger. I felt empty again. Filled with anger and bitterness. Hence I said nothing, and we traded looks in silence, sorrow unmistakable in our faces.

"Did you get his medicine?" Hannah said.

"Somethin' came up," I answered, trying to avoid the subject. Except Hannah wasn't done.

"The puppy?"

"I won't have an argument about it."

"It was irresponsible—"

"Then perhaps you should find work, so you can be the responsible party."

I then realized, regardless of my angst, my words were mordant. I reached for Hannah, but she waved me away.

"I'll set the table," she said as she walked inside. I stood there reflecting what an ass I had been. *How cruel. She still loves you, Irish. Speak to her. Tell her how much you love her. Quit actin' the maggot.* Those were Aidan's words. He'd used them a few times when he was alive. They came back just as he used to say them, word for word. I wasn't sure how I'd tell

Hannah how I truly felt. It seemed easy enough, but the truth was, it was too bloody hard.

Dinner had been pretty quiet as of late, other than talks about Cody and our money worries. Most of the time, the talk was about Cody's school, about the boys who had been bullying him. I'd promised Hannah I'd go to the school and straighten things out. So I did. Things settled a bit. But Cody told us he had still not made friends. People were afraid to touch him, afraid he'd break like a sugar glass. We told him to be patient. With time he'd make friends.

Tonight, I sensed we'd be having a different chat.

Four place settings were laid on the oak dining table. Hannah brought out a hot Dublin coddle and placed it on the table and sat, across from Cody.

I sat opposite an empty seat with a fork, knife, empty plate and glass, the vacant seat that would have been Aidan's. I wasn't ready to let go, hence, the psychiatrist, Doctor Lorcan, recommended Aidan's place setting.

I felt a knot in my throat and coughed softly. I drank tap water from my glass then nodded to Cody to proceed. Hannah and Cody bowed their heads.

I did not.

"Dear Lord, bless this meal. Bless those who have less than ourselves. And let Aidan's spirit rest in peace. In the name of the *Father*, and the Son, and the Holy Spirit," Cody said.

Hannah and Cody closed the prayer with the sign of the cross, "Amen."

I did not.

Hannah caressed Cody's hand across the table, who smiled thinly.

I watched in silence. They never complained. They simply carried on as we did each night at dinner and quietly passed the steaming pot around.

# 8

No crumbs were left in the pot. Enough of a meal was prepared to feed three hungry mouths; as weak as a salmon in a sandpit. Séamus wolfed down food from the pot I had put on his plate. Ten seconds. That's all the dog took to chomp it all down. Aidan's dish was bare.

I don't think I ever will let go. Hannah had dealt with Aidan's death quietly—not saying much. Perhaps her silence was admission of her guilt. Aidan's death became a taboo subject shortly after his death.

Somehow it was better that way.

I dodged the topic every time I sensed Hannah might have spoken of it. Really, I'd avoid it for the simple reason that I'd break her heart if she knew I thought she was guilty of Aidan's death. The empty plate was a simple reminder that I'd never abandon him, that I'd never forget him. Forgetting him would mean killing him all over again. I'd never settle for that. I had to remember. I had to be reminded that I once had an older son. His name was Cain Aidan Seamróg.

Cobbles are a favorite Irish meal, and it was undoubtedly ours. We dug in. Now was the time we usually talked about Cody's school. Somehow, I sensed the conversation wasn't heading in that direction. I tried not making eye contact with Hannah, anything to avoid what was to come next. I figured, better to avoid peeking into her spellbinding blue eyes. I stared down at my cleaned-off plate when she asked me to fill her cup with spring water. She had me—I looked up.

"Butcher came by again," she said.

"What for?" I asked, knowing the answer. He was our mortgagee. I figured I'd ask anyway to stall the conversation.

Hannah threw me a stare. I was trying to think of a way out when Cody chimed in, "Does that mean we have to give up Séamus?"

*Bloody, Cody*, I thought. *You're not helping.*

Hannah eyed me once more, the deep stare I was expecting and had tried to avoid from the very beginning, a look suggesting that buying the pet was not bloody wise. She knew where Séamus had come from. She knew the price range. She was smart. I'd say she probably guessed right.

Around seven hundred euros she must have thought. She knew we needed the money, but when she noticed Séamus lick Cody's face the thought of returning Séamus dissipated. Séamus had latched on to Hannah's affection—bastard knew the game.

*Well done, lad*, I thought.

"Séamus is family now," I said. "He's staying."

Hannah gazed down at Cody and managed a loving smile, then her stare returned to haunt me. I felt like a murder suspect during interrogation. I resented that feeling. Séamus made Cody happy. Why couldn't we agree on it, shake hands, and move on?

Then Hannah fired, "We're four months behind on the house. Your job isn't footing the bills. I can't work. Cody needs me. Perhaps a move back to Dublin isn't such a chancy idea? You could work for your father again."

"I'll get a second job. We'll manage," I said civilly when Hannah became aware that Cody had stopped eating. He had placed his fork on one side of his plate and his spoon and knife on the other. His glass of milk was half drunk. Plenty of food remained on his plate.

"What's wrong, muffin?" asked Hannah.

"I'll have the rest for breakfast," Cody answered.

"Are you unwell?" I asked.

"Is it your heart, honey?" continued Hannah.

I wasn't sure where Cody was going with this. He had always loved Hannah's cobble. Most of the time he'd wanted a third or fourth serving. I worried the loss of appetite was linked to his deteriorating heart. I thought about the death angels that carried Aidan's soul back to heaven. I thought about dying. I thought, *please not so soon. Not again.*

# 9

Hannah enquired once more, but Cody kept quiet. He wouldn't look up at his mommy. Where had his appetite gone? Cody looked at Séamus. A tear rolled down his pale cheek.

My heart was racing now.

Was this the beginning? Was frequent sleep next? Then what? Permanent bed rest? See, we had been forewarned. Cody's physician, Doctor Dermod, a peds cardiologist, who maintained a cardiology practice twenty kilometers from the hamlet and a second office in Dublin, had told us what to expect and how to deal with his condition should Cody's heart embark on a lethal phase of accelerated degeneration. The process started with a lack of appetite. Then frequent sleep.

Bloody hell.

Hannah held back tears. But she had to know. To be certain. She asked him again.

"Cody, honey. We've got to know if you've lost your appetite. It's very important. You understand that, right?"

Cody straightened up and surprised us, "We can save money if I don't eat as much."

I felt stabs of large knives repeatedly plunging into my heart. I couldn't breathe. Cody was stable, yet I was in the greatest pain I ever felt.

"No. You have to eat, Cody. Doctor Dermod's order. It will help strengthen your heart. Go on," Hannah said.

Cody looked over at me, seeking my approval. I was still in a maze of bewilderment, gratified that death hadn't knocked on our door. *We need more time with Cody. Spare him. I'll find a way. I'll find him a heart. Spare my child,* I said to the death angels I perceived outside our window. I wasn't sure if what I saw was real, or a figment of my imagination, but the words seemed to have pushed them away.

Cody placed his palm on my hand requesting my approval. I came back to the present and nodded quietly. Cody resumed eating; now so fast that Hannah asked if he'd slow down.

Later that night, I sat in the living room going over options in my head. I must have sat there for a long stretch, staring down at the receiver before I picked up the handset and dialed a Dublin number.

The other end of the line rang forever. Then there was a sudden interruption, a voice. Jack Seamróg, my father who I hadn't spoken to since Aidan's death, answered.

"Hello?" Jack muttered.

I listened, handset pressed against my ear. My aul man was responsible for Aidan's death. How could I possibly forgive him?

Never.

I still wished that he had been put behind bars where butchers belong. I hoped he'd rot in hell for what he did to my boy. Someone had to pay for Aidan's death. My father hadn't.

"Hello? Is that you, son? You've got to believe me... I'm really sorry about Aidan... Look. St. Paddy will be here soon. Bring the clan to Dublin. Cody needs to see his Granddaddy," Jack said.

I hung up before he could say any more. But I wanted to speak to him. I just couldn't get myself past Aidan's face ingrained in my brain. I knew my father loved me. I knew he had wanted us to start over—a family in high spirits once more. I knew he had forgiven me for the repeated insults and drunkenness before I had finally walked out of his life. I knew he was sorry. But so was I...

# 10

I pushed thought of the phone call to the back of my mind as I made my way to the bedroom two doors down the hall. Speaking to my father was no way to honor Aidan's memory.

I'll get help some other way.

I pushed Cody's bedroom door ajar. He was reading *The Lucky Bag* to Séamus.

I'd caught him a few times reading to something he'd call *Aidan's phantom*. I resented the joke. Cody was smart enough to know better, but the boldness in him tempted him, and he'd still do it every night.

"I'm not mocking the dead, Daddy," he once told me. "They like to fool around."

I thought it was in poor taste. I wanted him to respect Aidan's death. But I left it alone. I didn't push. Now at least he had Séamus. He could read to Séamus all he wanted. I was okay with that. So long as Aidan's remembrance was cherished.

I sat on the single bed beside Cody—Séamus at his side.

"Have you taught Séamus his Hail Mary?" I asked.

"I was waiting for you," answered Cody.

"Go on. Kneel," I said.

"Kneel with me, Daddy," asked Cody.

"You know I can't," I replied.

"God knows our pain. It's our faith that he wants to see," Cody said when he went down on his knees by the cot.

My eyes were wet as I looked away from Cody. How could it be that my little boy with the failing heart and the weak legs had so much faith? I said nothing but I took it all in. There was no way around it. His words weighed heavily.

"Come on, Séamus. Come on boyo," called Cody.

Séamus hopped off the bed and settled beside Cody who asked for my blessing with a quick glance—our nightly ritual. I blessed him, planting a kiss on his temple. Cody spoke.

"Hail Mary, full of grace. Our Lord is with thee. Blessed art thou among women and blessed is the fruit of thy womb, Jesus. Holy Mary, Mother of God, pray for us sinners, now and at the hour of our death. Take great care of Aidan for me. Amen," concluded Cody.

"That was grand," I said, melancholic.

"He says not to worry. He's with the angels now," Cody said.

"Who says?" I asked.

"Aidan," Cody answered.

What a boost to my low spirits. Cody had seen my eyes. He read them well. The words were a great solace. Cody couldn't stop surprising me. Perhaps he was an angel sent down from heaven to witness my faith in the midst of my tribulations.

"That's right, Cody. Aidan's with the angels. All right. Up you go," I told him.

Cody climbed into bed. I hated what I had to do next because I never knew what to expect. I had to do it regardless. It brought me comfort when I knew that Cody was safe.

*What father doesn't? Only an ape,* I thought.

"Let's see that heart," I said.

Cody pulled apart his martial arts pajama shirt. Shaolin's face separated—anything to remind me he'd want to be a professional fighter, Cody had used to his advantage. *I get it, but it's out of the question,* I told him repeatedly.

A holter heart monitor was strapped to Cody's chest, multiple electrodes plugged into his upper and lower body like blood-sucking leeches. The machine had an olive glow that blinked with each heartbeat. Doctor Dermod supplied the monitor after Cody suffered bradycardiac episodes for successive nights. I remembered asking Doc what the hell bradycardiac episodes were. "Low heart rate is the layman's term," he answered. I understood that.

"See. Beats like a well-oiled machine," said a comforting Cody.

I tucked him in.

"Tell us a story," asked Cody.

Cody was a fast reader. He had read thousands of books. I, on the contrary, seldom read—too busy putting food on the table. Truth is Cody should have been the one to tell me bedtime stories.

A few months back he'd informed me that Nat Dogg had died of congestive heart failure.

"His heart gave in. Sometimes dead is better," he concluded.

"No, dead is never better," I said. "And who is Nat Dogg?"

"The master of G-Funk... G-Funk Classics volumes one and two," answered Cody.

I was astounded at the depth of knowledge he had been exposed to at his age. He'd spend days at the local library and read anything he'd get his hands on. When the library closed, he'd read more on the now-and-then dysfunctional desktop we had planted at home. He was well-read.

My mind roamed in search of a story.

# 11

I had thought enough and couldn't invent a tale that would resonate with Cody. Every possible story he knew the minute I spoke the very first words. He abhorred tales that began with "*Once upon a time.*"

"They lack originality," he told me, time after time.

"What story would you like me to tell?" I asked, knowing I shouldn't have. I knew what he'd say.

"Tell us a story. One with lots of scares. Blood, gore... 'Course kung fu. Gunfights. It stimulates my heart," he said.

I frowned, and he smiled, acknowledging he'd made it that much more challenging for me.

"How about I tell you a different story? It'll still have lots of action," I said.

"Fine," he answered.

"Once upon a time—" I cut myself short when Cody glared, just like he always did on the many nights when I had not followed his specific story guidelines. On top of the list, in the first position, I was reminded never ever to begin his stories with, "*Once upon a time.*"

"I'm not a baby... Jump into the story."

*Yes, Father*, I thought. He was bossy at times. He reminded me of my father: short temper and uncontrollable mouth. I had disciplined him a few times. Most times I'd let him have fun with it. What else could he do? Who else could he boss around like that? He had no friends he could play *Master and Commander* with, except for Gilchrist who we hadn't seen for quite some time.

"All right then. The story goes, 'The giant Fionn mac Cumhail brawled...'" I halted when I saw Cody yawn, thoroughly bored. "So you read that one too?"

"A thousand times and more," he answered with an encouraging pat on my shoulder.

He yawned once more and stroked Séamus' fuzz. The dog had dozed off. All this time chatting with Cody must have sounded like a lullaby to teeny Séamus. Cody sighed. He loved a great story before he hit the sack, and I hadn't delivered. Somehow he forgave me. He knew living up to his expectations wasn't an easy task. Most times I'd rank six out of ten, and he assured me six was pretty good by his standards.

Hence I was pleased but this night, when he brought up two fingers then changed his mind and showed me a single finger, it was the lowest I'd ever received as his storyteller. Boy, was I blown away. Conceivably I'd had such a trying day that my right brain had an early close. But I was okay with one finger. That meant one out of ten. At least it wasn't zero out of ten. *I can live with that.* In his mind, I had probably failed miserably with a zero. I must have got one just for trying. He knew I had tried hard. When I thought about going through the same ordeal the following night, I felt dizzy. It was like going through tests of affection each night, each score tracking my affection for him. Higher translated into, "I truly loved him." Lower, well—you get the point. Cody's eyes were closed now.

"I'm sleepy," he said.

"Yeah. Me too."

"Goodnight, mate," he said when his eyes permanently closed for the night. I had wondered enough times if he'd wake up the next morning. And if what I had done was enough of a proper goodbye that I wouldn't miss him. A father should never have to think about burying his child, I thought.

"G'night, mate."

I examined his peaceful face. I thought how much I loved him. When he was awake, sometimes I'd wish he'd keep quiet. When he was asleep, I wanted to hear him speak to me.

How strange, huh? That's love. True love. I just couldn't live without Cody. I had made a conscious decision after Aidan's death that I'd dive to my own death at Moher if the death angels ever claimed Cody's soul. This night I was thankful they didn't save me from going diving the next day.

I kissed Cody's forehead. Hannah, who watched through the slightly open door, walked away.

# 12

Vaguely—I saw two preschoolers. And a park. I can't seem to remember the name of this place. I had spent much of my childhood here, an upbringing filled with much happiness. I must have been eight, maybe ten.

My father brought me here to escape the hectic life of central Dublin, a way for him to spend much-needed time alone with me. But though he was there with me, he seemed so far away—in a daze. I asked him about it sometimes. Instead of answering, he offered me a chocolate bar, his way to keep me at bay, keep me from digging deep into his state of mind. Then he'd always open his Bible on the *Book of Luke*. And he'd tell me to run about, that he'd watch me. I did, and his eyes always followed my shadow.

And each time he dozed off, I'd hear him utter the words "Put a ring on his hand." But he never did talk about what the words meant, so I never pressed on the issue as long as I got more chocolate.

Jack would walk me by the lake where Aidan enjoyed paddling. Yes, I had brought Aidan and Cody here. We held family picnics each summer when *Feilistrín gorm*, the native blue-eyed grass, bloomed. Hannah enjoyed watching the kids scamper about chasing each other. Aidan cared for his brother a great deal. He protected his brother from the gawking bastards that mocked him. A few times, we intervened and reasoned with the kids' parents. They'd apologize to Aidan and Cody, and things would get back to normal. Even with the bloody limp in his gait, Cody seemed happier.

When Aidan and Cody wrestled on the grass, Hannah cautioned they take it down a notch. I'd let them ruffle a bit longer before they turned into wild boars. They gave us love in return. We were the near perfect family.

*Sléibhte Chill Mhantáin*. I remember now. Forty kilometers from Dublin. Yes, Wicklow Mountains. I saw the two preschoolers once more: one taller, with blue overalls, the other in khaki shorts. They shoved each other, chuckled, and then chased after each other. I tried to see who they were, but whatever angle I saw them from, the sun seemed to obscure their faces.

Impossible.

My eyes followed them, playing *fox-n-rabbit*, free of blindfolds, along the grassy path near Reefert Church, still wondering who they were. I next remembered seeing the "Wicklow Gap" sign, then I saw the boys halt in front of the Upper Lake at Gleanndá Locha.

Taller took one step onward then dithered. He never looked back at his companion. Somehow, they resembled Aidan and Cody, but it was hard to tell and even harder to get to them. I tried lifting my legs, my arms. They were unmovable. All I could do was watch. I kept staring, unable to make sense of anything. All seemed so *not-with-it*.

I could still see the kids standing facing the lake, blue water radiating in the sun. I asked myself who they were and what they were doing here alone. Thirty meters deep was the depth of the mammoth lagoon. I became anxious. They stood there watching the lake. I tried calling out to them, but I had no voice. In some way, I had seen them before. I couldn't remember when or where.

Taller stepped forward.

"What are you doing?" roared Shorter. What the bloody hell was Taller thinking? Enough with the sports. *Be fearful of the monster. It'll swallow you*, I yelled silently. *Keep away. Step back*. But he heard nothing but the soft breeze of a cool spring when he jumped into the water. I shouted, devoid of a voice. Somehow I saw Taller drowning under water, but I could never see his face. I was underwater witnessing his fall deeper and deeper into the profound lake when I jolted awake.

Fuck.

I steadied my breathing as I stared at the picture of Aidan, on the wall. Then I gazed at Hannah. She was sound asleep.

Was it a warning? Was it Aidan's ghost haunting me?

I know not.

All I know was that it wasn't the first time I'd had the nightmares, and probably not the last. It was time to pay Doctor Lorcan a new visit.

# 13

I loathed visiting Doctor Lorcan's office. The place was depressing at best, somewhere that reminded you just how twisted you were. *Insane People's Office of Shrink Lorcan* should have replaced *Office of Expert Psychiatrist Oisin A. Lorcan, M.D., Ph.D*. At least that's how I perceived it in my delusional mind. Doctor Lorcan mostly saw patients who were arrested on criminal charges, really warped personalities.

I wasn't sure why I was here in the first place. But he was the best, so the townspeople said. At times I felt like one of those criminals. Most of his patients were referred there by courts for psychological evaluations.

I kept to myself and focused on the same picture on the wall, a weathered face of a chap in his nineties, I presumed. Gravity had contributed to his sagging facial appearance over nine decades. I thought about what I'd look like at ninety. I was pretty active, rugby. I'd say that was enough to stay fit. Then I thought of happier days as Dublin's Kickboxing Champion and former holder of the Golden Belt. I thought how mind-boggling it was that people had merely forgotten me, how the "Fighting Irishman" became a lost memory to so many fans. You never forget about those that brought you tremendous joy. Perhaps I never brought them the same kind of joy—I don't know. Aidan's memory crossed my mind again. I'll always remember Aidan. I'll never let him down. I was his diehard fan—eternally yours, Aidan. My mind returned to read the writing beneath the picture: *This man is forty-five years old. This is what your face will look like under severe stress. You're at the right place. Dr. Lorcan is here to help.*

What a gimmick.

My mind wandered again, this time about the doctor himself. What a pitiful poster! Was it pure ego or something else? That he had a five-star rating and that he'd helped so many people? I wondered about his life. How did he come to be Doctor Lorcan, M.D., Ph.D? Had he gone through a troubled childhood, one that he kept secret from everyone? I was not sure, but one thing is for certain. Shrinks, psychiatrists, soul doctors, whatever you may call them; they enjoy picking your brains. Some kind of personal satisfaction if you'd ask me. Perhaps a way to turn away from their own grief and ghosts. This was reasonable enough that I settled for it—they used us as their own medicine.

What I remembered next was the rotating gray ceiling fan...

"Irish, Aidan is no longer with us. We... you have to get past that. The sooner you accept it, the faster you'll be able to recover from the dreadful dreams," said Doctor Lorcan, slim, in his sixties. He sat with his legs crossed. I lay on the sofa, uneasy.

"The dream was different this time. He jumped into a lake. He never killed himself before," I said.

"How about Hannah? Have you told her?" asked Doctor Lorcan.

"She knows," I replied.

"About how much you love her?" he pressed.

I was deaf ears. He'd ask me this question many times. Frankly, I lost count. I wished he would remain focused on Aidan, the reason I was here. I wanted to curse him a few times for asking about Hannah—none of his fucking business. Then he'd probably never see me again. At least he was willing to listen to me rant about how I felt about Aidan's death and the recent nightmares. I avoided the question.

"The dream, Doctor Lorcan. It was different. Very different."

At this precise moment, the exact same thing always happened.

A clock beeped.

Doctor Lorcan glanced at it. I knew those eyes. I knew what would next come out of those lips.

"Time's up."

What followed *time's up* came unexpectedly:

"This is our last session. You must make an effort to—"

"I understand," I said.

"How's Cody?" asked Doctor Lorcan shifting topics to avoid further discussion, for which, deep down, I was grateful. Cody was a much-preferred area of discussion than my finances.

"I'm on edge all the time. Any day his heart might stop," I replied.

Our arrangement was strictly to have a one-on-one on Aidan. Though I always thought there was a possibility that Doctor Lorcan didn't care, never for one second had he displayed it. He kept the inquiry very professional—genuine. For what it's worth I didn't mind the next series of questions on Cody.

# 14

"The shots?" inquired Doctor Lorcan, referring to Cody's intravenous shots.

Again I didn't mind the question. I don't know, perhaps we had talked enough about Aidan. A bit of a chinwag on Cody could do no harm. Doctor Lorcan wanted to be seen as the compassionate psychiatrist. I let him.

"They keep him alive. But for how long? I just want him to be a normal child. If I could just—"

Doctor Lorcan, scribbling notes in my file, looked up.

"He's alive. That's what counts. Doesn't it?" he said before returning to his notes.

"Yes," I said.

Doctor Lorcan was still reviewing my file.

"I'll write you a prescription for the pain. These things take time to heal. You understand that?"

Doctor Lorcan was now eyeing me.

"Yes. I understand."

"Grand. This prescription will help you sleep better. Don't take more than two tablets at a time, always at the appropriate time, with a meal. You take too many you could experience side effects like loss of vision and—"

I nodded.

"I understand."

"It isn't all."

"Yes?"

"In some cases, you may experience dissociative identity disorder."

"Put it to me plainly, doctor."

"Multiple personality syndrome," Doctor Lorcan concluded. "Have I cautioned you enough?"

I nodded. Then Lorcan rose and showed me to the door.

He handed me the prescription, shook my hand, and I left. A practice that ran like clockwork. I loathed getting my prescription. A never-ending line of madcap patients snaked from one side of the hall to the twin hall and ended at the quadrangle window where a blasé chemist, chomping on lunch and a *Britvic Club* diet soft drink, filled orders. Forty-five dreadful minutes. Yes, that's how long it took.

I had skipped lunch to make a timely appointment with Doctor Lorcan, though when I arrived, the bloody patient before me stalled the doctor for hours. He had drowned his own son to death. Some squabble about human trafficking. Claimed he had seen the Devil in his eyes, the same evil spirit he'd then claimed to see in Doctor Lorcan. Chap went crazy and tried to choke the doctor. I had no doubt it was his last visit. He left sedated, in a straitjacket, straight to the mental hospital.

Never mind.

My prescription was finally filled. I barely said thank you and stormed out of there. I figured the chemist must have realized why—no need for further discussion.

I drove home and parked in the driveway. My eyelids shut; I must have been there for a while. A thought had crossed my mind. I had wished to live another life for a brief instant. Just to see if I had it that bad. I filed that reflection for later when I had a moment for further contemplation. Then I opened my eyes and appreciated the splendor of our home. Hannah's garden. Cody's unused hammock. I glanced at my watch. It was time to go inside. I reviled the idea—talks of Cody's heart and finances.

I went in anyway.

# 15

Vapor emerged from a stove-top steamer. Hannah glanced over, adjusted the temperature knob then returned to cut potatoes and carrots which she dumped into a large pot of boiling water. Condiments settled as she wiped the knife on her apron. Hannah loved to cook. Between the Mediterranean-styled kitchen and her organic vegetable garden, she made magical feasts. *Stobhach Tavern*, nearby, had always served astonishing Irish stews.

I'd imagine, had Hannah been its top chef, meals would turn from astounding to outstanding, she was that good. Culinary school was out of the question; she had never even considered it. She would have hated traveling back and forth to Dublin. Not without Cody. Hence, I never brought up the idea.

I pushed the door softly and entered. Aroma had a funny way of embracing my nostrils each time I entered Hannah's world, the kind that made your belly roar even when you were gorged. The kind that made men fall in love. So grand was the meal's aroma that it made me want to hold Hannah in my arms and kiss her keenly. I felt my heart beating, the barrier of silence I had built between us slowly melting away. *How did we get here?*

Hannah broke the silence.

"I'm making lamb stew for dinner. Will you stay?" asked Hannah.

As tempting as her offer sounded, I stood my grounds. After all, Hannah was still at fault. She had caused Aidan's death. *Why stay?*

"Connor phoned. A shark. No landing. No inspection. And a cash buyer—"

"It's too risky, Irish," said Hannah.

"We need the money," I replied.

Money was grand enough reason to escape Hannah's hold. I seldom made use of it. To keep it fresh and believable—no abuse here. Most of the time it worked like a charm.

"I'll keep a warm plate in the oven for you," said Hannah.

I gave her an insincere smile, hiding away all affection behind it. Best if she didn't know my real feelings. She'd hang on forever, knowing there was still a chance at true love. Had there no longer been a reason to be angry at her for Aidan's death, I'd hate myself. This was how I wanted to keep things. As they were. So long as I maintained our distance, Aidan's loss was given reason. Now and then I wondered if my deceased lad approved of my conduct. I knew it was the only way I could show him I was sorry by shunning the people who had caused his end. I hoped that brought him happiness, made him love me all the more.

"Where's the boyo?" I asked, recognizing Cody as the only subject of our friendly tête-à-tête. Hannah never looked back. She jazzed up *Knorr Aromat Seasoning* on steaming lamb stew.

"Out back with his new friend," she replied.

"I brought his shot," I said in a soft voice and placed the intravenous shot on the counter. "Same instruction. No more than one shot every twenty-four hours."

Hannah acknowledged and resumed to chopping vegetables, her back still turned to me.

"He reminds me of you," Hannah said, dumping more greens into the pot. "He'd be much happier if you showed him the way."

I didn't like where the conversation was going, moving away from the counter.

"He's been slow-walking," she added still busy at her task. "He calls it *fitt*—"

"I know," I replied.

"He wants to fight, like you did," said Hannah.

"He's your son," pressed Hannah with such conviction.

"We've had this conversation," I said, feeling my temper rise.

Then she stopped cutting.

"He has no friends... relies on those god-awful knee braces, and that thing strapped to his chest... He needs a reason to live," she settled.

# 16

Doctor Lorcan had recommended anger management courses, but I never attended. He stopped trying. Someway he realized it was a waste and I'd never grace with my presence. Without forcing me into punishment of a mandatory attendance, he just offered me a practical tip.

"When you find yourself boiling in feral anger, take a deep breath. Hold it for thirty seconds. Then let it out."

I had my share of fuming sessions after Aidan's death. It was my only way of coping with a never-ending grief. Anger was the least of my worries, but the concept seemed easy enough, so I tried it anyway. To my surprise, the few times I did, it worked beautifully. Yet the exchange with Hannah having Cody and martial arts in the same phrase had my temper rising so fast I forgot the doctor's tip and lashed out, "It's out of the question!"

Hannah turned to face me. Dreadful sorrow in her face. Last time we had an eye to eye was on Cody's birthday when I agreed to remain civil, and my emotions weren't boiling over. Some chinwag about Aidan's black belt that Cody wore pretending to be the karate kid. Cody dealt with Aidan's loss a thousand times more cleverly than both Hannah and I. *You've got to have fun with it, Daddy*, Cody would say. *Aidan likes it that way*. I ached that day but still played Dad well. Cody's party turned out a success. I'd give anything to relive that day for a moment. We were all smiles, and Cody the happiest.

But it was clear to me then as it was now. Anger was by personal choice.

I had chosen it as a path to my own salvation, salvation from contributing to my son's demise. Then anger turned into an addiction I couldn't live without. And every time I heard the words *death, heart, fight, money* reminded me of that. I was addicted to fury. And I knew then my extramural actions at Cliffs of Moher were evidence of a morphed form of my dependence.

Hannah wiped her hands on her apron. She fixed me with her stern stare. I anticipated her next words. They'd come crushingly heavy...

"You've got to let it go, Irish. Our son is dead. He's never coming back. Aidan's dead," she said.

How dare she demand that I'd bury my boy and release his ghost? How dare she, after taking my son's life, speak those odious words...

I felt my temper rise further.

"How dare you? He was just a bleedin boy. And you let—"

"Our son," interrupted Hannah. "Our son, Irish. He was our son. And he's gone. He's never coming back—"

"You made it so, Hannah. If you hadn't fed his ego. None of this—" I said with blazing eyes.

My temper had blown the roof off my internal rage meter. I stormed out of the room and slammed the door behind me. I never wanted this escalation of anger. But it happened. I had wondered how it was possible that secondary school sweethearts could end up in such unfriendly water. Climbing back up into sanity seemed insurmountable. Practically impossible.

I thought of married friends we shared who were still deeply in love, with healthy children. I thought: *Why us? Why our family?* We never hurt a soul. Why then were my kith and kin being punished? *Why?*

No answers ever came but the ghostly whispers of a dead son, and the reality of my surviving handicapped child.

I had witnessed the terror that murderers and rapists brought to families in Dublin as a child, yet those criminals were seldom punished with sickly broods. Most lived quite happily after their release from jail. I thought how come it was possible that men that brought hurt to the world were blessed with happy lives and I with such a curse?

*There is not a heaven,* I thought, as I hopped into my truck and roared off.

# 17

Times were hard. The few jobs that paid low wages had loyal employees avoiding early retirement. There was just no room for new hires. At times I agreed with Hannah, only I never let her know. Conceivably, moving back to Dublin was not such a bad idea, though what I found dreadful was Hannah's hope that I'd take back my job as boss at the "Shamrock," working under my father.

Gobshite.

Staying in the hamlet seemed a better alternative. I'd have to keep trying. Keep knocking on doors, smash them down if I had to. My luck couldn't possibly get any worse. Someone, somewhere, surely must have a place for me.

A few months back I had started with Conor, who had a local small-time fishing operation, *Conor & Fishing Co.*. He quickly became more like a father to me. Cody loved him dearly (but I must admit that in Conor's eyes, Jack, my aul man, was irreplaceable). Conor understood my circumstances—Cody's heart and my need to make ends meet. He loved Hannah like his own daughter.

I had met the guy through Goliath. He'd wanted to join *Dead Mate*. He tried rigorously without success. I figured the chaps simply wanted him away from hardball rugby—*his damn mouth*. He talked a lot of shite on the field.

Once in a while, we'd let him scuttle when he wasn't running his fishing business. I, for one, loved his style. His clatter-mouth was a smokescreen for the strong legs he lacked. Most of the gang outran him. Yet at seventy he performed skillfully. I enjoyed playing side by side him. Except I had a unique talent, a gift that allowed me to do what most men were terrified of: I wasn't afraid to die. And that's how I found work with Conor: heavy machinery lifting no one dared to take on—seldom required but when needed I was the man. Made perfect sense—the job was hard labor. In a sense, it was like dying or, better yet, a near-death experience.

Conor had a full crew on board. I was there merely as Conor's attendant. We'd drink *leann dubh* (black ale—Irish stout), while the crew tended the net. When we went for the big fish, which was only once Conor's forecast called for it, the crew was limited to two—Conor and myself. He figured I was worth a hundred of his best crew. I was okay with that so long as I got paid my habitual bonus, which always came in handy (enough to cover arrears). It meant that Hannah was able to buy more seeds for her garden, a great way to save on vegetable shopping. Conor loved fishing. However, today was unlike most days. Conor predicted we were going after a great one, one he hadn't seen in over five years. Conor had a simple formula that predicted when shark fishing was apt—*Croí na Mara Ceilteach,* Heart of the Celtic Sea, proper marine weather and the good Lord on our side. We had caught a lot of small sharks. Guess his forecast had worked its magic. This was very different—a bigger fish meant more money, but we had to operate illegally for this arrangement. No landing onshore for fin inspection. This was a large cash deal, and we imagined we were efficiently prepared.

Latitude— 49.070512

Longitude— -8.250254

*Heart of the Celtic Sea...* Conor's archaic fishing boat floated in the presumed center of the ocean. The Irish sun slowly faded into the distant horizon. Waves were getting rougher. Off the edge of the boat, Conor, the old fisherman, cast off a considerable quantity of bloody fish scraps, a magnet for thresher and porbeagle sharks. When we ran out, I'd bring more fishing pots, and we'd empty more seafood into the sea. Conor loved our quiet time together like father and son, a son he never had. His wife passed three decades ago on the operating table while giving birth to his babe. He never recovered and never remarried. He was forever bound to his fishing operation—the love of his life—a proper Irish fisherman.

"There's a storm coming," said Conor.

I followed his finger pointing at the dark low clouds looming in the distant skies.

"You said light rain... Goddammit, Conor."

Perhaps it was a warning that his forecast was way off and we'd be better off heading back to shore.

"You want cash?" said Conor pulling down on cargo straps. Conor was a confident fisherman. He knew precisely where to cast the net; when, where and at what precise time to go for it. He had been fishing all his life: knew nothing else, really. His forefathers' fathers were all in the fishing business.

But things had changed drastically as of late. Less fish. Most that were caught were no good. Mostly dead from the nearby oil spill from a five hundred and fifty thousand deadweight tonnage Arab crude tanker *Ab Mukhtar Al-Arab* with busted oil tanks. Nothing like the Gulf of Mexico's catastrophe of the past but enough that we felt the impact on our pay. Ireland cleaned up the mess rather impressively. However, the side effect in dead cods caught once in a blue moon was still a reality we faced. I let my mind wander a bit till my reason returned to remind me of my purpose of being here on Conor's boat: Cash.

Catching the big fish was an excellent opportunity to make some good money. At least enough that'll cover a few expenses and a sizable down payment on Cody's heart transplant if his heart condition didn't improve.

Transplant seemed like the only way. I had already made up my mind. If things went belly up with Conor's business, I'd find work elsewhere, and I was prepared for anything.

But now at this very moment, we were on a mission. To catch the bloody shark. At two hundred euros a pound of fin on the black market, Conor estimated we'd bring in a generous profit given we'd sell off the whole fish to meat smugglers. I was to claim forty percent of the share. That was fair. I focused on the money, on Cody's heart, on his ugly knee braces, on our finances. Money was necessary, and I was prepared to face the beast. I'd do anything to get my dying son a healthy heart.

"You sure you saw it here?" I asked, gazing at the ocean.

"Sure as Fomor's blood runs in my veins. It was clear as day. The-son-of-a-bitch was as big as I'd imagined. A fish like that... We'd really do well.

Put a smile on Hannah... C'mon. Let's cast that line," shouted Conor as the wind gusted.

I hooked a large lump of cod on it and cast the line overboard.

The wind got stronger, and then, without warning, heavy rain began bucketing down on the boat.

"I'll keep an eye out," I shouted to Conor.

"I want to see the beast," answered Conor.

"Go inside, Conor," I insisted, waving him away from the outer deck.

"I want to see the bloody shark," shouted Conor, tying together a fallen barrel with cargo straps.

"Jaysus. Visibility is a bleedin bitch," I shouted, shaking my head.

Conor hung on to the ropes as the wind blew harder and the boat suddenly experienced a wrench.

Conor and I exchanged an excited look.

"It's on the hook!" Conor pointed at the stretched line from my rod.

I felt my adrenaline rise—the same kind of thrill I felt just before our deadly rugby matches. Better yet my kickboxing days.

The moment we've been waiting for...

# 18

Conor's eyes gloated in awe. In all his years in the business at sea, he had never sensed a wrench that massive. The most he had felt was ten times lighter, much smaller sharks. From the uncertainty in his eyes, I knew right then. We were both novices facing an unpredictable predator, and one Conor had underestimated. I could cut the line, but I needed the money. If it meant dying for Cody's sake, I was ready. I gazed back at Conor with his hands clamped on the line. He breathed in air of confidence in his large weathered lungs.

"Reel it," shouted Conor when a loud thump erupted throwing Conor and I off balance.

The line tightened. I dashed over to Conor while hanging on to the rod that nearly pulled my arm off (except I was unlike most chaps with the strengths of a thousand men).

"You all right?" I asked.

"Go on. Reel the bloody fish," the aul bastard answered. "Do ya smell the cash? I smell it, Irish. I smell the fuckin' cash."

"Grab the wheel," I said when the line hardened, and I felt a sudden pull.

"Reel it. Reel the bastard," shouted Conor.

My attempt at reeling the bastard did nothing.

"Rod's jammed," I shouted back, pulling with incredible strength from my arms. The very bendable rod flexed its muscle. So did I. I imagined a lesser mortal would have lost both arms. The pressure was intense, but I'd managed to reel in four inches. The bloody shark felt like it weighed fifty tons. I flashed back to my younger days when I'd pulled a forty-four tons locomotive with my bare hands—hardly a challenge.

"We're going to need a bigger boat," thundered Conor, dashing into the cabin.

"We haven't got a choice. We must tow it back to shore," I shouted with my palms pulling inches from the line. I wasn't letting go of our cash. I saw again images of devilish kids cackling at Cody's knee braces as he crossed a path, escaping into the murky neighborhood woods to find refuge, a tear trickling down his pastel face. *Crutch boy*. They chuckled. All the more reason to hang on to the line.

I pulled with all my might. A few inches gave. Yet the bastard shark had us prisoners like teenage lads on a water-skiing dare. A thought crossed my mind: let it go. My arms were in unimaginable pain, pain I had never felt my whole life. I wanted out. Then I thought of Butcher, the mortgagee. How he had come by recently and made Hannah uneasy with his demands.

Conor brought me back.

"Can't take it back to shore. We'll be put in handcuffs and handed to Garda... Hack the line. You're going to get yourself killed."

*What about Cody?* I thought.

"I need the fuckin' money."

"For Christ's sake, Irish. Hack the line," Conor shouted back when the cargo straps snapped, a barrel smashing at his frame. Conor fell to the deck.

"Dammit, Conor," I said, not sure if he was severely hurt.

"Conor?" I called out. Then loosed my grip, grabbed a blade and swiftly cut the line, which whipped into the stormy water.

"Fuck!" Conor said, rising back to have another go with the escaping beast. I felt my money slipping through my fingers...

Without thinking, I dove into the gloomy sea.

"Irish!" Conor shouted.

I blacked out.

# 19

A flashing fluorescent golden glow with capital letters S-H-A-M-R-O-C-K, shed light on the blackened sidewalk on cobbled Fleet Street, south of the Liffey.

The green-painted brick wall had a series of large windows. It was a pub in the heart of central Dublin, where a black and white sign dangled on a teeny see-through suction cup plastic hook affixed to one side of the double wooden frame glass doors of the front entrance, indicating "Closed." Inside, a row of tall chairs lined the bar. Fat beer kegs sat beside the storeroom door, awaiting the next day's wave of Irish "black stuff" lovers. At the bottom of the large mirror facing the room, half-empty glasses dotted the granite countertop.

There were four chairs to a table, and opposite the bar, was a stage where local talent performed on busy nights. Beneath the large glass windows overlooking Fleet Street were booths for patrons who sought more privacy and comfort, perhaps even horny pupils from the nearby boarding school who, every so often, would make out in darkened booths.

My father once told me the story of this place, which he summed up in two threads: "Your great-grandfather's father first opened this tavern in sixteen ninety-three. Dubliners loved it so much they dubbed it Seamróg after the clovers that grew in the tavern's front yard, a proper landmark for famished and lost patrons, and in due course, we came to be known as "Shamrock." Good, fit, and proper." The family's real name was lost to history and replaced with Gaeilge Seamróg—Shamrock, a name that brought the family pride and success, a name many before me went to their graves adoring. Seamróg had, most importantly, a most distinguished meaning at least to me—great strength.

Silence was nonpareil after hours. Typically not even a squeak could be heard. Yet a muffled human shout echoed from upstairs. A door was closed shut and tight, on it a sign, "Office."

Shrieks of agony came from behind the door.

Inside were a mahogany table and a most fitting leather chair where a man, dressed in an expensive suit and black leather gloves, sat comfortably, legs crossed, his features buried in the shadows. His suit was probably Italian, worth no less than a few thousand euros, fashionably pinstriped, balanced with gleaming leather designer boots.

Opposite the unknown person was a battered Jack Seamróg. His gore stained a smooth-edged card table where his head lay, looking like a dead man. A large man in his seventies, Jack's broad face bore a full bloody beard that used to be gray.

"Yes, Jack," the unknown person said. "Micheál, Liam, and Tadhg are pretty sick bastards."

The trio of Micheál, Liam, and Tadhg were the mystery man's brawny enforcers. Explicitly, Liam and Tadhg were Micheál's torpedoes. Resembling *Marvel Comics* villains, the triad all had chiseled jaws that brought terror to their victims.

Micheál's knuckles were bloodied. He had been doing the pounding. People such as these were only in such a place to inflict pain in exchange for whatever, largely money or information. Yet, pounding on Jack's face had got them nowhere. Jack was a tough bastard, but he had lost plenty of vital fluid.

"I can make it stop," the perfect stranger announced when Jack spat on the floor in a show of might.

The uninvited guest motioned his right hand to Micheál.

Micheál lifted his fist and then, in a deliberate blow, dropped it fiercely on Jack's skull, smashing at it with the strength of a giant. Bloodstains grew larger on Micheál's fist, but Jack was digging deep within himself and seizing a breath of strength. In a flash, Jack snatched the shooter from the goon's waistband and fired five rounds into Micheál's chest before Tadhg pulled the back of Jack's hair and smashed his head on the table, causing

Jack to let the gun fall to the floor. Micheál dropped while clutching his bleeding chest. He struggled to grab the gun at the base of the poker table, but his head fell askew, and the hardchaw exhaled his last breath.

"Fuck," said Tadhg, a mass of a chap, six feet tall, with the build of a machine, stooping to check Micheál's vitals as Liam, cheesed off and more, charged from behind Tadhg, raising his fist to join in the beating.

"Enough," said the man obscured in the shadows, extending his hand to Liam. "Your gun."

Liam paused, and handed over his weapon, turning his gaze to Micheál who'd hacked and drowned in his own blood.

"He's dead," said Tadhg to Jack.

"Settle down, Tadhg," the concealed man said while Liam restrained Tadhg. "Settle down."

The assassin trained Liam's gun on Jack.

"Jack. Tell me where I can find it—"

"I take your sins to be mine," Jack slurred, fluid oozing from his nostrils while he coughed blood insistently.

"Tell me where!" the mystery man said firmly.

"May God have mercy on your—"

The man, rising from his place of harbor, fired.

The smoke at the far end of the double action handgun barrel marked the end of Jack's life.

The light in Jack's eyes steadily faded and he slid from the chair.

The executioner moved toward Jack's body, stroked Jack's thinned and grayed hair and then lifted Jack's left hand. The executioner's gaze settled on Jack's thick ring finger. He struggled to remove an old gold band with a Shamrock clover engraving; Jack's finger was thick. The executioner dropped Jack's hand to the bloody floorboards where it belonged. He kissed Jack's brow gently.

"Put a ring on his hand," the executioner whispered to Jack, "*Slán leat*."

"Get me the ring. Make it look like a break-in. And find the *deed*," the man said, tossing the semiautomatic pistol in his hand to Liam and walking out. His face forever obscured in the shadows.

# 20

"Father!" I bellowed as I awoke on Conor's boat.

We had anchored. But I remembered hearing my name called out a few times. Must have been Conor. I remembered being hauled out of the deep with a lance. I had never blacked out in my forty-plus years. I had the strength of a god...

"Irish."

Conor loomed over me.

"Thank the heavens, mate. You bumped your head. A drifting buoy... Fish got away... I'm sorry, but the buyer called off the deal. We'll have to try again when the weather is fit," said Conor like a caring father.

Yet, for some odd reason, I felt I had just seen my father, Jack. His presence felt real. My chest felt heavy as if sheathed in lead. But my thoughts were hazy, and whatever I had seen I didn't remember.

But thoughts of Jack crept on for a while 'til I thought of Cody's heart and how I had let him down. I thought of Hannah, how she'd remind me about Butcher. I thought of Aidan once more. Was this how I had let him die?

I thought, *Fuck.*

Hours later, just outside my front door, I pondered. How could I return home after a long day's work without a bloody copper-covered steel coin in my pocket? I had turned down Hannah's invitation to stay for lunch and left her in our kitchen suffering unbearable anguish, in the hopes that some money would subdue some of the pain we both shared. Money, no matter how risky the enterprise, would make her forget just how boorish I was to her that morning, would dampen Butcher's excessive harassment. And there might one day be enough to fix Cody's heart.

I thought how the beast had slipped through my fingers.

Rugby balls had never fallen from my hands. Kickboxing contestants had never put me down on the floor.

*Never.*

How then had the bloody shark escaped my hold? I felt low, really low. I considered how much of a disappointment I'd be when Hannah heard the news, how she'd give me the distant stare, one that deemed me a failure, an absolute piece of shite of a man. I dreaded opening that door.

My hand rested on the doorknob for what seemed like an eternity. I thought of a thousand combinations to break the news to Hannah. None appeared proper. I thought of how I'd reassure her that I'd find a second job to make ends meet. Truth be told, I was running out of options. Returning to Dublin as the Shamrock's boss seemed a tempting prospect. Then again the inspiration brought me further rage when I thought of Aidan. I quickly filed that imagination where comparable opinion belonged.

*Bloody hell.* Hannah had to know.

Perhaps she was in bed asleep, like most nights I was out with Conor, fishing. Right now I hoped she was resting in the comfort of our queen-sized bed. I'd devour whatever ration of food she left in the oven and head straight to bed with no questions asked till morning. That was a better deal, one I'd settle for. I wasn't able for a full-scale quarrel at this late hour of the night. Once Cody had woken up to one of our debates. I had raised my voice a few times, and so did Hannah. We swore never to repeat it. Tonight was inevitable. *Let her be in bed*, I wished when I turned the key in the knob and entered the hall.

My heart jumped when I found Hannah standing there, stock-still, inside the doorway. Saint Nick hadn't granted my wish. Pity, never believed in the chap anyway. *How devilish*, I thought. Then something awkward struck me. A tear unhurriedly rolled down Hannah's cheek, cordless phone in her hand, a disconnected tone distinctly audible. Surely, she can't have been in tears all day? By now, I'd imagined, passage of time should have helped sooth this morning's debacle.

So what then? Was Cody all right?

"It's Jack," said Hannah.

Long ago, my father suffered two heart attacks, underwent a triple coronary bypass, quit smoking and in the process turned vegan when it wasn't so fashionable (although only for ninety-six short hours; the aul man couldn't give up meat). All the same, in more than a decade he had been in great health. I vividly remembered training with him for some of my best fights. I owed my championship title to his wits. He was no fighter but knew the form and unofficially made a remarkable trainer. But enough of that.

What about Jack?

I gently took the phone from Hannah and held it to my ear. I wanted to make sure Jack wasn't on the other end. Though I heard the noticeably clear cut-off tone, I wanted to be sure: perhaps a chance to hear his voice again. Let bygones be bygones. Embrace life with its imperfection and let a fresh start be the resolution of our past offenses.

*Hannah, I will make that call. I will call my father*, I remembered thinking. Then I hung up the phone.

Hannah embraced me, and her words sent a chilling sensation down my spine.

"He's dead. Jack's dead, *Cain*," Hannah said, snuffling. She hadn't called me *Cain* for ages. That's how I knew it to be true. My father was dead.

I felt my world crumble into pieces. I was bereft yet again. I lost my ma at five. Aidan had passed less than eighteen months ago. Now my father had died. And I never had a chance to say goodbye, a chance to make amends. *Had he really killed Aidan*? I questioned myself. I knew the truth.

Everyone knew. Yet I made Jack bear the burden of a guilty man never proven guilty. I felt a sharp pain in my chest. I wanted to die. I heard Aidan's voice once more. *Quit acting the maggot.* Yes, I was the maggot. Refusing to let go.

I thought, *why?* I should have called my aul man long ago. I should have forgiven him. I heard my demon laugh, *alas...* Then I felt a contact, a soft brush, alongside the nape of my neck. Maybe a goodbye from my father, Jack. Perhaps not. I stood there, motionless, assimilating what had transpired.

My father, Jack Seamróg, had left us. Jack, broad face and full white beard; my own daddy was dead—RIP.

Twelve hours passed. It was first light. Rays of the Irish sun pierced through our bedroom window where Hannah packed garments in a suit-case. Cody was sobbing. He sat on the bed calmly with Séamus.

I walked in, phone to my ear.

"Hold please." I then lowered the phone to my thigh.

"Pack lightly. We're only going to bury him. We're not staying," I said to Hannah.

"These are Cody's. You know how he fancies his Shaolin pajamas," said Hannah, planting a gentle kiss on Cody's forehead. I said nothing else, shamefaced, with a mild grin at Cody.

We had to put my father in the ground. How else but to return to Dublin, the city I had buried after Aidan's death?

# 21

Black-Headed gulls whistled past Clontarf Cemetery's gate, landing on a cedar tree overlooking a burial procession beneath them. A small crowd dressed in black assembled around a cleanly dug out oblong hole, deep within the earth. A silver casket had been lowered into the damp earth, resting above the bottomless pit. Onlookers sobbed. A few gazed down into the abyss where Jack's coffin would come to rest. A Catholic high priest ended a blissful prayer of absolution, "... *in nómine Patris et Fílii, et Spíritus Sancti...* " followed by making the sign of the cross. The crowd blessed the dead with "Amen."

Three old-timer pipers, entirely clad in traditional Irish dress, played the bagpipes. Two altar boys passed white baskets to the crowd. A hand wave from the cleric suggested the time had come. Four stout Irishmen lowered Jack's casket into the ground with solid cords that ended in the hollow as their last resting place.

Séamus barked as, one by one, the crowd flung shamrock clovers from their bowls, parachuting atop Jack's coffin, a symbolic green bouquet honoring the dead.

A brief moment of silence elapsed. Soil would fill the grave. Like my ma and Aidan, Jack settled to rest in peace six feet under. Jack had departed.

All the assembled embraced, doling out words of encouragement, wishing me and my kin their heartfelt pity. Then, like ants they dispersed to their own sheltered lives. Such was the way of the world. Cadavers watched their own.

"*Slán, Athair,*" I whispered.

I offered my last blessing and walked to the adjacent tomb. On the stone, the inscription read:

"Cain 'Aidan' Seamróg, Jr.

Our Beloved Son

A Fighter. A Champion. Rest In Peace."

Hannah and Cody looked on, standing by my old truck. I knelt. Séamus licked my face then ran off to Cody. I touched Aidan's Celtic cross tombstone. I sensed a huge energy transfer into my body. I knew it was Aidan's spirit, telling me it was time to let go. I fought my mind. I felt one more. I knew then without a doubt Aidan was speaking to me from the depth of his grave. *Father, let go... Let go...* was what I remembered when the psychic energy in me left, just as it had entered my frame.

A tear ran down my face. I felt at peace, peace I hadn't felt in a long while. A burden lifted off my shoulders. I could breathe...

Before I kissed Aidan's stone, I gave my word to never forget him, and that I'd love him forever. That I'd start over with Hannah, Cody, and Séamus. I had ended a war with my father and myself. I was whole again when I kissed Aidan's rock once more. Then I rose and blessed my ma's tomb.

Hannah was taken aback. I hadn't been present at Aidan's funeral. She knew what this meant: forgiveness and a chance at a new life, all four of us. We'd start slow, but we'd get there for certain. She would be content with that, no matter how long it took. She'd stick it out. She'd be there for us. She had never stopped loving me. And now our love would flourish even more. She'd given me enough space, but she knew I'd come around. She struggled to contain her tears. They came anyway. Cody hugged her dearly and offered his grand comforting smile.

I walked over and embraced the three of them. Séamus licked my features once more. I ruffled his fur. He barked. Cody grinned when I kissed Hannah on her temple. A tender kiss she hadn't felt since Aidan's death...*Damn.*

# 22

Patrons crowding Fleet Street hurried into the busy Shamrock. Hannah, Cody, Séamus and I pulled up in my truck and paused to watch the gathering through the Shamrock's large glass.

Inside, a mixed mob dressed in black and traditional attire—kilts, arans, fringed cloaks, chunky wool sweaters. The place was heaving. Punters were served Jack's specialty: mutton stew, malt, and stout.

A band of locals playing Irish trad faced the crowd, some of whom were seated at booths, others at center tables, plenty at the bar.

The place was lively, as it had been for decades, even centuries, a place well known to Dubliners as the iconic Gaelic tavern of the capital. Tourists and natives alike frequented the Shamrock for a taste of Ireland's best, time-honored cuisine and brew.

Business never slowed down. A drunken midget leprechaun played the bodhrán, having a good craic with the band and the patrons.

The double doors that made the entrance to the Shamrock opened. Hannah, Cody, Séamus and I entered. Séamus disappeared into the crowd. The music stopped at once. Everyone stared, sorrow in their faces, yet rejoicing in the full life that Jack had lived. A year or so ago, I had left without warning. These people knew me well. I'd gone in search of a new life in the hamlet, a simple life without being reminded of my shortcoming—Aidan's death. And now, I felt a warm welcome by the people I imagined would have strapped me to the cross and crucified me for what had happened to my son.

Gilchrist, my childhood ally and Shamrock's new boss after my abrupt disappearance, held it together. He had a much softer side, which I witnessed when his grandfather passed. They were close, as close as Jack and Cody. He never knew his father who deserted him, and his ma left when he turned one. Today, he wanted to be strong for me, so he held it together.

"Great to see you," said Gilchrist, embracing me like his own flesh and blood, his strong hands grasping my shoulders. "You look grand."

"You don't look so bad yourself, mate."

Gilchrist smiled, but he was never skillful in hiding his sorrow. I saw the hurt in his eyes. He loved my aul man like his own.

"I wanted to be there. But you know. He was such a stubborn bloke. He made me promise. If he ever—"

"I know," I said. I was sincerely happy to see my aul mate. We shared many great memories together.

"Happy Birthday," I said, kissing his forehead like I always did. Gilchrist had just turned forty. Today we'd celebrate his birth and my father's passing. We'd have a grand party like Jack always enjoyed.

Gilchrist hugged Hannah and planted a soft kiss on her pallid cheek. He ruffled Cody's chestnut hair.

"Sailor," said Gilchrist, saluting. Cody smiled.

"Aye-aye, Captain," said Cody, jumping into Gilchrist's arms. The two did the same each time they were in each other's company. Gilchrist was a great friend and spoiled him like the uncle Cody had never had.

Each person touched Hannah, Cody and I as we marched through the throng, a touch that meant we were loved.

When Aidan passed on, we had gone through the same line, except I never set foot in Clontarf. And I never thought of Aidan on that damp day but of the bastard lad that took him down on the mat, the blue mat. Perhaps even indigo. I could still see the blue mat, evermore ingrained in my mind. When we made it to the bar, Gilchrist motioned to the bartender, a youngster who had been working as a barman for longer than I care to remember, a mate with a good heart. He lit up when he saw my face. He had worked for me while I ran the place as Shamrock's boss.

"Bleedin great to see ye back!" the lad said. I nodded.

The truth was, I was pleased to be home. This place was where I spent my childhood. If I rewound the hands of time, I couldn't remember a time I lived in Dublin without the Shamrock in it.

*Home sweet home*, I thought.

"Johnny-jump-up?" asked the bartender. I shook my head.

"Straight vitamin G. And a glass of hot chocolate for me chiseller," I said.

The bartender handed me two full pints of Guinness. I gave one to Hannah. And a goblet of hot chocolate that the barman pushed across the counter went to Cody.

We raised our glasses.

"To Jack," I said when everyone cheered, "To Jack."

"Happy birthday Gil," I followed, and the crowd went berserk, cheering and hollering. I motioned to the band. The four musicians resumed their playing. The drunken midget leprechaun hugged me, bodhrán in hand, and then carried on. Gilchrist smiled with a sense of pride. Hannah gazed at me. This was a moment she had been longing for. I read her lips.

*I love you.*

I stared pensively at my wife. I felt the same, yet all I offered was to gently stroke her face.

Hannah broke into a grin. She knew with time I'd come to share once more those cherished words that formerly bound us—"I love ya."

Only time will tell.

"Help your mommy settle upstairs," I said to Cody, who grabbed his mother's hand in his.

I watched Hannah walk away with my son. Séamus in tow.

"She's more and more beautiful," Gilchrist said, and truth is, she was. And I wanted desperately to tell her. Nevertheless, I knew we had plenty of time. I figured let the dust settle.

# 23

I had spoken to the Gardaí early that morning about my father's death. They suspected a burglary gone badly wrong. A ballistics test conducted at Dublin's police crime laboratory wouldn't be released till the following day. I was told not to have high hopes; no gun had been recovered from the scene. But I knew something had gone terribly wrong. No way in hell this was a burglary gone wrong. It felt downright awkward. I couldn't come up with an answer. Standing at the bar, I turned to Gilchrist.

"The Gardaí say nothing was missing, other than Jack's ring finger. Anyone you can think of who would have wanted to hurt my father?"

"Jack was a holy Joe. You know that. Never hurt a soul. Everyone loved him," Gilchrist said.

"It's just that... two dead bodies. And cash in the till. Six thousand euros untouched," I said.

"Why cut off his finger?" said Gilchrist.

"I don't know, but he bore a rare copper Celtic ring," I said, staring at my own reflection in the large mirror atop the bar before me. "It's been passed on by my family for generations."

I tried to visualize my father's last moments. How he must have felt hopeless.

I imagined how he'd want to see Cody and embrace him and give him a goodbye kiss before that bullet ended his life. How he'd wished he could tell Cody how much he loved him.

Then I thought of the prick. The coward that had taken my father's life. I considered how I'd crush the guilty party if I got hold of the somewhat improbable piece of information from Gardaí, how I'd end the bastard's life slowly, ensuring he felt a thousand times more pain than that endured by Jack. *Fuck kneecapping. I'd use Chinese punishment—rat torture.* Let wild rodents feast on the living bastard. Then I'd beat him to death. Yet, in some way, I regretted that thought. I didn't enjoy the way it made me feel—like them, a cold-blooded criminal.

But it was foolish to assume a junkie had done the deed. Six thousand euros in the till was proof enough. But how could I be so certain? I wasn't.

"Cheer up. Look. Stay in Dublin. This is your aul man's place, and now it's yours. You tell me what you want done. Whatever you want," Gilchrist said.

"May I count on you to keep it open?" I countered with a melancholic grin.

"Done."

Gilchrist tapped my shoulder; *I'm here for ye.* And I knew he meant it. He had always been there for me. Besides Jack, Gil was one more who had contributed to my championship win while at the kickboxing tournament in Belfast in Northern Ireland. He was the brother I never had.

"Let's have another drink in Jack's honor," said Gilchrist.

I hadn't seen Gil in over a year. I was happy he was here in my most difficult times.

I waved at the bartender for two more. He went by so many names I hardly kept up—something about talking to different lasses at the bar. The one I remembered was McCauley. Hence I called him by his name. I enjoyed the way it sounded—McCauley—very Irish. McCauley smiled like he always did, appreciating that I remembered one of his multiple names. He delivered two pints of the black stuff filled to the top. Gilchrist gazed at me. He had more to say.

*Spit it out* was the expression he read on my face.

"When you left, your father hired aul man Abel as his trustee. Called me yesterday. He wants to see you," said Gilchrist.

"What about?" I asked.

"He said nothing," offered Gilchrist.

"Okay," I said. "I'll go and sort it out."

"Grand," said Gilchrist.

We said nothing else.

I looked at Gilchrist thoughtfully, then gulped down my tipple.

# 24

bel's office was down the street from the Shamrock. He had been Jack's chum ever since I can remember. As they aged, most of their mutual friends had passed. Somehow Abel got stuck playing trustee unofficially for the dearly departed's estates. Three years back he had retired from government service as a law clerk—a career he despised for as long as I can recall. Following his retirement and due to increased demand for his trustee service, he opened a trustee company with the slogan, "Your future. Our care."

Abel made more money than all of his forty years of service to the Irish government. He was quite gifted at it. Perhaps it was a career he should have considered long ago. He would have been happier sooner. *Live and learn.*

I made my way past commercial mailboxes up a staircase.

When I walked in, Abel embraced me like his own son.

"How's the form?"

"I'll live," I said to my aul man's mate.

In the past year, he seemed to have gotten a bit younger. I wasn't sure if it were the dyed hair or what looked like a facelift. Remember, Abel was my father's age, around seventy, almost certainly a little older. Anyway, I said nothing, but he still guessed, I suppose from the look in my eyes. So it came out anyway.

"I've got the best plastic surgeon. If you ever need a lift—"

I waved him off—not interested. He knew I wasn't here for a casual chat. Candidly, I didn't care. He looked great, and I was happy for him. Hell, he had been single for three decades. His wife committed suicide when I was in primary school. She fell for another chap. The unfaithful promised to leave his wife for her. He never did, so she took her own life. Abel never really recovered. Hence, I was glad he wanted to move on.

But I wasn't here to chew the fat or to reminisce about his wife. I couldn't even remember her name, it was that long ago. Anyway, Abel was ready to perform his task. He asked me to follow him into a room, and then he locked the door behind us. He proceeded to a large safe at the rear of a Picasso painting.

"Nice portrait," I said.

"Everyone knows it's a fake," said Abel.

I didn't care. *The safe, please.*

Abel opened the safe, pulled out stuff.

"A Bible. And a picture of your sons, Aidan and Cody. Jack always spoke so fondly of them," said Abel.

I nodded and flipped through the bible. It was bookmarked in the *Book of Luke.*

"Son," Abel said, wavering. He'd seen the edginess in my eyes.

"Son. Your father's will and the deed to the Shamrock have vanished," said Abel, showing me an empty folder with the inscription "Jack's Last Will."

"Vanished?" I asked.

Abel nodded, a pang of guilt in his eyes.

"How?" I said.

Abel shrugged his shoulders.

"Damned if I know. Maybe your aul man took it from the safe. Never even got a chance to read the bloody thing, so my guess is as good as yours. Shamrock must be yours."

I was dazed. How could Abel be so careless to let my father's Will disappear in a place that had more locks than keys? Then again he had done his duty. I focused on that to subdue my temper.

"Abel. Thanks. I'm sure he'd still be proud. You're all right with me," I said, gathering all of Jack's things into a medium duffle bag.

"People tell me your kin's cursed. I tell them to go to hell and kiss my ass," said a grinning Abel.

I smiled thinly, "*Slán leat*, Abel."

Abel patted me softly on my shoulder.

"You know the way out. Lock up when you're done. I'll see you 'round."
He walked off.

I stared at the duffle bag, wondering why Jack's Will had vanished.
I couldn't make anything of it. A missing ring finger. A lost Will. I was
no detective, merely a layman with a sick child and a grieving wife. Yet it
seemed, in the vein of plots and twists, straight out of a mystery. This was
no fantasy. It was as real as it gets, my life somehow in the hands of a pup-
peteer. Just what the bloody hell was my father involved in? What kind
of trouble was he in? I thought of every possible illegal scheme my father
could be involved in—drugs, money laundering, gambling. Nothing
made sense. No way would Jack get involved in such pettiness. He was
Roman Catholic, after all, a man with a deep faith who never missed Mass
on Sundays.

My thoughts ended back where I started—nowhere.

# 25

On the second floor of the Shamrock was Jack's office. Down the hall and up little stairs was a fully furnished four bedroom apartment, one he had renovated beautifully with Bella, my ma, in their favorite colors—gold, emerald, and pastel. It was where I had lived all my life till I married Hannah.

When I pushed open the entrance to Jack's office, the place had been cleared up. Yet, the smell of cheap cigars hit me. Jack had been a light cigar smoker for many years. He'd plant himself in his reclining chair and puff while I counted the day's receipts. On some nights we'd play poker with Gilchrist and a few chaps who patronized the business. On several occasions, Aidan and Cody had joined to watch. Each time, Jack had cleaned up. He'd claim his grandsons brought him luck.

I missed those days.

I gazed at walls lined with old Irish beer posters, frames of Aidan, Cody, Hannah, Bella, me as a young lad and one of his idols, St. Patrick. I sat down in Jack's reclining chair, and I felt the leather armrests under my palms.

I imagined the murder. The pain my father must have endured just before the killer pulled the trigger. That brought me resentment. I wished I'd been there. Might I remind you? I had a gift. Not a superhero, but close enough that I could cause significant damage and instant death. Perhaps a gift from heaven. Perhaps from the gates of hell. I don't know, but I knew I had lost faith in the Man above. He had taken Aidan away from me. That was what I felt. The fact was Aidan roamed among the dead—not the living.

I thoughtfully eyed a picture of Aidan in my palm. The world would never be the same without him. But I had made peace. I had made a promise to Aidan. I would live up to that pledge.

I glanced at the German clock on the corner: 1:11PM.

I pulled out a prescription bottle from Doctor Lorcan, dropped two pills of Seroton in my hand and swallowed.

Hannah appeared at the door.

"I'm taking Cody with me. His pulse dropped. Probably just fatigue. I've called Doctor Dermod. He's aware. I'll have him checked," said Hannah, in a Celtic shawl, looking more radiant than ever.

"Let me take him," I said, rising to my feet.

"We'll be back in a jiffy," she said with the most delicate smile. Then she turned to leave. I gazed at her intently. I had made up my mind that I'd tell her how much I truly loved her. I'd go *at it* that night. Something we hadn't shared since our son passed. Perhaps we would try for another child a few short years from now when Cody was in much better health. We'd start over.

"Hannah," I said when she turned back.

"Yes?" said Hannah.

One way or another I felt nervous, like a boy asking a girl out on a date for the first time. I don't know, but it felt like a rebirth, a chance at an opportunity to make things right once and for all. Nothing needed to be rushed. There was time. Perhaps I'd tell her when she returned. I'd sit her down, and I'd ask her to marry me a second time, to renew our vows. She'd love that, I was sure of it. I rubbed my sweaty hands and swallowed with hesitation.

"I... uh... I... "

"What is it, Irish? Cody's waiting," said Hannah.

"It's nothing. I'll be here. I'll wait for you," I said with a smile that almost brought her tears as she walked away.

Then I was forty kilometers from Dublin. Yes, the Wicklow Mountains. I saw two preschoolers once more—dimly, one taller with blue overalls, the other in khaki shorts was slightly shorter.

I felt a danger and called out but couldn't make a sound. Taller marched on.

"What are you doing?" cried Shorter.

What was Taller thinking? *Keep away. Step back.* Except he heard nothing but the soft breeze of a cold spring when he jumped into the water. I screamed soundlessly.

I saw Taller drowning under water, but I could never see his face. I was underwater witnessing his fall deeper into the fathomless lake when I jolted awake.

Bloody hell. Not again.

# 26

I perceived an ominous mechanized sound. The robotic echo belonged to the nearby phone that rang endlessly. Somehow, I was glad the bloody thing brought me back among the living, though I admit I wanted to smash it for being so loud and sudden. Nonetheless, that wasn't the chief obstruction. I knew I had been dozing for a bit surrounded by the silence of muted ghosts.

I wiped haze off my gaze and eyeballed the clock, which read 4:11pm. Hannah had been gone for three hours. She had never been gone so long for Cody's health check. I wanted to dial her number except Jack's damn phone nearby kept ringing anxiously in need of answering.

Irked, I picked up.

On the other line, Gilchrist's voice was hardly audible—with ample static.

I pressed the handset closer to my ear.

"I can't hear you," I said, moving away to the nearby window. Then I heard Gilchrist's voice turning frenzied. I realized something had gone wrong. I wasn't sure what. But I kept it together.

"Hold on, Gil," I said, shutting off any noise in my left ear with the palm of my hand. "Now, tell me... what's happened?"

Gilchrist's voice was more audible, and what he said next sent my blood pressure through the roof. It hit me like ten thousand cement blocks.

"She's dead," he said, not even having the chance to tell me *who* when I dropped the handset to the floor and stormed out.

In the car, I couldn't let my foot off the bloody accelerator. Speed was imperative. The damn banger never delivered. Taking me places had never been a quandary. Getting me there at record-breaking time was always a snag. Bloody engine lacked raw torque. However, I didn't mind so much before. Now I minded immensely. Something had happened to my kith and kin, and I had to get to location *X* before it was too late.

On my way, I acknowledged I hadn't a clue where I was heading. Hence I phoned Gilchrist. Twice the yoke went to voicemail. The third time Gilchrist answered. His speech shaken as he passed me the address. "Chatham Street." Tires screeched when I hit the brakes and made a U-turn. I had just passed Chatham Street. How could I? There were more spectators than at a Conor McGregor match. I felt the butterflies in my belly. They'd stay with me for a while. I tried ridding myself of the bloody feeling to no avail.

When I parked, I saw a mob of Gardaí two-bulbs and ambulances. Officers barked into microphones. I bolted out of my ball of shite and pushed through a snooping crowd. An onlooker whose shoulder I brushed cursed at me. I didn't care, or perhaps I hardly heard him. "Ball-bag!" I wasn't sure what I heard. Wasn't important. I had to get to Hannah and Cody.

I reached the edge of the crowd, sealed off with yellow crime scene tape. There in front of me lay Jack's overturned Rover, smashed into an Eircom phone booth. The back of the vehicle was severely crushed as well.

I saw a body bag being wheeled on a gurney to an awaiting coroner's van. Gilchrist escorted the body, his face in shock. Part of me refused to take another step. I called out to the Man above. I asked and pleaded that it not be true. I didn't pray the Lord's Prayer. I plainly requested that he'd show me a favor. Then again I thought how I'd lost faith.

*Could the prodigal son be in his favor?*

I thought there was always a chance. Perhaps he'd forgive my sins and bless me with a heavenly miracle. But then again why was I asking for favor? Nothing I could see led me to believe favor had been required. Who had died? There was no affirmation of it yet. Perhaps Hannah had picked up a friend of Gilchrist. She was known in Dublin and always played

Good Samaritan. At least I denied it to myself. It just couldn't be. My ma. Aidan. Jack. Perhaps Abel's acquaintances had been right. We were cursed. However, I ditched that thought quickly. It just doesn't happen that way. No way was Hannah gone. No bloody way. I had to be sure, but I didn't want to face reality. I fought through a crowd of Garda. Two tried to stop me. I was ready to launch a blow that could prove deadly when a headman, Detective Laughlin, in his forties, clean-shaven, thick eyebrows, a proper Jackeen (as culchies named Dubliners), waved to let me through.

Gilchrist saw me and attempted to restrain me from getting any closer. I tackled him, causing him to fall hard on the pavement. I asked if he was okay. He nodded a yes. I didn't wait. And stormed off to the body bag and waved for paramedics to unzip it.

# 27

Dying people often claimed to see their lives flash before their eyes. In my case, I saw mine flash, and I wasn't dying. My heart pounded, my chest ached.

I couldn't breathe. I knew then I was experiencing a panic attack. My palms were moist. The world around me spun and turned up-side-down, like a youngster on a boundless but silent merry-go-round.

I dreaded gazing down at the corpse in the body bag. I wished the paramedics would talk me out of it; "You'll have to present yourself at the morgue." That they'd stall me, delay the process. Enough that I'd hang on to that bit of hope that grew inside of me. Hope that Hannah was still with me. Alive. Yes, hope was grand. Gave me something to hold on to, something to live for.

The bloody medic complied without objection. I guessed they'd recognized my face. Cain 'Irish' Seamróg, the Fighting Irishman. Best to step off and let him deal his business.

One of the four medics unzipped the bag.

Don't let it be Hannah, I remembered wishing. Don't let it be my beloved. I haven't said *slán* (goodbye).

I felt the hair rise on my arms. I just couldn't look. I dared not. Maybe best if I didn't know. At least I could still hope. Again, hoping was better than knowing. Something to grab hold of was healthier than certainty.

The medic pressed me, "Sir, we've got to clear this place. Please, is this your kin?"

My heart dropped to my stomach when I made out Hannah's exposed, still features.

I fell to my knees, palmed my mouth, pressing hard. No words, just undertones. I cursed the Man above as tears welled in my eyes. God had let me down.

There is no heaven. There can't be a heaven. How could I suffer from so many curses? There is no heaven...

I found a little strength and rose to my feet. Perhaps convincing myself there was no heaven brought me strength, in that I'd no longer be account-able to the Man above and unleash widespread curses on those who'd taken Hannah's life.

Had I been a bad son, husband, and father? I had loved *Pádraig*, yes Saint Patrick, like my flesh and blood.

Why then?

I had my doubt about the Church and faith. Now even more than ever, the whole lot was out of the window.

My God, why hast thou forsaken me?

I stared back at Hannah for a moment, not believing she had walked out on me.

I rested my hand on my wife's brow and gently caressed her red hair. At last, I found the words I'd been trying for close to two years to tell her. They poured out of me and felt guilt-ridden that they never arrived earlier.

"I love you. I love you so much," I said, kissing her temple, not once but twice or more. All the while the world spun around me. Nothing was steady, but I held it together nevertheless. The medic zipped shut Hannah's body bag.

I scanned my surroundings, searching and found nothing. When the medic turned to leave, I held his shoulder.

"My son?" I asked.

Surely, Cody cannot be dead. I would jump to my death at the Cliffs of Moher. This was certain. I dared the Man above.

I'd take my own life this time. I had enough of *His* tests of faith. Death was not a game, at least, not to me. Why then was He persecuting me? Again I swore I'd dive at Moher. Perhaps then I'd meet my Maker head to head. I'd give Him a piece of my mind. Only I questioned whether my suicide would land me in Hell first without a pass through Heaven. That was more angst for my consideration.

73

The slim green-eyed paramedic brought me back.

"The ambulance just left. It's headed to St. Luke's Hospital," he said.

I offered nothing back, storming off. I hadn't even found whether Cody was still alive. I just knew I had to be in his company, whatever that meant.

"Mr. Seamróg. Hey!" Detective Laughlin called out, pausing from his interrogation of Gilchrist.

I ignored him as I did Gilchrist.

I jumped in my truck and sped off.

In the car, Hannah's still face flashed in my mind like a distorted film, and I began to weep like a child. Hannah was dead, and I'd done nothing to prevent it. I was appalled at the level of my recklessness, but then my mind's attention returned to the road ahead when I had to maneuver around speeding cars that honked avoiding a collision.

My weeping turned into annoyance and then rage when drivers slowed my advance.

Passengers stared at the crazy—me.

Drivers stared, cheesed off they couldn't mimic my driving, too chicken they'd be pulled over by hidden traffic Gardaí.

The difference between them and me was I didn't give a shite. I was after Cody. Nothing could stop me, not even the Irish gods. Besides, I was neither at war with them nor the heavenly King. He had left me with nothing but sheer sorrow. Yet I was ready in case of a face-off. He had blessed me with a gift, the strength of a thousand men. I intended to use it. Even if it meant confronting his cherubs of death if they were sent to reclaim Cody's soul. The last of Seamróg. I was on a mission. And I intended to give my life in exchange for Cody's immortality.

I zoomed my vision at the traffic ahead and perceived not a single ambulance in sight, all the while oblivious to signs lining the roadside: one with a construction worker holding a flag, several with "Construction Ahead." I was in a zone that needed no disruption. And I intended to hang about in my zone till I found my son, Cody.

I wanted to know he was alive. I wanted to know the ambulance hadn't been carrying his cadaver. Though Hannah had departed, I found hope in Cody's continued existence. He had to be alive. Or else hell would break loose in the whole of Ireland. I'd shake the island till God himself descended to answer my grievance.

Then again I wondered why Jack's SUV had hit a phone booth? How was it possible that Hannah had been so negligent to drive herself and our sickly boy to near death?

Somehow I knew Cody was alive and I hadn't a chance to think of other queries when I fled the crash scene. Only unanswered questions crowded my mind. I should have asked, I thought.

Why had Hannah died?

Again I thought how Hannah was a more skilled driver than I was, a more responsible one. She had never, ever, been in a single fender-bender in her whole life. No way had she driven that car into the booth. No bloody way. Then I thought of the smashed rear of Jack's vehicle. Soon I'd find the why. But now I had to find Cody.

Was he alive or dead?

All I knew was the bloody ambulance had taken him to St. Luke's Hospital, Dublin's finest. Hell, I had to be sure my sickly boy saw my face and knew I would be there for him.

"Cody," I said. "*Fan.*"

With that, I pressed once more at the languid accelerator.

# 28

My mind was on a one-way street; get to Cody and assure myself of his wellbeing. I was utterly oblivious to how fast I'd been driving—least of my worries.

Nevertheless, my eyes, as curious as they'd always been, glanced just below the windshield for less than a quarter of a second. Yes, I'd been that skilled, able to spot menace from afar, a skill learned only during my instructional days at the most prominent martial arts club of South Dublin.

Master Hachirou, a retired martial arts champ, taught me it only took a second to grasp an aggressor was upon you. A quarter of a second was needed to wreck the attacker ahead of their assault.

"Irish, you must seek the attacker with all your senses. Again," he'd demand, "try again."

I'd become great at it, part of the reason I became Dublin's Kickboxing Champion, a sport I'd fallen in love with. Though I'd never made use of my unique God-given strength in all fairness to my opponent, I knew when to call upon that extraordinary strength, which came naturally in high moments of extreme adrenaline charge and moments of great threat.

But enough of that.

The point was that besides my natural flair, I was a skilled martial arts fanatic, and used my skills quite successfully even when chopping scallions.

And now I was on a trail to find my boy's ambulance. A simple task so long as I kept my foot pressed hard against the accelerator demanding high speed.

A thought recurred—the speedometer!

Bloody hell.

I was maintaining a hundred and ninety-three kilometers per hour in a fifty kilometers per hour zone, a major offense. Yet I didn't give a shite and felt I needed more speed. I wished the banger had wings. I wanted more power.

Ahead, construction machinery dotted the pass, and again more bloody signs as I flung past them like flies.

One particular I had registered yet ignored read "One Lane Road Ahead." I floored the accelerator pleading for more speed, banging on the steering wheel for the sluggish engine to pick up. The tachometer's hand ventured past warning yellow into risky red. The truck gave me just a bit more horsepower.

My vehicle's bumper must have been a few yards from impact when I sighted a blue-hatted, hi-viz–wearing road worker holding a stop sign ahead. I honked, waving off at the chap who held his ground, signaling that I halt.

"Get off the bloody road," I barked, and he finally listened, diving off aside as I flew past him.

Directly ahead, a construction truck backed into the one lane from the twin closed lane where men worked the pavement, pulling sliding cement from a concrete mixer truck into the potholed dugout road.

I honked the horn forever, alarming them I wasn't stopping. Cody's face flashed past my thoughts, and the honk only got louder. I wasn't letting off.

The construction truck's driver saw my four wheels approaching like a menace to society. He dove out of his vehicle, rolling on the pavement. The bastard had thirty seconds to dispose of his banger cleanly, yet chose to abandon his giant truck. *Pity.*

I had but left and right to go and ten seconds to make that judgment. Left were construction and heavy machinery digging, moving dirt.

Straight ahead was the clunk of metal the construction worker had skillfully abandoned. A reminder that hell existed and was calling me to drive straight on and smash into the vessel that'd transport me straight to oblivion.

*Fuck hell.* I wasn't ready to die. No, not now. I had to locate the ambulance. I couldn't be but a few kilometers behind.

Ten seconds had passed.

I forced a risky right past green shrubs into the other side of the interchange on N81 traveling the opposite way, back to Dublin city center.

Cars skid far and wide on the pass, smashing into each other, missing my cataclysmic truck just inches.

One of the drivers cursed me as he honked vehemently. I was flipping him the bird when ahead I spotted flashing hazard lights on an abandoned ambulance on the other carriageway. The rear doors of the ambulance were flung open, and I couldn't make out any detail.

I remembered how my heart dropped fearing the unknown, fearing the worst. Bloody hell. Why me?

Sometimes I wanted to trade places with others just to see how bad I had it. My circumstances had to be pretty shitty. The average family must have never felt my pain, oblivious to the cruel world outside theirs.

But I had to keep it together for Cody. Consequently, I forced a left turn almost smashing into an approaching crock of shite and made for the Tallaght Pass traffic pouring in the proper direction.

My truck skidded to a halt just to the rear of the ambulance.

I jumped out.

# 29

As soon as I entered the back of the ambulance, my reflexes went to work. In a quarter of a second, I made out two paramedics onboard. One dead. The other still breathing. The driver had a bullet wound on the back of his skull that went through the windshield. He must have died straight away on impact. Doubtless the best way to go. Zero fear. Zero stress. Just a clean shot to the head. Yet my first observation less than one-fifth of a second after boarding the ambulance was that Cody was gone. As much as I worried, I must have felt that he was still alive.

And I had to be sure. I had to find out.

I grabbed the dying paramedic by the lapel of his shirt and propped him up. My inquisitive mind knew to do the rest.

"Where's my son?" I barked, shaking the man, who was losing blood rapidly. I had to act fast, no time to apologize.

Wouldn't you? I had a missing child.

"Water... " whispered the delirious medic, gushing blood, as Gardaí sirens loomed.

I figured I only had another second before the Gardaí arrived. I slapped his face.

"Stay with me," I said. "My son. Where is he?"

The paramedic studied my face, "Water... please... "

I scanned around under medical supplies and equipment of all sorts: a defibrillator, syringe driver, suction unit, high flow CPAP, CPAP-helmet, more syringes and needles, lots of drugs, immobilization equipment, medical gloves, ventilator. I yanked a drawer open, more equipment; infusions, intubation. I wrenched the emergency suitcase and backpack. There was a container with water. I reached out and grabbed it, propped him up once more and brought water to his lips.

He drank with difficulty, coughing more blood with each sip.

"Help's on the way. But I need to know where my son is. Please," I insisted when the cocks of a thousand guns echoed.

"Put your hands where I can see them. And step out of the vehicle, slowly," shouted Detective Laughlin.

I was fucked. The Gardaí were here, and I hadn't made any progress with the dying medic. When I stared into the soul of his eyes, I knew he had seen my son's taker. I had hardly a second before his lights went out. I had to act quickly.

I gazed back, over my shoulder. What I saw made me think twice about what I would have done. A mob of the Gardaí Regional Support Unit, guns drawn, lined the road outside.

Except I was never afraid. I returned my gaze to face the paramedic.

"Who took my son?" I asked pointedly but what I heard was Detective Laughlin's aggravating voice once more.

"Seamróg," said the detective, meaning business. "If you want to live, I suggest you step out of the vehicle. Now!"

I gazed back again.

Fuck.

I had to lose this battle for Cody's sake. Alive I had a chance of finding him.

"I'm steppin' out," I said, exiting the ambulance, my hands up just above my cranium.

Garda grabbed me and shoved me against the hood of a police vehicle and handcuffed my wrists while paramedics from a second ambulance rushed to the first and transported the dying paramedic to the waiting vehicle.

Detective Laughlin hovered over me in an until-proven-guilty-you're-still-guilty stance. I resented it. And I surely didn't enjoy him invading my personal space. But I had to remain calm. That was the best way to ensure that I'd find Cody.

I stared back at Laughlin over my shoulder while Garda pressed my shoulders against the hood of the two-bulb.

"My son's missing," I said calmly. "The medic... He saw who took my son. Please, detective. I need to—"

"Don't try anything foolish," said Detective Laughlin, turning to the paramedic wheeling the dying. "Hold it."

Detective Laughlin waved to a Garda to let me up. The paramedic on the stretcher was still breathing, though with grand effort.

Laughlin nodded at me. I went for it—no time wasted.

"I should have been more thoughtful. But my gasún's all I have. I need to ask again... " I said.

The man nodded okay. He was going to let me have that answer, and I was already grateful to him for that. I mean the chap was trying, and I acted like a bastard, not even calling out for help. I was terribly remorseful. And I took it he felt that in my voice. He was willing to blather, hence I asked one last time.

"You've seen the people who took my son. Were they wearing masks?"

He strenuously shook his head, "No."

"So you've seen their faces? Haven't you?"

He nodded yes.

I felt my heart race. But I had to keep the inquiry simple.

"They came in the ambulance. Shot the driver. Shot ya. And took my son. Am I right?" He nodded yes.

Now, I figured the chap, who'd been grandly psychedelic, had less than twenty seconds to live, so I had to lay it on him quickly. Hence I went for the kill.

"Who took him?" I said pointedly.

The man studied my face again; stunned I had asked that question. His lips came apart slowly with each fraction raising my anxiety. The words finally emerged much to my dismay:

"You did... " said the paramedic, exhaling his last breath—dead with no room for a comeback.

Detective Laughlin looked at me, all his doubt eradicated. I was guilty. Only he and I heard the dead. But that was enough that he'd find a way to get me convicted. The arrestable offense? The kidnapping of my own son. How ridiculous!

How could I have possibly taken my own son? It made no logical sense. I'd have to be a god to be omnipotent. I indeed wasn't one.

Perhaps it was Doctor Lorcan's meds. Perhaps they created an illusion, as you might say, a double personality? One of whom I knew; the other I wasn't aware existed. But how could that be? Then I questioned my father's death. Hannah's death.

I thought of Aidan's too...

It was impracticable. I had been there when Aidan passed. No way would some wicked alter ego of mine have slain him. Then Doctor Lorcan's words returned to haunt me: *In some cases, you may experience dissociative identity disorder... Multiple personality syndrome.*

*No, it can't be*, I thought. It was the mat where he landed that shattered his spine. I was sure of it. Absolutely certain. I'd been prescribed the meds after Aidan's death... And Jack. Hannah. They were partly at fault. Though I knew deep down, I no longer believed that as well. It was just my way of clearing up Aidan's death.

My mind jumped on Jack's night when he was killed. I wanted to be sure. I was with Conor, on the boat. I thought of the bloody shark that slipped through our fingers. I went back in time and thought some more of the time I blacked out. Surely I wanted Aidan's death avenged. I just didn't have the blood of a killer. Surely I blamed Jack. I knew I loved him too much to murder him. He was my father for Christ's sake. Therefore I dismissed that hypothesis. I couldn't have been there. Plus Dublin was two hundred and sixty kilometers from the hamlet. I'd have to be a conjurer to be there in seconds and do the horrific things done to Jack. Multiple personalities—no way!

My mind jumped to Hannah's crash. I had dozed off. No way to prove my whereabouts. But I remembered the boys. The lake. *Sléibhte Chill Mhantáin*—Wicklow Mountains. I remembered calling out. Then Jack's phone ringing gallingly off the hook. I couldn't have been there. Surely my wife was as guilty as Jack. But I did not kill Hannah. I loved her dearly...

"Take this filth away from my sight," said Detective
Laughlin. Garda escorted me into a two-bulb.

The cars stormed off, trailing behind me, sirens blaring through the tranquil neighborhood.

# 30

The interrogation room at Pearse Street Garda station smelled of cigarettes and musk. I dreaded inhaling for more than I had to each time I took a wheeze at the appalling stench.

The room was square with no opening to the outside world but a bolted entrance and four low cemented walls that ensured one's provisional imprisonment.

A plain table and two opposing chairs made for dull embellishment. I sat on one of the hard chairs. Aside from all the dinginess and shabbiness, a large tinted window faced me. It was so damn obvious some cowardly Gardaí watched me behind the bloody veiled curtain the saps called one-way glass.

I had always wondered why the darn thing was tinted. It wasn't like the detainee was oblivious to the fact that he was being watched. But again I didn't care. I focused on Cody, and I knew time had elapsed. I understood kidnapping was no laughing matter. People who dealt in this trade meant business. And time was always a factor that played against you.

I had to find a way out of this bloody secure unit. Except the grilling had started.

"Retired kickboxing champion," said Detective Laughlin, setting up the habitual cross-examination he so loved. "Between these four walls, I am God. I am the law. It begins with me and ends with me."

Laughlin lived for his profession. He had no children and no wife. Not even a mot. At times he was a real brute. One of his colleagues, attempting to test his street fighting skills, found out the hard way. He was beaten practically to death. Gardaí got involved due to the chap's fractured skull. Nothing could be proven. Eventually, following the chap's recovery, the two made amends, and the chap requested the investigation to be brought to a halt. They became *auld segotia*—as Cody'd say, B.F.F., best fucking friend. Yet the "friend" knew never to fuck with Laughlin again, a real brute that often operated above the law. Yes, *above the law* as in, "whatever it takes." And it hadn't been the first time Laughlin had pulled such stunts.

Rumor had it a chap, Kerrigan, late forties, of Finglas, had dispatched a hog's head to Laughlin's house. Instead of letting the man appear in court to be appropriately charged with posting a rather threatening message, Laughlin had the chap bludgeoned by some local heavy in exchange for hallucinogenic mushrooms. An investigation into the chap's death was launched and found groundless. When Laughlin took matters into his own hand to rid Dublin of the likes of Kerrigan, he was skilled to leave no loose ends that would lay the blame on him. He had always been smart at the task. Somehow, I was okay with that. Thugs as in Cody's takers who caused harm to the innocent had to be punished. If it meant the law had to be broken or bent a few times, it had to be done. There was enough hurt in the world, and dead, the goons would hurt no more. But I was no criminal. I hadn't done any wrong. The problem was that only I knew that and only I could prove it.

Detective Laughlin's technique always started with him inquiring about one's profession, but I said nothing. As far as I was concerned, I was innocent. There was no way I had my hands in this, the kidnapping of my own son. Cody was my offspring for heaven's sake. How could I?

Laughlin thought otherwise.

"Ballistic test was inconclusive. We can't trace the shells to any maker... You've got to give me something. Confess to the crimes—"

"You're wasting your time and mine," I said calmly.

Laughlin didn't like my comeback. It diminished his ego.

He had to come back stronger, perhaps intimidate me: a true battle of testosterone.

"Unless you're an ape, you'd understand the gravity of this situation. You're looking at possible life in jail for a double murder and a kidnapping.

And believe me when I say your punishment will be much more severe. I will see to it myself," said Laughlin.

He had scored a point or two. That resonated. But I was innocent. And I was sure of that, something I maintained and tried to get across. Candidly, my patience ran low.

"I did not kidnap my own son. I did not kill my wife. I loved her!" I said, staring straight back at sharp-eyed Laughlin.

"And your father? You loved him too I suppose?" the detective said, studying my reaction.

I knew what he was after, but I remained calm in his attempt to test which buttons would get me going. I plainly maintained my innocence. And I had figured what button to push to make him squeal. Hence I went for it.

"Detective. My son was abducted. And I intend to find him. Every second I spend here debating with you while you feed your ego with hypothetical horseshite is endangering my son," I said, letting the words hang.

For an instant, I regretted the *ego* part when I saw Laughlin's face. His eyebrows furrowed. His lips pressed together. His face deepened to the red of his tie. I knew then I was going straight to lockup. Undoubtedly solitary confinement for insulting a Garda. Then I realized his ego was bigger than I anticipated. Laughlin had always been in control during his interrogation. Not giving up so quickly was his strength. He fancied a thought-provoking exchange, and I brought that to the table.

So he settled with, "Watch your gob. You're on my turf."

Somehow I was relieved. But I had to convince the bastard I was guiltless. And my internal clock reminded me time was ticking. With every second Cody was further from me, it would be more difficult to find him if ransom was not the business of the kidnappers. I had to find a way out of this bloody borough.

# 31

Detective Laughlin's words were pointed when he flung my file on the table.

"Unless you make a confession, you're going to be my bitch, and you'll do as I fuckin' please," said Laughlin, hands in his pockets.

"My son has a deteriorating heart," I said without a flinch. "If I don't find him within the next twenty-four hours and give him his shot, he will die. The men who took him, they probably want money."

Laughlin didn't buy it. He had a gackawacka grin on his face, one that suggested he was in charge. Hence he pressed.

"Money, isn't it? This is what it's all about," the narcissistic bastard said.

I said nothing.

"I pulled your biometric record. Squeaky clean it is. Your biometric record that is. Flawless," said Laughlin, repossessing my file. "The other chap. Do you happen to know him?"

I shrugged a resilient no.

"Perhaps a hired gun when you couldn't kill your own father?" attempted Detective Laughlin. But I knew he was having a go at crushing my spirit, his way of getting at the truth. I still shook my head in disbelief.

Hence he went on, "Yes, I know. Your scheme is rapidly unraveling—"

"Detective," I said.

He raised his finger.

"Kill your father and collect from the insurance," said the detective. I shook my head once more.

"You're grossly insolvent and need an out," said Laughlin proudly pacing about with my criminal file in hand.

"... only the insurance is tied to little junior, your son, which brings us to the kidnapping," said the famed detective. Elated to have decoded my life's conundrum in no time, it all made perfect sense to him. A double murder and a kidnapping. Only I was in his custody. How would I cash out?

"You shouldn't speak of things you don't understand," I said to Laughlin who shrugged offhandedly.

"You should keep your mouth shut."

He grinned knowing he had struck a nerve but pressed on once more for yet another round.

"I wasn't finished," said Laughlin. "You hired a hardchaw we can't identify to do the job. To kill your aul man."

At this point, my temper was rising. There was nothing I could do to control it. I was nearing the danger zone. I had to keep my cool if I were to get out of this spot.

"Enough," I said acknowledging that response was pretty lame and it never would have stopped the detective with his grand ego. It was worth a try. Yet Laughlin pursued. Somehow trying to catch me in a fib. Perhaps I'd give in and admit to my guilt.

"But your father and the unsuspecting hired gun go at it, killing each other," said Laughlin, persuaded of his own piteous hypothesis.

I had heard of Laughlin as a kickboxer. I had heard how he was. How he had never lost solving a crime. He had a perfect record over the years as a highly decorated Garda detective. He had solved a hundred murders over the course of his somewhat short career, and doubtless ample more success ahead. And I happen to be one more of his thought-provoking cases. It raised the possibility of the case being solved quickly. Even if in the end I was to be found culpable I would settle for that. So long as Cody got to be alive, I'd happily rot in a dungeon for the rest of my days for the murder of Jack and Hannah.

Hence Detective Laughlin's involvement brought somewhat of a reassurance that either I'd catch the bastard "whodunit" or worse, Laughlin would beat me to the punch. But I hoped to nail the gouger on my own. It could have severe implications if at the end the perpetrators weren't brought to justice or killed. So with Laughlin, I was ahead of the game.

The story goes, so I'd been told, one of Dublin's elite kickboxing club bosses had killed Laughlin's partner to have a larger percentage ownership of a thriving martial arts club with grand sponsorship from some notable billion-dollar corporations.

Millions of euros in sponsorship funneled through the club for advertising and promotion. Nothing new. It was business as usual. Lots of money was being made. Enough that Ultán wanted most of the club's bottom line for himself. So he hired a gun and had Laughlin's partner killed. Laughlin demanded he'd be assigned to the case, and resolved it in record time. Ten minutes. That was his best, one that landed him in the official Guinness World Records for solving a murder case in six hundred seconds. The story made front page of *The Irish Times*. A mug of Laughlin hadn't done him justice. But he loved a grand publicity. Somehow the celebrity that came from cracking murder cases was like no other.

A mistake had been made at the murder scene. The gunman was high on cannabis when he carried out the job.

A blunder one never made was to leave gun shells behind. Bloody things were traced back to the killer's strung out *aul wan* who gave up his son in exchange for two euros worth of *sneachta*—cocaine.

That's how fast Laughlin was able to crack the case. Yet in my case, the gun shells found sent the detective on a wild-goose chase. These were no ordinary shells. Nothing traceable. Perhaps ones from Polish smugglers. Perhaps Dublin's notorious mob. Perhaps, on level pegging, Al-Qaeda. Though he gave up this idea as swiftly as it came to him. Why would a former champ be implicated with a terrorist group? Made no sense.

Polish smugglers were likely. A group of unlawful immigrants in Dublin city center had been known to manufacture and sell firearms on the black market, a way to earn a living in a chaotic economic climate.

The early hours of investigating my case had left Laughlin stuck in a dead end street. A first in his rather successful law enforcement career.

He had hit a serious roadblock. So questioning me was his best counter strike at solving the murder. But I was seriously losing my patience.

"Perhaps a group of Poles owed you a favor. They're known to be active in the sports betting circle. Perhaps they owed you for an old match they'd bet on. So you settled to have the slates cleaned if they'd subscribe to have your father murdered?" said Laughlin.

"That's enough," I barked at Laughlin who pressed on pestering me with probes that led us nowhere but all with me as the prime suspect. A total waste of time. I began to question my limited faith in him.

But the detective ensued with his grand hypothesis, trying to ensure that he maintained a successful record of cases efficiently cracked in record time.

I, as the prime suspect and given my financial calamity, made perfect sense.

My motive—the procurement of money at the death of my kin—sat right with Laughlin. No question about it. Plus the dead paramedic had clearly identified me as the son's kidnapper seconds before he passed.

How was I to contend against the word of a cadaver? Detective Laughlin felt obliged to raise the tension for Jack and Hannah's justice. Someone had to be found guilty. And I was the easy quarry. He knew that. I knew that.

Hence, he launched yet another, "So you hire someone else to finish off your wife. And you kidnap your gasún who will likely turn up dead so you can collect whatever money you have tied to—"

"Detective. I've had enough!" I barked once more. This time really got to me.

I meant it when I felt the pressure blow the lid off my temper. *Son* and *dead* in the same phrase was a combination I loathed to hear after Aidan's death, something Doctor Lorcan and I had worked on endlessly during many psychotherapy sessions to overcome. Yet this bastard caused all of my effort to be undone in less than a second.

Laughlin had said enough. And truthfully I was fuming when the knuckles of my fists banged the table with such ferocity that it broke in half, sending Laughlin jolting backward in awe.

# 32

Nothing else was said. Detective Laughlin had realized the incredible strength; perhaps the so-called gift everyone had bragged about me. He experienced it first-hand, quite frankly enjoying that he had witnessed *Irish*, the Fighting Irishman, without having to pay front seat at one of my kickboxing matches.

But the silence between us was temporary when the bolted door to the grilling room flung open.

A Garda clerk entered with a document in his hand that he promptly tendered to the detective.

Laughlin scanned the document hastily. A smirk appeared at the edge of his lip.

"Astonishing!" yapped Detective Laughlin. "I must admit you've made quite an impression on me, Seamróg."

I wasn't sure where he was heading with his sarcasm.

"I'd taken you for the sloppy kind. But you're very good," said Laughlin.

"Detective. What's this about?"

"You planned it all in your head," said Laughlin. "You knew we would arrest ya. That was part of your grand ploy. Wasn't it?"

"I don't know what you're talking about," I replied, earnestly dismissing whatever the detective implied, frankly oblivious to what he was getting at.

"You knew we would have no evidence," said Laughlin. "Do you know Chief Superintendent Ceallaigh?"

"I honestly don't know what you're saying... But you must let me go," I said.

Earlier, following my arrest, I'd been passed in front of Chief Superintendent Elizabeth Ceallaigh. Though Detective Laughlin had many pulls, unbeknownst to both of us, Chief Superintendent Ceallaigh was one of my loyal kickboxing fans long ago. Since my interrogation had led to no substantial results, she issued an order for my immediate release on conditions of house arrest within Dublin city limits until some evidence was brought forth, which Laughlin settled for privately with her ahead of my arrest. Somehow she believed in my innocence. Yet Laughlin was persuaded of my guilt. Hence they had settled at that.

The condition of my freedom I'd found interesting. No armed Garda to watch me. How would it be that they'd keep an eye on me? I could ditch Dublin, and they wouldn't know. I thought Laughlin had always thought of everything. Why then had he neglected to leave me unguarded, if I was to be free subject to a botched interrogation? I thought again and parked the thought for later—not my problem.

As always Detective Laughlin had promised to deliver Chief Superintendent Ceallaigh evidence linking me to the double murders and kidnapping. Truthfully, he had always delivered, and the chief knew that. Hence the chief agreed to the interrogation for no more than an hour, then the condition of my release would go into effect should nothing surface from the cross-examination.

Then again, I thought I had to find Cody. Otherwise, I'd end up in lockup as I knew Laughlin would find anything to maintain his reputation as Dublin's chief crime solver. Anything to keep his good standing and put me away for good. Innocent or guilty didn't matter. Laughlin loved to win.

My face had made the Breaking News home page of *Independent.ie*, causing the story to go viral. I was once more Dublin's famous kickboxing champ. Only this time for the murder of Jack, Hannah and Cody's kidnapping. I was petrified.

The heading read: "Former kickboxing champ, Cain 'Irish' Seamróg—The Fighting Irishman, arrested for suspected murders of wife and father and son's kidnapping." On the photograph, Laughlin had been portrayed with one of his trademark grins, one that suggested he had already solved the homicide. I hated him for that.

Yet upon examination of the record from the Garda clerk, Laughlin must have felt that he was losing ground quickly when he tossed the document in his hand on the broken Gardaí table.

"Well, Chief Superintendent Ceallaigh certainly fancies you. She's requesting your immediate release. Bravo!"

I was flabbergasted, yet part of me was thrilled. A way out of this bloody borough. I could now go after Cody's takers.

"Remove the handcuffs," said Detective Laughlin.

"I intend to find my son. And kill his kidnappers," I said without flinching.

"Congratulations." Laughlin clapped. "That makes two of us."

I shook my head, "Check your ego, Detective. You're after the wrong fella."

Being that I was to be released by order of Chief Superintendent Ceallaigh, I meant every word of it. Frankly, Laughlin was not moved. He merely stared, but I never anticipated what he was to say next.

# 33

Detective Laughlin's look was cold and stern. He meant every bit of what slipped through his lips. Besides, he didn't have to do much convincing.

"You're free to go. But you so much as skip beyond the city's limits, that little band on your ankle will transfer toxin like a thousand volts into your body, rendering you dead within seconds," said Detective Laughlin.

Whatever that meant I hadn't the faintest idea. But my memory was refreshed when I gazed down at my ankle: a tiny band wrapped around it like a serpent squeezing on my ankle. I hated the sensation. I had always been a free man, roaming the scenic seaside landscape in the hamlet. Yet with this gizmo strapped to my ankle, I looked like a wild animal. Detective Laughlin's grin returned to show me he had won. He had always been the victor and being on the right side of the law had its benefits.

"We have the best weaponry. We'll be on ya. Literally," said Laughlin.

Touché.

I had struck out at dice. Though I was being released, he still had the upper hand. And to him, that felt great. Reminded him of his days at Dublin's 78 Club where he'd become known as the connoisseur.

How had he slipped the bleedin thing on my ankle? A quarter of a second was needed to wreck the attacker before they struck. I had failed

Master Hachirou. But again Laughlin was known to manipulate outcomes by making use of illegal maneuvers. Being *drugged* while in transit on my way to the interrogation was always a possibility. Still, I was impressed, but I never showed it. Doing so would have magnified his already grand ego.

"Clever," I said, without saying more.

"We are, after all, Ireland's most elite guardians of peace," said the prideful detective, except I had already exited through the egress which was left flung open.

When I walked out on Pearse Street night had already fallen, reminding me I had lost ample time in a futile debate with a big-headed Garda who didn't know his ass from his elbow. Yet immediately that became the least of my concerns. Was Gilchrist out there waiting for my release? To the best of my knowledge, Gilchrist hadn't a clue I was in custody. Following the debacle between us at Hannah's murder site, he'd gone to Saint Patrick's Cathedral to pray. I'd found out through Laughlin on our short trip to the Garda station that he had interrogated Gilchrist earlier at the crime scene. He knew that Gilchrist had offered to drive Hannah to the clinic. And when she'd passed on his offer, Gilchrist had never insisted as he always had. As when he did, she always gave in, except this time he felt she needed breathing room. So much had happened in so short a time. Perhaps she'd wish to be on her own. To think things over. Think of a better future for us. How she'd do things differently for Cody and me. How she'd start fresh.

Accordingly, Gilchrist figured he'd give her breathing space, enough to get herself together. But then again I was cheesed off at the bastard for not pushing. I knew Hannah would have been alive had he pressed her to tag along—if he had protected her as he always had.

Outside the Garda station, I scanned the area, and much to my anticipation I saw no Gilchrist. I thought perhaps the guilt must have been unbearable. He just could not face me even if he knew of my whereabouts. He had done the same when Aidan passed, feeling responsible and grieving for two long months.

I felt culpable a few times. Gilchrist mourned Aidan's death with more passion than I'd shown. It was embarrassing at times. People thought he was the father. Bollocks! He literally ached. At times he'd get more hugs and kisses because of his distress, as if he'd lost more than I had. But I understood he was made that way. Our hearts reacted to the same thing differently. Perhaps that was the reason he'd been my playfellow since childhood. Yet I remembered telling him to tone it down, take it down a notch or two. He understood and went along. That's what friends do. They listen without question. Hence he did, and I blessed him for it.

Gilchrist wasn't here, but I didn't have to wait long before a young lad approached me. He was all business.

"Hey, top man. I'm Peter. The smartly dressed bloke over there told me you'd pay me fifty euros if I hand you this mobile," said Peter without flinching. He meant every word, particularly about the fifty euros.

The lad must have been no more than ten years old. The *gasún* waited impatiently in an, "I don't have all day" stance. I stared into the distance. Peter pointed to an overdressed chap in a blue trench coat with pulled up sleeves who walked away.

Bloody hell.

Who was the mystery man? All sorts of questions boiled in my head. I sensed I had to get to him quickly. But I had to get rid of Peter.

"I don't have cash," I said.

"He said you'd pay," said Peter. "It's about your *gasún*—"

Peter needn't have said another word. I snatched the phone from his hand and dashed across the street after the man in the trench coat.

"Hey! How about my money?" barked Peter.

Frankly, I ignored Peter. All I could hear was Cody's voice screaming in agony for not receiving his shot in time, a cry loud enough that I thought it was real. But it was all in my head.

I had made up scenes of Cody in his hell. I'd imagined how he needed me, how he wanted me there with him, how he had been disappointed I had not found him. And each time I thought of the pain he felt in an unfamiliar and chaotic world, I thought of crushing his takers' skulls with my bare hands, something I was very capable of. But I asked my mind to take a back seat and be patient. I would find Cody, and I will make his kidnappers suffer till their dying breaths.

But I was not fast enough to catch the chap ahead of me who moved like lightening without breaking a sweat. He never ran, yet his stroll seemed like a jog.

"Hey. Stop!" I said, pointing to the chap in the blue trench coat.

Bloody chap never looked back.

# 34

By the time I had started to gain on the man he had turned the corner of Pearse and College Streets. I followed and collided with a cyclist. I carried on without stopping to help the fallen biker.

"Asshole," barked the chap, and in a flicker, when I had turned back to ensure the cyclist was all right, the chap in the blue trench coat had vanished—a major faux-pas.

I had to think fast.

I glanced at the phone in my hand, the one Peter had surrendered to me. A bulb went off in my mind. I had to be fast. Time was passing quickly, and with each tick, Cody was moving further and further away from my grasp.

I dashed to the nearest electronic store. All sorts of apparels and certain unusual items were sold in the warehouse. Even Barbie dolls. Bloody hell if I knew where they'd gotten those. I didn't care.

But I cared about the salesman being tied up with patrons bombarding him with whatever queries came to mind. I couldn't understand why they'd ask a million questions with no intention of ever acquiring products in the first place. One particular shopper barked for sixty-five seconds about how the newly released *iPhone* couldn't fit into her holster and then refused to purchase the phone when the salesman proved the mobile fit correctly. She shoved the holster back in her faux Coach bag and hoofed off claiming she'd changed her mind.

I pitied the salesman. He had almost certainly become accustomed to this form of abuse from crazed shoppers, and his indifference was evident when he mimicked the ganky woman behind her back, laughing his cacks off with a colleague.

It was my turn. There wasn't much time for a chat. It was as if the lad read my mind when I pulled out the cell from my chinos and presented it to him.

"Yes. Definitely a prepaid," said the salesman.

"And you sell these?" I said anticipating a yes, which would end my search right then.

"No. Best if you try another store," said the salesman.

"Thanks," I said.

"Sure," said the lad who walked to the next patron in need of abusing his time.

I left.

I must have scoured all the electronic shops in Dublin before I came across a young fella who held a phone resembling mine plugged into his ear. I knew then I must have been close.

I asked the young lad who promptly directed me toward yet another store. Except this was a vintage store, unlike the others.

Before I entered the shop, I thought of Séamus, for some reason. Yet only for a second. Then my mind jumped to Cody. And my heart lurched. I felt sharp pains shooting to the side of my shoulder up to the nape of my neck.

I knew I must try not to think of Cody. It felt wrong, but it was necessary to get me through the next ordeal.

I marched into the store, and in a quarter of a second, I had scoped the whole place. There were no mobile phones. Still, something was odd. I could tell I was in the right place.

# 35

A vintage electronic store. Freakish dark overtones loomed as if it was a mortuary dwelling where the weird worshiped the Devil.

Eerie gothic music blasted from ceiling speakers, almost deafening. It felt as though the bloody vibrating roof could crash down on me any second.

How was it that the glass window at the front of the shop hadn't shattered with such devastating noise? How could these youngsters be so entertained with such blaring beats? The bloody music was just too damn loud.

The Harry Potter Generation was one I struggled to understand, though Cody had attempted many times to educate me on the matter. They were different, they were technology savvy, fast thinkers, brash, and they spoke a language of their own. Cody had been my mediator. Now more than ever I needed his voice. Except he was the one I was searching for. And the clock was ticking. The more I shilly-shallied, the more Cody distanced himself from me.

A long line of young gothic bargain hunters trailed at the mouth of the aisle.

I gazed around the room. There were morse code units, sound/light translators, ancient light bulbs, tube-type AM radios, stereo receivers, dual-trace oscilloscopes, VCRs, monitors, vintage comic books, even a section with modern PlayStations, Xboxes, flat screens, MICs, PC games, and adult movies.

A few bowsies, clearly underage, discreetly entered the adult section of the store. No one cared.

When I first entered I'd noticed large TVs mounted to walls in all four corners of the store that showed off muted shoot-'em-up video games. Heads and limbs were blown to pieces, and digital blood spurted on monitors.

Two kids, planted in front of one, watched with pleasure as zombies got their legs shattered. The sprogs couldn't be more than ten years old. Still, their thirst for carnage glowed in their eyes.

Was this the world we lived in?

Perhaps the thirst for butchery has always been in us, part of our humanity, and these lads were simply exuding their prime instinct. I'd looked at the lads too long; they both flipped me the bird and bolted out. I sighed, watching them leave. Then again, when I looked at the clock tick, I was reminded I had to find Cody.

I looked away from the clock and my eyes settled upon a young couple making out in one of the aisles.

Watching them would cause me to be portrayed as inhuman if their bond didn't spur loving thoughts of Hannah. In spite of everything, Hannah and I had been secondary school sweethearts. Seeing those two kids smooching took me back, yet not for long; the lad behind me tapped on my shoulder. The line had moved in front of me.

I glanced at my watch with tormented eyes. A salesman waved me to approach, "Next."

I fast stepped to the counter, with each step feeling closer to finding out the truth about the origin of the phone in my pocket.

I hadn't spotted any similar phone on any of the display shelves. Yet deep down I knew I was at the right place. I didn't know why.

The place was creepy enough that I'd recognized only such a depot could produce the type of smuggled phone that a kidnapper would use. Plus they'd most likely frequented a store that reminded them of just how wicked they were.

I pulled out the prepaid mobile and presented it to the unfussy salesman. "You carry this?"

The lad, pierced nose and dark eyelashes and lipstick, a heavy-metal disciple, examined the mobile.

He shook his head, "Nope."

"You sure?" I said.

"Positive," said the lad.

I felt my chest clench. Air compressed from my lungs. I hadn't many clothes on but felt inundated with layers that I couldn't shed. I quickly reverted to Doctor Lorcan's thirty seconds breathing exercise—breath in, breathe out.

That helped.

"Thanks," I muttered as I stepped off, still not convinced.

"Next," called out the salesman as I headed for the door. My mind was engulfed with thoughts of a kidnapped son and not a dime in my pocket when a chap, sixteen or so, a real heavy-metal punk, called me, "Pssst!"

I glanced to the side at him.

The boy's eyes were intense, like those of a much older chap, like he'd had a rough life, forced to grow up quickly, something I understood. Now and then life forced you to mature at an exponential rate. Fuck puberty. Straight to adulthood without a clear transition. Such was life.

His eyes were locked on me.

# 36

The young lad nodded for me to follow. I wasn't sure what he wanted, but I felt that he knew something about Cody's hard luck. I didn't grasp how; I just sensed it. One thing was guaranteed. If he tried something foolish, I'd have him up high by his Adam's apple and crush the life from his lungs. He'd not stand a chance. He must have known not to muck around. I was bigger, stronger. I don't suppose he recognized the Fighting Irishman, and that was grand. I wanted to keep things that way: maintain a low profile. So I followed him as we retreated into a corner, poorly lit.

The stranger pointed to my phone.

I hadn't the slightest idea how he'd known. But I said nothing. I paid attention.

"You don't want sneachta," said the punk. "But you want another phone?"

"Yes. Tell me," I said, anxious to hear his comeback.

Anything to lead me to Cody.

"I can get you the same," said the lad.

"That'd be grand—"

"But it'll cost you," said the punk, dulling my short-lived gladness. Of course, I knew that. Everything in this bloody life cost money when you were fishing for information. I hadn't a cent in my pocket. But I had to play along if I was to find Cody. I sensed the lad would lead me to my son's abductors. He had identified the suspicious mobile in my hand without my asking. He had made the first contact. Hence I knew whoever had taken my son had formerly made contact with him. And if I were to get information out of him, I'd have to play along. So I did.

"How much?" I said, pointing to the bait phone in my hand.

What I heard stunned me.

"Hundred euros—"

"For this piece of shite?" I barked when the lad placed his forefinger before his lips, "Shhh... you want to be discreet. Don't ye?"

"Yes."

"Then it'll cost you a hundred. Take it or leave it."

Such was the cost of commodities on the black market.

Prices would ebb and flow from one maximum to another based on the smuggler's perceived necessity of the patron. And from the pained expression in the depth of my eyes, the punk had noticed my desperation. So it was. He hiked up the price, at once. I had no intention of paying, but I had to play along. I had to find Cody before it was too late.

"I'll pay. But I don't want the phone," I said.

The lad looked puzzled and tried to work out the mystery of the man before him. Apparently, he must have seen I didn't give a shite about the cell in my hand. I was after something else. What was I after?

He eyed me yet again. Studying my anxiety. Perspiration. Sweat glands. But he just couldn't get a reading. He pondered once more. *Why was the chap after anything other than the commodity he customarily traded?* It was a question he'd shortly have the answer to, so I talked.

"I want a name and address."

The lad's response was curt and forthright.

"No."

A big mistake on his part. I was done larking about. I hadn't time for some fool's game. Cody could be dead. The more I thought about him, the more my rage intensified.

"I'm not asking," I said. "I'm making it easy."

I must admit the sprog had balls.

"Or what?"

"I'll break your neck," I said calmly. I'd learned the expression from Cody, one that Millennial Generation understood.

He knew I meant it. He'd seen the Devil in my eyes. He knew I meant business. He had to deliver or be *márbh*. Yes, dead. Death was inevitable.

The punk toppled a rack of DVDs by the side of me. I leaped forward, and my fingers missed the lapel of his shirt by millimeters.

The lad was agile, dodging me and bolting out.

I recognized he must have been a traceur. Only one with that skill could escape my assault. But I was up for the challenge. I'd been active in parkour, commonly known as PK, for many years, as early as age six. Perhaps seven to be exact. No, this was no senseless, free-running workout. It was all competence and alacrity, and I'd mastered both on the rough streets of Dublin where corners were landmarks for more than a few middle-class sprogs' muggings.

I'd been beaten up a few times. Hence, to elude the packs of juvenile ne'er-do-wells, who hung around on street corners, I'd mastered the ways of PK. It was a style I'd embraced, whereby I'd jump over buildings to escape from a horde of attackers. I'd become quite skilled and later combined it with my martial arts, and my natural God-given gift.

I'd become a natural killer, a gifted pugilist, and the punk escaping my onslaught reminded me of my younger days.

Fuck it.

I had to catch the lad and make him talk, by whatever means. And I was prepared and well equipped to inflict pain if necessary. The punk had made his bed in his anarchic existence crammed with fiends. And I was there to make him sleep in it, except I had to grab the nimble bastard. Hence I stormed out and hunted him.

# 37

The punk exited into North Wall Quay, proceeding west. I trailed him as he dashed across the Sean O'Casey Bridge into traffic on City Quay, dodging fast cars. He bolted into a urine-smelling deserted alley.

I chased behind; cars honking wildly.

The lad showed off his PK skills—leaping upward and over an out-sized dumpster, literally airborne, never touching metal, an agile and fast rocket. Then he bolted sharply right, entering a series of gin mills, leaving mayhem behind him. I tracked him, as a pissed-off tavern boss let off two rounds in rapid succession from his get-the-hell-off-of-my-porch twelve gages double barrel shotgun. A volley of gunfire soared, slinging past my bloody brains.

The lad leaped atop a progression of festooned tables decked out with highborn-on-tour-patrons feasting on Ireland's best. The punk's waders splattering their meals on their most beautiful fabrics as they gasped in shock. The bourgeois clientele frowned, their faces crammed with appalled dismay and rage.

My trailing behind made matters even more complicated, as if before-hand they hadn't had enough of the lad's pandemonium; I served them some of my own.

I watched the lad ahead of me. He entered a shabby apartment building, with faded paint and shattered windows.

I raced in, following.

I had crossed the threshold of the grungy edifice when I gazed up the long flight of stairs. The punk leaped over a set of steps, in a flash. Unbeknownst to the caffler, I had a secret of my own. I was born with a rare knack, one that rendered me neither human nor superhuman (maybe sandwiched somewhere between the two of the Almighty's divine creations).

For each step of advance the lad made, my divine gift permitted me two steps. And given the lad's own natural talent, I considered mine heavenly or perhaps earthly, as my faith in God had vanished long ago.

I nearly caught him, when the punk put his boot in my face, sending me flying back a few steps down the stairway. He scampered speedily up the stairs.

I chased.

The punk's boot smashed open the exit into the rooftop.

I chased.

In a neat maneuver, the minor leaned on the palm of his left hand and leaped forward above a massive spinning fan, reaching the cement edge of the roof, the replacement for Nelson's Pillar, the Spire of Dublin, evident in the far distance.

Nowhere to go but down thirty meters into certain death.

The punk halted.

I made my way out of the stairway into the rooftop, past the barricade.

The sprog hauled out a semiautomatic pistol. Like a shot, I grabbed it and spun the lad about. He almost immediately recognized the barrel of the shooter resting in his trap—the junior member of the Dublin criminal underworld had been slow on the uptake.

"I want a name and address," I said with an expression of fierce intensity on my face.

I realized the punk couldn't possibly speak with the barrel shoved in his mouth. I flung the revolver off the roof into the alley below. The boy threw me a look—*fuck-ye-did-dat-for?*

"Guns destroy human life every day... Now, name and address," I said, handing the boy the cell from the mystery chap in the blue trench coat.

The punk examined the cell.

"Each one sold has a tracking number on the back," said the brigand, flipping the mobile on its backside.

"Right here. I'll have to cross check against my database."

"That'd be grand," I said. "So where to?"

"My flat," said the lad, pointing beneath us. "One floor below."

I was in no disposition for further mucking around. I'd been fair. If he tried anything thoughtless, I'd put an end to his life. I didn't care about his age. I only cared about his connection to Cody's takers. If he brought me an inch closer, I'd forgive him his sins. Right now, I desperately needed information. Even more, one reflection had entered my mind, which brought some senses into my present psychosis. *I can't kill him now. Not now. I need him alive. I need to find Cody.* These thoughts brought me some sense of much-needed calm.

# 38

I gazed deep into the punk's eyes. He was telling the truth. Don't ask. Sixth sense shite. Took a trice to get to that inference. Nevertheless, I had to be cautious. The lad had been nimble. Losing him for the second time was always a possibility. Surely, after giving me the jog, I was not up for a new marathon. Not that I was out of it; I just had no time for a bloody five-k run. Cody had to be saved. And the bloody unnatural tick-tock in my subconscious that never let up reminded me of just how fragile Cody's heart really was, a heart that'd give at any moment if he hadn't been given his shot. Dr. Dermod's words returned and lingered.

Yet again I was reminded just how agile the punk was. Grabbing him by his jacket's collar was a definite way for the criminal to evade my grasp. He'd swiftly drop, roll, backflip and dive into empty space down thirty meters landing each time, feet first, on a fire escape staircase; settling undamaged on "liberty" alley where he'd run off to a place of escape. Never to be found.

So I grabbed the young fella by the nape of his neck and shook him to his core.

"Be smart, or I'll wring your neck," I said.

He nodded, recognizing the seriousness of my voice. He'd also seen the death wish in my mug.

*I want blood.*

We moved off the rooftop back into the building. Somehow, I felt closer to Cody once again. I didn't know why. I just did. Felt as though keeping the punk alive assured me of Cody's survival. Perhaps it was the boldness that hope brought. The prospect of seeing Cody again. His frailness. His knee braces. His shortness of breath. His funny walk. His limpylegs. As warped as it seemed, I didn't mind them at all. In fact, I missed it all. I missed the whole of Cody. My boy. My Irish sprog.

When we crossed the doorsill into the con man's dwelling, my investigative instinct kicked in. The lavishly furnished place gave reason to my suspicion. The lad was making cash trading black market wares and making a killing. Such was the life he had chosen. I wasn't judging. In fact, half the stuff in his lair I couldn't afford, especially bringing home the dismal minimum wage from *Conor & Fishing Co.*

The flat was decked out—in a manner of speaking—in money: all-in-one revolving small circular kitchen, glass-mirror-TV, Italian designer furnishings.

Damn that.

I couldn't care less about the lad's lavish lifestyle. I wasn't after his wealth. I was after the bastards that abducted my son. I crushed the lad's neck. He yelped and pointed at a computer on standby.

I shoved him to the ultra-modern workstation and planted him in the three-sixty-degree-swivel leather chair.

"Type!" I said.

He took a breath then paused, searching his soul for what, I had no clue. With no holds barred, I had no time to squander. My large hand clamped down heavily on his neck. I was capable of crushing it if needed. Now was neither the time nor the place. Nevertheless, the act was effective.

"I can't think if I can't breathe," uttered the punk.

"Now," I said, loosening my mortal hold.

A login window blinked impatiently.

"I said now."

"Give me a bleedin second," said the fella. "I can't remember the code."

*Horseshite*, I thought.

I grabbed the punk by his Adam's apple and literally yanked. He begged for release, and then straight away went to work. My violent gesture had refreshed his amnesia.

I released my grasp.

The boy entered a secret code. The full screen appeared.

The boy brought up a file and at once scrolled down a long list of trans-actions on his monitor.

Then he stopped—another login. Nervily, he stared back over his shoulder.

Alas, I hadn't vanished. I was still planted there; waiting and wanting intel. Anything that could point me in the right direction.

*Bloody hell*, he must have thought.

I shoved him—"Pull it up."

He proceeded and logged in a number.

A message flew across the screen and halted mid-center:

"Cash Transaction."

*"Shite,"* reacted the punk.

"What does that mean?" I said.

Frankly, I had no tolerance for more bullshite.

"No name. No address," the edgy teen said. "He paid cash."

I gasped and looked away for a second. I tried to contain the bloody rage that beat against my cranium. At any moment, my wrath would burst. Then an unexpected beep brought me back.

"What's that?" I said, pointing to a blinking Windows folder. I was no Windows expert, but I knew a few things of my own. Plus Cody had shown me a few tricks on my second-hand personal home computer.

"That folder's blinking," I said. "What's in it?"

"Nothing," said the concealing punk.

Unfortunately for him, I'd grabbed his writing hand, twisted his arm, locking it up. Any more pressure and his humerus would snap.

"You'll never type the same again," I said.

"Arrrgh!" screamed the belligerent con juvenile.

"I'll rip it off—"

"All right," begged the lad, "he was desperate—"

"Desperate?"

"Yes," said the pained boy.

"Who?" I demanded.

"The chap," said the teary lad. "There was another purchase. Non-cash. No name but an address—"

"Show me," I snapped. "Pull it up."

"Here," said the punk, pointing to an address on-screen.

# 39

I wrote the address on my palm.

"About the money," said the lad, glancing up.

The resounding clatter of the pen I once held in my hand hitting the marble floor filled the dead air, and I left. Not a farewell. Not a thanks. Not a word. Staring down at the palm of my hand, I found hope. Hope that I desperately needed to carry on, and belief that would bring me the strength and courage to bear vengeance and destruction upon the guilty who had kidnapped my child.

I reached Parliament Street. The sun had come out, perhaps a sign from heaven? The weather had been pretty grim and arctic. But in any case, I had lost faith in the Man above.

Once more I read off the scribble on my palm. I cross-checked the address. A perfect match. This was it. A semidetached house. My heart pulsating out of control, I must have felt Cody's heart beating as well. I was here. This was as close to Cody I imagined I had been.

I went in. A depressing narrow hallway led to two tightly shut doors. Each heartbeat was a constant reminder I was getting closer and closer to the grand final—the grand reveal. The truth was locked away behind one of those doors.

It was unbearable, but I thought of Master Hachirou. In all instances, one must remain calm.

"*Irish*, you must seek peace of mind. Only through serenity can one find himself. Again. Try again."

The words resonated. I had to remain tranquil. Except that didn't work.

I halted a quarter of the way down the hallway, at two chipped and rusty mailboxes. I scanned for any practical information.

No names. Just occupancy numbers: 13-31A and 13-31B. A thought struck me. Long ago, when I turned seven, I was diagnosed with triskaidekaphobia. I was terrified of number 13. My father blamed Cunningham's slasher film *Friday the 13th*, which he judged had given me my morbid fear for the number 13.

See, I'd been seven when Gilchrist and I snuck into Savoy Cinema on Upper O'Connell Street to watch the film's early theatrical release.

Maybe Jack had been on the nail. The flick shook me to the core to the point of becoming terrified of everything 13.

Dr. Ríoghnán—my psychiatrist who had also been a qualified neurologist—was a long-time friend of Master Hachirou. They met while they attended Keio University in Tokyo in the early sixties. At the counsel of Dr. Ríoghnán, Master Hachirou had endorsed Ríoghnán's advice to manage my paranoia through martial arts, which was how I became an apprentice of Hachirou. Except operating under severe stress, made matters worse. The phobia overpowered my nervous system. I could not bear it.

I forced a thought on my bloody brains to kill the angst I felt, enough to calm my senses. Anything to distract me from thinking "thirteen," or of Cody's agony. A juvenile thought entered my mind. I wondered if the mail carrier was ever annoyed at delivering parcels to mailboxes with no names. Except that didn't work.

I tried to think of something else.

I was human after all. And my senses reminded me of it. Tension mixed with my fear. Perhaps I should give in to my fear. Perhaps that was best, keep me on edge and ready for anything. I felt sorry for whoever would be heir to my fury. There will be bloodshed. *Someone must die.*

I gazed back at the scribble on my palm: "Thirteen Parliament Street." Bloody hell.

So 31A or 31B?

I was at a loss. I reasoned. *Patience, Irish.* I retraced my steps.

Back on Parliament Street, I spotted an internet café across the street.

Inside, I planted myself in one of the computer lab workstations facing a large glass window through which I could see the house and settled in to keep watch.

I must have nodded off. The café's worker tapped me on the shoulder. It was stiff.

"Sir, you've been at this station for over an hour. You can't—"

"Swipe the card," I said, extending a worn-out prepaid debit card, dismissing his petulance.

He took it and went to the till.

My gaze returned across the street. At the sight of a man in a blue trench coat entering the semi, my core shook like a massive underground eruption.

I rose to my feet with every heartbeat audible. The donor of the mobile phone in my pocket, the one linked to Cody.

This time I was leaving nothing to chance. I dashed to the door and made for the house.

# 40

It hadn't occurred to me that I'd abandoned something behind.

"Hey," barked the internet café worker after me. "The the card was declined…"

I was deaf to his aggravation. I was entering the house.

Inside the semi, I found myself where I'd been; the narrow dismal corridor. Before me, I watched the door to flat 13-31B close abruptly.

I checked to see if the place was rigged for security measures. My head tilted aloft—a camera.

I lowered my form and headed for the door, with every step imagining this was the place where Cody had been, imagining he would soon be in my arms. That felt grand. Only that part. Except my twisted mind's eye also forced my imagination of a Cody who'd been roughed up—mishandled.

That brought me further rage, which caused my calves to thrust my legs into further motion and advance rapidly upon the kidnapper's front gate.

I nudged the door a bit. It was shut, but unlocked. I twisted the door handle. The thick steel entry opened. Loud death-metal music emerged from within. I went inside.

Shadows loomed far and wide. The place, dimly lit, was closed-in, claustrophobic.

I stepped further into the entrance hall. The music was too damn loud.

I moved carefully, one step at a time, with each footstep, readjusting my posture in readiness for an assault. I was prepared, my eyes permanently scanning, assessing, and reassessing.

I moved into the first room. All sorts of medical devices were stained with human blood—aged and fresh. Stains spread to the four corners of the long oval oak table, a corroded metal sheet fastened on it with hexagon head bolt screws. Leather straps were secured on each side.

A spine-chilling thought crossed my mind; a human was butchered here...

I held my hand over my nostrils. The stench was unbearable—the stench of the dead.

I moved past the dining area, music blaring in my ears, into an adjacent room, when the death-metal stopped.

Dead silence.

I halted—not a sound.

I searched my surroundings, ready for whatever.

Shadows crept around, desolate. I thought I saw movement, but it was mostly my imagination.

I tried listening—not a sound.

Where had the bloody music gone? Why had it stopped so abruptly?

The tang of danger lurking, I felt a presence, a sense that someone watched from the hellish shade. A wicked soul waiting to strike. Except I was a chap unlike most. The only problem was which side they'd come from; the room was almost pitch dark.

I slowly walked toward the back of the room when a rusty thirty-inch threaded rod swung at me. I ducked. The rod flew across the room.

A light bulb flickered. I caught a glimpse of a chap's face before a strong jab knocked me out and one of my own instantaneously striking the assailant—an even boxing swap rendering us both K.O.

We were both on the floor, knocked out cold.

My assailant, down for the count on the floorboards next to me, I had never met and never knew.

Why had he been linked to Cody's abduction?

# 41

Yet again I was forty kilometers from Dublin in the Wicklow Mountains. I saw two preschoolers once more—vaguely. One Taller with cerulean overalls. The other in khaki shorts was slightly Shorter.

I felt a danger and called out, but my vocal chords seemed dormant.

Taller marched on.

"What are you doing?" bellowed Shorter. What was Taller thinking? *Keep away. Step back.* But he heard nothing but the soft breeze of a cold spring when he jumped into the water. I shouted, devoid of a voice. I kept trying till I felt my throat burn in excruciating pain from my extended cry.

I saw Taller drowning under water, but I could never see his face. I was underwater witnessing his fall deeper into the deep lake when I jolted awake.

Not again.

I returned to life to the smell of raw fuel.

The flat was in flames.

My head ached. Thick, heavy smoke overpowered my senses. I covered my nose, scanned the room.

It only took half a second to realize the worst; the man in the blue trench coat had vanished.

A large white ice box was wide open, covered with blood stains. I was nervous, but I had to be certain. I searched inside and found nothing. One way or another I was relieved I hadn't found my own flesh and blood in pieces. I scanned the room once more. Impracticable to stop the fire.

I had to get out of there alive. Cody still needed a *fella*.

I spotted a door that was hidden.

I elbowed at the bloody thing with the strength I'd been given at birth. When the door swung open a dead body collapsed to the cement floor. I jumped back at the sight of Abel, my aul man's trustee. The stench of the dead competed cheek by jowl with the overpowering fumes. He'd been dead for a day. Two at the most. His heart, teeth, and eyes had vanished.

*Bloody hell*, I thought.

Just what had Jack been involved in that got my son kidnapped? I hadn't the slightest idea. But the sight of Abel, dead, brought more mysteries than I could find answers to—I was utterly lost in a web of questions.

Who was Jack, really? Who was my aul man? Had there been a darker side of him I'd been shielded from? Had he been involved in a shifty deal? Had he owed some people money? Had he done business with the Devil?

I couldn't make sense of anything. Except I had to get the bloody hell out of there. The house was blazing, with me in it.

I thought it over once more. I had to get back to where it started—at the Shamrock.

I escaped through a broken window.

Soon after, I had made it undamaged back to Jack's office at the Shamrock. The place was a mess. I'd been pulling out drawers and dumping all the contents on the floor.

Precisely what I'd been looking for I hadn't the slightest idea. Yet I scoured the space for the irregular, anything that appeared out of the ordinary.

I rummaged around—beneath Jack's desk; over it. I yanked out a sizable drawer from the nearby armoire. Pictures parachuted onto the floor.

I halted my fury and squatted.

Photographs of me and my dead son—Aidan—working martial arts, running, hugging, messing... Then me as a fifth-degree black belt champion recipient.

I lifted one photograph up, of my folks. We were all smiles. I was caressing Hannah's face when the wood floor squeaked.

I paused and gazed back. No one.

The wood floor squeaked once more in a rhythm of footsteps rising up the set of steps, unhurriedly; watchfully. *They're here* was the first thought that crossed my mind... *here to take life... to kill Irish...* was what I concluded. I'd be damned if I wouldn't take some of them with me.

I clamped a butcher's knife in my fist and stood static by the open door where darkness loomed.

I watched a shadow cross the threshold.

On the double, I grabbed the trespasser and ensconced the butcher's knife on the chap's gullet that at once did away with his hood.

"Jaysus!" said Gilchrist.

"What are you doing here?"

"In case you're off your nut, you bloody ask that I keep it open," said Gilchrist. "Settle down!"

"Make yourself known next time," I said, disposing of the slayer blade in my hand. "Or I won't be so careful."

"If you care to hear my opinion, you're losing it," said Gilchrist. "You should consider—"

"Abel's dead," I said. "Tortured to death. And no. I don't want your opinion."

"Christ," said Gilchrist.

"I need to find Cody fast."

Gilchrist drew near and tried to reason with a whisper, "You need to let the Gardaí handle this."

"Piss off! You expect me to be a fuckin' jibber?" I barked to my childhood mate.

The mobile in my pocket came to life, ringing—insistent. Gilchrist and I traded looks.

This was the call I'd been expecting. Either Cody was dead, or the kidnappers had settled on a payoff. Either way, they had the upper hand. I had to take part in the bait.

First thing, I had to answer the bloody handset. I gestured Gilchrist to hush up.

I pulled out the cellular from my pocket and pressed the answer key.

A mechanized voice spoke evenly, "You'll keep your gasún alive so long as you follow our instructions. The abandoned flats. Nephin Road. Fifth floor. Ten minutes."

The mobile went dead. Not a chance in hell for a rejoinder. I boiled

117

inside, and I had my punishment face on—all senses operating on a bursting reservoir of rage.

"Rescue missions are for the police," said Gilchrist. "And vengeance for the gods—"

"Then I must be a Garda demi-god," I snapped, bidding Gilchrist farewell.

"Close the place for the time being and stay off Dublin 'til I can sort this out. And take care of Séamus."

"Be careful, mate," said Gilchrist to which I nodded as I headed for the door.

# 42

Seconds later, my banger had flown past Cabra Garda station on Nephin Road, Dublin 7. I mulled over informing the Irish police. The idea was grand except it would assure me of Cody's death. Gardaí would take matters into their own hands, dispatching their bolshie negotiators, and fuck up any chance I had of saving my son. A possible solution was to force the Gardaí's hand in dispatching Garda Síochána *Aonad Práinnfhreagartha*—Emergency Response Unit, Ireland's most elite armed killer unit, fifty strong. I'd have a fair chance with them. I knew of their training with the FBI's Hostage Rescue Team, America's notorious *Servare Vitas,* counter-terrorism paramilitary branch.

Still, I wouldn't chance Cody's life in the hands of Gardaí. Detective Laughlin would demand he'd be involved: a way to keep the scores of his successes in the public eye. He was an officer who'd chance everything in exchange for further media coverage and futile accolades. I was having none of that.

If I'd get my son back, he had to be breathing. Even with a weak heart, I'd take him—my only path to permanent sanity. Aged Nephin Road dwellings zoomed past me. I'd driven past this neighborhood many times before when I lived in Dublin, except during happier days with my folks. Aidan and Cody would stare out the window for hours as we drove past neighborhoods and tell Hannah and me how one day we'd have a four bedroom detached bungalow like one of these on Nephin Road. One with a two-car garage, a porch, long hallways, timber flooring, open fireplace, bay window, and a bath with a shower accessory. One where a Jack Russell would run about freely with the boys in our rear garden.

I had cherished their dreams. They brought me such pleasure and hope that I needed to carry on. Sadly, those memories were short-lived, as the Man above had claimed Aidan, then my folks, which brought me back to my present-day pursuit and pressing charge—to find Cody's abductors.

I had arrived.

It was a decrepit and forsaken building, hideous, that offended one's sense of calm. I stood facing the menace, wondering if this was yet another Parliament Street: a safe house for the hostage-takers.

I scanned the area. High voltage overhead power lines, aluminum warning signs—"Unauthorized entry strictly prohibited." Soaring weeds and rubbish on all sides.

*How had it been that the Council had allowed this place to get in this state without OCU—Garda's Organized Crime Unit—eyeing the place for society's rabble-rousers?*

*Fuck, I'll handle my own affairs, for Cody's sake.*

One section, on the far side of the building, had a tiny old cottage, reminiscent of a maid's quarter.

I felt adrenaline kick in. The time had come.

I pushed through the dismal, rusted-iron front gate, vengeance in my clenched fists.

Inside the scruffy lobby, a gigantic flight of steps stood before me.

I reckoned they would be at the top. Accordingly, I went for it, rushing up long staircases passing a series of ghastly halls. A thought crossed my mind; this had served as some sort of nursing home at some point. Abandoned beds and wood chairs crammed bone-chilling dusty halls. I didn't know anything about this place or its perhaps once-glorious history, and frankly, I cared not a single bit. After all, if this were where Cody had been kept captive, I'd demolish the place, bringing it down to its knees like a giant crashing down to its earthly rooted dust with its residents—the hostage-takers—returning to the hellish hole from which they material-ized, the depth of agony.

I entered the fifth floor. I tramped past a series of opened doors to class-rooms with broken windows, floored with ancient dust.

A series of lockers lined the hall.

I halted when the mobile rang. The outlaws had known of my presence. I answered.

"Locker three fifteen. Your dead son's birthday. He would have been twelve. Are you going to let this one die too?" said the mechanized voice. That struck a nerve. My facial appearance had turned ill-tempered except I had to maintain my calm.

"I need to know he's alive—"

"Open the locker and follow the instructions," the voice said.

"My son's ill. I'm willing to deliver his shot—" The connection went dead.

*Calm, Irish*, I told myself. *Keep calm.*

I unfastened the locker.

A black leather manila envelope was inside. I retrieved it and drew out a document. The post-it note read: "Endorse where indicated."

I lifted up the note. Underneath, the title of the document read: "Last and binding will of Cain Angus Seamróg."

*What-the-bleedin-fuck*, I thought as I scanned the document.

Words jumped out at me: "Beneficiaries: I surrender every one of my property to the following persons:

Every part to Fharma Holdings plc and percentages—100%." A retractable ballpoint pen from the envelope fell onto the cement floor. I hunkered down to reach for it when two bulky chaps ugly as sin turned up at either side of the hallway. One had a deformed methhead-like mug, a birth defect.

The skin of his neck was like plastic. The other, bare-chested, was scarred from his jaw down to his torso.

I had finally set eyes on the guilty that might have taken Cody. Vengeance boiled in me, and I was high on intent for destruction.

"I love my gasún," I said, plainly spoken.

They stared, stiff as *Sorbus hibernica*—Ireland's whitebeam tree.

"He may not mean anything to ya. But I'm giving you an opportunity to live," I said, addressing both.

The contenders stared at me like zombies, immovable.

*Had they been doped?* I didn't care. Perhaps they had no knowledge of me and my strength.

"Give me the location of my son and of the ball-bag behind my son's abduction," I said, pitching the envelope and deed back into the dim locker.

Both men hauled out daggers, pommels hand-carved in bone skulls.

121

"Suit yourselves," I said, pitying their corpses for what they'd endure as I unleashed my wrath.

The men charged to the fore.

One smashed his dagger into the hard metal lockers.

I bent backward inches from the blade with a boot to his jaw while I spun back to face the other menace who clobbered the steel blade past my crown.

I clutched the pen in my hand and jammed it into the chap's crotch then promptly grasped his collar and snapped it plainly like a hen's neck.

I gazed down at the dead on the floor, annoyed I had disposed of my first informer. The other thug, gagging, made for the edge of the hall and ran up the stairway. I chased behind, pledging to my sprog that I'd grant the chap a proper judgment the second time around—only not ahead of finding out of Cody's whereabouts.

A cat and mouse chase ensued up the flight of stairs when the man exited into the top floor. I chased behind and crossed the threshold. The man's dagger flew past my face, thudding into a wooden beam.

I snatched and flung it back, pommel first, at the man's skull, knocking him down on impact.

"I'll ask only once, but I'll kill ya either way. Where have they taken my son?"

The man laughed wildly.

"You're dead, Irish," cackled the crazy, exposing his rotten teeth. "You're dead!"

I sliced off his ear with the dagger. He shrieked in anguish.

"I won't ask again."

"There's no escape," yapped the half-amused, half-weeping psycho as if he'd been drugged.

"The chap you bludgeoned. He had a detonator in his chest that will set off. That was sixty seconds ago. You have sixty seconds left. We're all fuckin' dead, mate!" chortled the nutter.

"Wrong," I said. "You will watch me live while you die." A loud growl echoed.

"And that mate, is the snarl of the beast..." chortled the bleeding thug. "You can't save your son. He's already dead!"

A wolf lunged in, jaws snapping. The dagger in my hand swiftly cut the side of the dying chap's throat, fluid squirting in all places, appealing to the bloodthirsty wolf that assaulted its own master, pinning him down to the floor and taking a large bite out of the man's throat.

"Eejit! Some kind of loyalty your beast has. Fuckin' waste," I said, never pitying the dying.

My clenched fists shattered the glass wall to smithereens; and I leaped out through the broken glass, just as the building blew up.

I crashed onto the maid's quarter's rooftop, bounced, and slammed hard onto the grass in the bounds of the cottage.

I rose and raised my chin, gawking at the height of my plunge.

I made my way out into the open air when pelting bullets skidded past me.

A rapid volley of gunfire was unleashed.

Two more enforcers were firing, sequentially reloading as I jumped for cover, diving in the shades of high grass. I'd seen a motorcyclist turning the corner of Nephin Road. I dashed past a dirt field, yanked him off the Triumph Scrambler like a child, flung him off to some green pasture, jumped on the bike, and raced my way off down the adjoining street.

The hardchaw, yes, the man in the blue trench coat, and a second hardchaw he called "Liam" climbed into a sports vehicle—a silver Volvo hatchback with black rims. Tires burned the pavement as the car sped off while the enforcers fired away.

I bent sharply right onto the next street. The enforcers' V8 pursued and chanced a risky right. Cars honked madly.

I blipped—revved then released the throttle. The bike took off.

Two sheets of plywood had been propped at a forty-five-degree angle outside a house. Some kind of half built ramp structure. I heard the men's barks—cascades of fatal gunshots never ceasing. I advanced, straight for the plywood. The scrambler took off into the air, into empty space, and over the house's top.

Assassins launched a frenzied gunfire assault. I had landed in a back garden, raced my way out of the rear garden, the landlord's dogs woofing their lungs out.

I saw the blue trench coat fella that Liam called "Tadhg," in the passenger's seat, point, "Make a left!"

Liam turned the wheel and bent the paved street with a sharp tire-screeching left.

Liam was irritated, banging on the passenger airbag compartment. Liam said, "I don't see him."

"We'll flush him out!" Tadhg said, scanning the area.

Liam was gunning the hatchback when, from the left, I flung past, the car missing me by just a few meters. Liam slammed on the brakes and accelerated in reverse.

Even now shots flew past me.

I braked, clutched, shifted, and forced another right. The sports vehicle still in reverse drew near swiftly then halted for its passengers to look at the street where I had forked to find an empty road. From the turn of the road, I snuck a quick look. Liam slammed on the controls.

Tadgh pointed ahead, "Drive. Drive!"

"Where to? He's gone," argued Liam, irate.

"Just drive!" barked Tadgh.

The eight-cylinder tank-like engine roared. The car broke the speed limit, racing straightforward, on the narrow street when my frame came into view, from where my motorcycle crashed, a filthy pail in hand, and I pitched dirty water at the bloody windshield. The vehicle lost control, smashed against a massive industrial waste container.

A metal tube had impaled Liam's head, but even now he refused to give up the ghost. He bawled, shrieking from the depth of his lungs like a werewolf in agony. He pulled on the tube that gradually slid out of the hole in his bloody head, but it was too much, and it was then that death angels drew closer to claim his existence. *Bollocks!* was his final expression as he caved in and gave out his last breath.

Straight away, the trunk popped open. Tadhg's hand reached out from the passenger's window and released the door. He climbed out, marched to the back and grabbed two semiautomatic shotguns.

I jimmied into a Mini Cooper. I climbed into the vehicle and worked the engine to life.

Tadhg, looking like the *Terminator*, armed and cheesed off, opened fire, ejecting shells onto the cobbled pavement and squandering multiple cartridges with every trigger squeeze.

I took off.

Tadhg turned the previous corner and gave chase.

I floored the accelerator, and the Surbiton-born rear-engine marvel gripped the street and raced.

Tadhg entered from the adjacent street. I jammed on the gas. The coupé almost flew.

Tadhg shouldered one of the semiautomatics and with precision fired at one of the high-performance tires.

The car flipped into the air, landing on its roof, and skidded down the street at astoundingly high speed.

Facing the auto straight ahead was a cement platform paralleling the Liffey; the river that flowed through Dublin. I shouldered the door which never yielded. At the same moment that I glanced past the shattered windshield to the front, the car at once struck the curb, flipping midstream into empty space. I leaped out and dove into the water inches from the car that landed, almost burying me in the river.

Behind, Tadhg fired then calmly vanished when a Gardaí *two-bulb* siren approached.

# 43

I had been in the icy river—the Liffey—for a beat. Reeling back from the depth of the black pool where I'd been kept captive from the vacuum-like effect of the car's descent, I emerged and climbed back out to life on a busy street, unnoticed.

I hauled out the water-resistant mobile from my pocket and rang a number.

A beep—the cell forwarded the call to voicemail.

"I need a returned call right away. It's important. Hold..." I instructed into the cellular, while I searched the cell's recall. "A Belfast number. Four four oh two eight nine oh one eight triple oh one."

I hung up and lifted my damp chinos enough to peek at the tamper-resistant lethal weapon on my ankle. The tether was unmistakably still there. I'd known Detective Laughlin had been knowledgeable about my whereabouts from the radio frequency the bleedin thing emitted back to the Gardaí. And I'd been curious why he hadn't apprehended me following the fracas I had caused in the city. Nonetheless, I cared nothing of it. I was ready for him had he attempted to make an arrest. I was clear in my mind.

Moments later, inconspicuously, I exited a clothing store where I lifted a fresh set of wears.

I felt a vibration, then the receiver in my pocket rang. I picked up; it was Gilchrist.

"We've got a problem. The kidnappers left a note at the Shamrock. You've got forty-eight hours to endorse the document, or they kill Cody. That was twenty-four hours ago."

"Are you safe?" I asked.

"Yes."

"Séamus?"

"He's fine," assured Gilchrist. "We're at Granny's old cottage. Northside, Clontarf."

"I don't know who they are, but they tried to kill me—"

"Who'd bloody want to kill *Irish*?"

"I don't know. But I'll sort it out. Don't call unless I call you first."

"Irish..." said Gilchrist. "Doctor Dermod phoned. Test results from Cody's last visit came in. If he doesn't get an implant in forty-eight hours, his heart will stop—"

"Stay off the line," I said, then hung up.

I spotted an internet café nearby. I fast stepped into the place. I watched a lady leave her computer station for the jacks. I posted myself at the station. I figured I had approximately two minutes before she returned. Maybe less. My fingers went to work. I googled *Companies Registration Office of Ireland*.

A hit—grand. I performed a company search for Fharma Holdings.

Another hit. *Fharma Holdings*. My eyes scanned the profile, but there were no address details.

I sighed and thought for a moment. A new Google search of *Fharma Holdings* and *formation*. My fingers typed and scanned down then stopped midway.

Bingo.

An entry. A telephone number and a name, Barrister Simon Donagh. Listed as a high profile corporate counsel for an international commercial law practice, Walsh & Partners. All of my attempts at the hyperlink landed me on a page which no longer existed. I scribbled down the telephone number on a post-it note when the lady exited the jacks.

I walked off into the street where I phoned the number. A receptionist answered, "Hello, Walsh and Partners."

I went for it, "Ma'am. I need to speak to Barrister Donagh."

"Simon Donagh?"

"Yes. Specializes in company formation?"

"Oh, yes. The womanizer."

"Excuse me?"

"He's no longer with the firm. He pensioned off a few months back."

"Would you happen to have his direct contact? Or where I can find him?"

"If you can keep a secret," the woman hushed. "Can you?"

"It's a promise."

"That bastard," the woman said. "Try the Merrion Hotel. You can't miss him. He takes all his mistresses there."

"You've been a sweetheart."

"My pleasure."

I hung up the phone.

I had arrived at the five star Merrion Hotel on Upper Merrion Street in Dublin 2.

I duped a valet into believing his *fella* had endured a massive cardiac arrest. I was his long-lost nearest and dearest. In return, I'd offer to stand in while he'd visit his aul man at the Mater—*Ospidéalan Mater Misercordiae*. I'd been convincing and passed on that all telephone lines were busy. When he attempted the call, I was fortunate the hospital phone lines were in fact busy, which saved me from having to put him to sleep.

I was in a proper valet uniform greeting a moneyed patron, Barrister Donagh, and his blue-eyed, blond, young mistress exiting their vehicle, an impressive Maserati GranTurismo. Cherry interior. Seventy-two hundred rpm. A real bastard engine.

I thought how fair life had been that my chiseller needed a heart I couldn't afford while shams like this divil dropped cash on conspicuous consumption—*gobshite*.

The Irishman laid his keys and a danny boy on my palm. I climbed into the posh car and drove into the hotel's garage.

I scanned the vehicle for anything apparent. Nothing out of the ordinary. I hastily exited the car.

In the hotel garage, I punched the up button at the lift.

The steel door opened. I exited the garage into the lift.

Exiting the lift, I made my way into the private hotel suite where a young lady of the night, in lingerie, see-through black leggings adorned in square patterns, cuddled. There was no doubt she was a harlot, selling her goods to the highest bidder. Her beauty was unparalleled—a real bit of skirt, a mermaid among the living. That further enraged me. I thought it was possible she was a good girl at some point in her life with ambitions of her own, but that then life had been hard on her, forcing her to resort to selling her good nature to pedophiles with fat pockets and more money than they knew what to do with, so bored that they had to resort to such extramarital behavior to keep their egos happy. These were men that exploited young girls, possibly their own daughters' ages, which made them feel like kings and gods among peasants and those unable to do for themselves. She leisurely throbbed on top of the wealthy weathered-faced punter, gently caressing his temple, working through his fine hair. His eyes were covered in a sleep shade. He moaned eagerly—his behavior lechery—wanting naughtily to escalate to the next step, intercourse.

"Want my big *knob* ..."

In her Dutch accent, the whore worked her benefactor to arouse him, "You big *fella*—"

The rage I felt seeing her and thinking of Cody's disappearance brought me the strength and insanity to proceed with what I was going to do next.

I promptly hushed the lass who nearly jumped at my sight. I moved her away from the tycoon and hopped on the man's chest. My knees pinned against his shoulders, obstructing any ill measure by the criminal.

"What the bleedin hell?"

At that, I countered squarely, "Barrister Donagh. I don't have much time. My son is in great danger. I'll ask you one question which will determine if you get to live."

# 44

Men like Donagh knew of men like me—downright unwavering. Yet we were of the same make. Except on opposite ends, serving gods poles apart.

Barrister Donagh seized the sleep shade, attempting to remove it. I wasn't so docile when I detained his wrist.

"I wouldn't do that if I were you," I said irreverently.

"What do you want from me?" said the bewildered pervert.

"Fharma Holdings. You arranged its formation two years ago. I want to know who owns it and what kind of business they're in."

The cream of the crop's retort surprised me the least. Straight from the shoulder, I anticipated the rejoinder from the want-to-be tough guy.

"Whoever you are and whatever you seek, I don't care, but if you leave now, you will *live*."

The bravery of him was astonishing. A chap in a compromised position, blindly staring up at the mug of a huntsman bearing vengeance and zero forbearance for patronizing scum.

Did he know about me? Had he heard of Irish, the *Fighting Irishman?* A chap with the strength of the gods? A chap with the gift to crush skulls with his bare hands? The maker of Ireland's wicked and most lethal game—*Dead Mate Rugby?* One who'd played the game of gods in the depths of despair, a chap who had lost the tang of life and would lay his life on the line for the existence of his kin? A chap with a thirst for blood and revenge.

"Wrong," I answered to the man, blindfolded and glued to the king size bed. "You're not in a position to negotiate. I am. And I need an answer in three seconds, or I'll cut off that which is precious to your mistress."

I let the words hang a bit for more intense effect, just enough that he'd digest them. Process them in that psycho scumbag mind of his. Let it marinate. Make him aware of the repercussions of fucking with a fella with a death wish, one who'd kill just to be heard, one who'd seek the face of hell to save his chiseller. My effort had almost efficiently marinated, except the bloody whore had interrupted my brilliant performance.

"Please don't hurt him," she murmured from her point of view beside the regal custom-made silk curtains. "He's got a new heart."

I gazed back at the mistress.

"Excuse me?"

"He's my cash. If he dies, he's no good to me," said the whore to whom I acknowledged she'd been on the money. If the barrister gave up his ghost, he'd be of no further use to her, or to me. All my effort to locate Cody would have been in vain. So there was an incentive to keeping the bastard alive. He'd lead me to the villain who held my sprog hostage. Right now I held the upper hand. I would make him suffer slowly to get him to spill whatever confidences he kept in his head. Secrets of Cody's whereabouts. Secrets of things perhaps I ought not to know, which would render me a danger to whatever cloak-and-dagger circle he belonged to because I would then know too much. In due course that would turn me into a target, conceivably for the rest of my living days. I understood that, and with no holds barred I had settled with myself that'd be the price I'd pay for Cody's freedom. Cody's location was of greater consequence. The rest I'd attempt to flout, save for the fact that, I'd be born to a new existence— a new-found world I never knew was real—very real.

Fuck.

The price had to be paid. I had to know. *Except the whore must go.* That was the least I could do. Trade her life for mine. She was youthful and had plenty of life left to live. So long as she could clean up her act. Start brand new and never look back. She had to be gone—now!

I gazed at my side and pointed to the barrister's wallet.

"Take the money and leave. His wife won't miss it. There's plenty more where that comes from."

The streetwalker snatched the linchpin's wallet and took the

131

money—most of it. Without warning, the call girl tenderly kissed my rugged cheek, leaving a mark in cherry lipstick. Her scent made me choke; she reeked of cheap counterfeit Chanel, like the kind sold by nomadic road vendors for a quarter of the price. Yet all of this happened fast, and as she made for the exit, I knew what the kiss meant—perhaps she would chance her luck at a new life, one devoid of the demands of being someone's *bitch*. That felt grand. Except the barrister had forewarned:

"You're making a big mistake."

I was no longer up for the advice of counsel. I was the interrogator. I wanted to make it crystal clear. Hence I gave him a jab in the ribs, a jab that was meant to be a warning, hard enough he'd get the point. And he did; gasping for air.

"I'm running out of time. I'll kill you if I have to. Now Fharma Holdings. I need a name and address," I said calmly.

If he'd thought I was bluffing, he'd laugh-out-loud and stick me the finger. He knew better. That was best.

"All right," said Barrister Donagh, "I need to check my phone."

Master Hachirou's teaching had been ingrained in me.

"Irish, ten seconds. Again. Try again."

I could see how this would play out. He'd politely ask that I hand him the mobile. He'd punch his password and open his contact list. He'd pretend to pull Fharma Holdings while he'd, in fact, transmit an electronic mail to his security while whining for twenty minutes that the contact was in fact on a different phone—at his place of business, or better yet at his home office in a safe place. All the while his gang of tough guys would creep into the hotel lobby, rush up the emergency stairway, unnoticed, while avoiding area surveillance cameras and dismantling all emergency exits alarms as they made their way into the hallway, weapons ready, hidden beneath patrons' towels they'd sequester from hard working Bulgarian immigrants who they'd kill with bullets in their skulls. Then rough the door, surprise me and put two in my head and six in my chest.

I wasn't having that. Hence I brewed a strategy of my own.

"I'll do it. You'll give me the password."

The barrister must have been stupefied. His ruse had been utterly dismantled with no opportunity for reinforcement.

# 45

"Make it fast," I uttered, grabbing the cell by the elegant Celtic lamp on the cherry-finish nightstand.

"Password's *pussy*," said Barrister Donagh with a mortified grin to which I shook my head in disbelief.

The barrister was as deceitful as I'd imagined, wedded and with kids probably. I knew he was married from the rare and skillfully crafted artisanal platinum Claddagh wedding band on his ring finger. A true symbol of love, friendship, and loyalty, which connubial faith and vow he'd royally breached with great insolence in the arms of this hooker.

I'd known about his kin from the wallet photograph that found its way on the *sex* hotel carpet while Gisela, the hooker, had seized the chap's cash.

I entered the sinful password and logged on to the barrister's iPhone.

I flashed the mobile screen at my hostage, removing the sleep shade.

"What next?"

"Find the contacts icon."

I did.

"What now?"

"Enter Fharma. It'll bring up what you want," said Barrister Donagh.

My fingers worked swiftly. I'd typed fast enough that I'd dig up the information rather promptly. Plus my boundless angst brought me the speed and efficiency that only a person under these circumstances could achieve. I briefly thanked the universe for the acute anxiety. That felt grand when what I hunted for flashed on the mobile phone's screen before my eyes. I thought the barrister had done right by me. Had he not, I'd done much worse than what I was to do next.

"How easy was that?" I said with a sarcastic smirk.

I believe Barrister Donagh fully expected what was to happen subsequently.

In the twinkling of an eye, I grasped the chap's collars, with the back of my hands at opposite ends of his neck, in a sleeper hold, feeling his life and blood pulsing, and I squeezed while clenching the back of my hands together as I pulled on his top causing temporary oxygen saturation.

Barrister Donagh was out in seconds. I knew the blood choke was momentary. His carotid arteries would in time expand, his brain would flood with O2, and he'd regain consciousness shortly. So I had to carry on the high-speed action. Just then I noticed a long and freshly healed scar down the bastard's sternum. One that appeared to be a vertical inline incision—a median sternotomy, one where the sternum had been cracked to access the heart and lungs for whatever patch-up they required.

I was reminded of Cody and his diseased myogenic muscular organ.

Why had this man recently undergone corrective surgery?

I was a strong bloke. Even so, my stomach twisted into knots, which caused me to nearly gag. Save for the fact that I had to hold it together for Cody. He needed me most. Still, I realized a mistake I made was to put Donagh out ahead of grilling him on the matter. But I hadn't the time for an inquest. I had the information I needed, and I was to decipher the mystic conundrum on my own.

I flung the mobile on the informant's chest, punishing him some more, after jotting down a name and address for Fharma Holdings that was unfamiliar to me. Yet naturally, these unfamiliarities had become a common trait of the mysterious world I pursued in search for Cody. I was aware I hadn't seen the last of it. I figured there'd be more like it.

I grabbed Donagh's wallet, extracted the last of the currency Gisela hadn't seized, and I headed for the door.

In the hallway, I snatched Ishka *spring* water jugs, splashed my face, wiped off Gisela's lipstick from my cheek, and consumed the remainder, which rejuvenated my organs.

I pressed the lift's down arrow button, which lit up. I then heard footsteps. The room service attendant, in black chinos and black top with short sleeves with a slick black bun updo, who had delivered a meal to one of the guest rooms, exited into the hallway to reel the pushcart to the opposite door and provide meals to more hotel patrons.

Very soon, the attendant would make it to Donagh's room. I forgetfully left the do-not-disturb hanger inside the barrister's room.

Now the lady attendant was knocking on his door and turning the knob. Best if no one knew I had been here.

Just as the hotel worker crossed the threshold into Donagh's room, the lift opened wide. I quickstepped inside and pressed 'P' for Parking.

When the lift opened onto the parking level, I remembered I had kept the barrister's car keys. I pressed a key that forced the alarm on the Maserati to light up the darkened underground carport.

Dreaming of driving one of these had never entered my mind. Perhaps as Europe's kickboxing champion. But it hadn't happened. I retired after Aidan's death, at what the public and Dublin media considered the defining moment in my career, a time that would have elevated me among the elite of the sport. Money was no longer to be the object of my worries. Alas, with Aidan's death, all these seem so fruitless. I had quietly walked away, never looking back.

As a worker for *Conor & Fishing Co.*, the dream of ever owning one of these sports vehicles was utterly a castle in the sky.

It followed that, in some twisted way, I thought of Butcher, my bastard mortgagee, and then of Cody and his heart.

My brain had been zoning out; wandering a bit. So my thoughts weren't too sharp for a second till I forced my mind to focus.

I was reminded that time hadn't been a friend—*Cody!*

My son's remembrance pumped the adrenaline through my veins. Enough to regain my spirit.

Hence, I jumped into the patron's sports vehicle. I switched the ignition on. The robust engine roared as I revved to ready its compression gates.

I had a name and address—O'Laoghaire—North Dublin.

I was to find Cody.

Tires skidded, blazing across the pavement and leaving marks of ghost tire tracks behind.

I was headed for Cody's takers.

# 46

The Maserati GranTurismo pulled up to the side of a mansion in the countryside—just shy of the boundaries of Dublin, yet local enough that I'd have not a worry about Detective Laughlin's lethal contraption on my ankle to consequentially activate.

I scanned my surroundings.

A grouping of stunning gently sloping sea-green hills, with neat multi-million euro homes and farmhouses that spread out uniformly across Gaelic lands. They were indisputably not *nouveau riche*, but old money.

I checked the address against my note.

I blew out a breath of relief, yet I was still filled with butterflies.

The address checked out, except there was something peculiar about this place. In some way, I remembered being here before. I searched my soul and could not bring up any information about the memory of this place. Nevertheless, I trusted my photographic memory. There was a reason. Had my remembrance of this been a déjà vu or just something of a real memory recollection? I just couldn't pinpoint precisely how or why. Had I been here in the physical or the mental? In my dreams, perhaps. I couldn't remember. Why had this home been memorable when its occupant, its address, and the name 'Fharma Holdings' had no connection at all in my mind? Not a single connection to my current and prior life—whatever that meant.

Enough, Irish.

I had to find an entry to the unknown manor.

Promptly, I hopped out of the barrister's car. I progressed stealthily, looking for somewhere I could break in without a shatter of high-priced treated lowlight glass window.

Following my forced entry, I crossed the threshold into a finely ornamented home office.

I glanced over pictures of a handsome—prejudicially criminal-free—couple who were in all the photographs lining the wall.

I wondered why such a cheery couple was serving the Devil in a manner of speaking. I wasn't sold by their make-believe smiles. In spite of everything, they'd been associated with Fharma Holdings, the only link to Cody.

In my mind, the pair was responsible for Cody's disappearance. And for all it's worth, I had made up my mind to slay the bastards after extracting from them my son's exact location.

A fast but sore death awaited them.

One detail was certain, I didn't recognize their faces, and I'd been lost in the authentic texture of their joyful grins. Nonetheless, some way, their faces seemed well known.

I had to find out more.

I unlocked a center drawer from the reddish-brown desk and was searching it when I sensed a presence crowding me.

Someone was standing right behind me.

I knew this from the staunch smell of rot and the tobacco that reeked of the goon's breath.

The intruder to my personal space, as it were, although I was *trespasser* to his lair, swiftly announced his intent:

"I've been diagnosed with a rare form of Parkinson's disease. So my finger won't hold much longer on the trigger. You've got two seconds to tell me what you're doing here... take longer, and you're a dead fella."

I had to see my assailant. I had to see his eyes when I was done punishing his bloody bones following his torture with multiple deadly blows from my vengeful fists.

Yet from the hoarseness in his voice, I recognized the chap was upwards of eighty or ninety years of age. Perhaps even throat cancer judging from the excessive coughs. A much older man than the gentleman in the picture.

Hence, I could frankly slaughter his shell with my back turned if that'd be his choice.

In spite of that, I felt I had to face the *dodgy bloke.*

Promptly, I turned to face a butler in a brushed-cotton flannel shirt with low-back denim overalls and garden boots—hands shaking.

The manservant struggled to keep erect a twelve gage thirty-six-inch barrel bolt-action goose shotgun while he aimed it at my skull.

His diagnose had been on the nail. Surely it had been Parkinson's disease. The lanky chap must have been living his last days. He could barely move, and when he did, he was all but steady.

All my bitter judgment dissipated. Somehow, I knew this mate meant no harm. Maybe he could offer a clue or two about Cody.

It was best to get on with it.

"My son was kidnapped two days ago. The only clues to his where-abouts point to this place." The man stared at me blankly. I gathered he needed to hear more. Bring him up to speed.

"The couple in those pictures. They must be the O'Laoghaires?"

The man lowered his gun.

"They are," said the butler then he paused and looked down as if to bless the dead with the sign of the cross.

"Are they dead?" I said, anxiety quickly re-entering my bloodstream.

"Both died six months ago."

The life in me almost bled dry with the thought that the only link to my son had been shattered months before Cody's kidnapping.

*Had this been planned ahead? Had the kidnappers known I'd get this far, and eradicated all clues that would lead me to them?*

I felt as though I was losing my mind, and fast.

"Car accident," the aged houseman said, "still under investigation. A suspected homicide."

A murder?

Why had the O'Laoghaires been suspected victims to a bloody murder?

Questions that flooded my mind were left unanswered.

Uncertainty followed...

"It was all over the news. They were a high profile couple, a High Court judge and a stellar plastic surgeon," the butler said.

I nodded calmly while I battled to answer a thousand questions and more. I now remembered where I had seen the O'Laoghaires' manor and the couple's memorable faces—RTÉ News Now.

Yet, I considered, surely this servant must have heard something.

"Does Fharma Holdings ring a bell?" I said, evenly.

"No."

To which I nodded once more.

"Forgive me, sir, but you can't stay here. This place will be auctioned off today," said the rickety gent when I spotted a torn envelope in the bin.

I recognized Abel's trustee company's slogan, "Your future. Our care."

*Fuck.*

Abel was linked to the O'Laoghaires, but I understood it to be a trail gone cold—he was dead. The kidnappers had been ahead of me, ensuring me of no further contact to pursue my own inquiry.

"All personal effects were turned over to their trustee," said the butler. "There's nothing else here."

I believed he was telling the truth. He'd looked me right in the eyes throughout. He hadn't at the slightest instance fidgeted or broken a sweat: not even a tiny bit of nervousness in his delivery.

"Thanks for not blowing my head off," I offered.

"Wish I could be of more help," the old man said and gave me a weak yet genuine grin.

"*Sir, dea-lá.*"

"Good day." I bade him well, and left more bemused and depressed than I'd come in.

# 47

On my way to the Maserati, I suffered a sudden panic attack, a reminder of ghostly memories and realities I was unable to escape. In vain I tried blinking off those memories to focus on Cody. Nothing gave. I had lost my ma at the young age of five. At the advice of my M.D.—a pediatric specialist with the responsibility to manage my sanity and the emotional wellbeing of my aul man—I had been heavily drugged following my ma's death, which resulted in losing all memory of most of my childhood as if it was a vacant black hole. I remembered nothing.

The fear of the unknown had suddenly gripped me and shook me to the core.

Will Cody live?

In quick succession, I had lost Aidan, Jack, and Hannah without a chance to grieve properly. *Had the Man above dared to test me beyond my loss of faith?* I had no further intention of becoming once again his loyal adherent. He had failed me completely and utterly. He would have had to raise the dead should he want my regained faithfulness.

Fear of Cody dying forced me to collapse to the ground at the same time as my brain suffered a debilitating migraine-prone vision. It was otherworldly, yet felt as real as my intense trepidation.

I felt my heart being compressed with every attempt to stop it dead.

I saw *Taller* once more. Yes, the lad in my former visions, drowning in the stream, his face hazy to my eyesight. He was drowning as before, except for one further factor—his hands were hot crimson-gold flames.

I never jumped out of the protracted trance, but I did gasp for oxygen as the air within my lungs dissipated with each increasingly larger burning flame. It was as real as if it was happening right in front of me.

Was this a sign that Cody's life had ended?

What the bloody hell did these visions signify?

I wondered once more if the Man above had been so displeased with me that he had resorted to prosecuting me. I searched my soul long and hard. In all my life, I hadn't done any wrong to any living soul. In fact, my limited existence had been filled with grand deeds.

Why then was *He* on my ass?

I shook off my spiritual deliberation and tried to regain my sense of calm, to concentrate on saving Cody through fire and water, when the *divil's* cell phone in my hand buzzed.

It was time to face my son's takers yet again.

The mechanized robotic voice was mordant and undoubtedly made its point.

"Well done on locating the foundation of Fharma Holdings. Quite evident. Owned by the O'Laoghaires. There are nominee corporations, trusts and more persons involved than you can ever imagine. Of course, you are too self-important to endorse a simple record and save your *gasún*. Instead, you squander valuable time chasing ghosts. Why don't you try saving your son for a change? Endorse the record and your son lives, and yes you'll die. But you'll die knowing you saved a life for once."

He had a point.

"What do you *really* want?"

"Return to the city. Further instructions will follow," said the voice.

With this last bit of command, which had left me feeling like the kidnapper's flunky, I had wrongly assumed the exchange had ended.

There was more.

"A piece of advice," said the bastard.

"You have my attention."

"Take your medicine."

Then the connection went dead.

I thought, *Bloody hell. How had he known?*

# 48

My head spun. Each time I'd have a vision; my bloody brain would ache like a billion pins jabbed at my cranium—more so in the bounds of my skull. The hurt was so intense I could barely set eyes on the road ahead. And now, I suffered a minor nose-bleed which I wiped away with the back of my hand.

The forty-two hundred plus cubic centimeter V8 engine I navigated meandered the countryside road and into the city of Dublin, where busy streets exhibited no mercy and called for precise driving or else collision. I had no time for a motor vehicle pileup. I had to be in the business district, at the ready for Cody's takers' further instructions.

The bloody migraine was utter agony, repeatedly beating my head at every chance, reminding me how I had failed to feed its own addiction with prescription meds. Somehow I was offended by the alien migraine. It had engulfed me, manifesting itself from nothingness. More so I was cheesed off at Dr. Lorcan who had turned me into a freak, a med-addict. Perhaps I had been a mediocre patient and had deviated from the good doctor's strict orders to take the meds in sets of two at appropriate times. I couldn't remember if I did or not. The bloody pounding in my skull was just too painful. It was eradicating all possible opportunities for my applying logic, to think clearly.

But again, I was Irish: Cain Angus Seamróg, the Fighting Irishman, the chap with the rare knack: a gift from the gods to achieve heroic deeds. It was the strength of Samson and more.

I parked hastily in an empty space on Ellis Quay facing Dalbhach Pharmacy in Dublin city center.

I opened the vehicle's heavy driver's-side door, my head pounding.

I flung my body out of the automobile, falling to the footway, only to get back up, shutting the door behind me, and make my way to the drug store's entrance, all the while bumping into people who marched into my unpredictable walking lane as I staggered toward my destination, grasping my skull.

Suddenly I felt as if I was suffocating. I halted and tried to breathe. Air wasn't reaching my lungs, and the pounding in my head wasn't letting up.

I entered the chemist's, past drug aisles.

I forced my legs to move rapidly as I made my way to the counter, but still, each step felt as slow as an old man on a walker. Finally, I arrived at the counter where I'd get my meds and rid myself of this calamity, this cancer that had dragged to a halt my daring act to find Cody.

I was relieved at the sight of the apothecary in his pallid lab coat working carefully behind the counter. Soon, I'd regain control of my senses to redeploy my get-up-and-go to saving my son, Cody.

I tapped the chrome service counter call bell ring, fixed firmly by the flip-up countertop door.

The druggist stared at me, annoyed. I couldn't understand it.

Why was he so irritated at serving the people he had solemnly pledged to aid? Wasn't it the purpose of attending pharmacy school, after all, to help those afflicted in need to satisfy their man-made drug addictions? Not merely to be clad in a lab coat and end up in the register of pharmaceutical chemists?

I understood one thing very plainly from my secondary school psychology course. Folks at all times veered to those who fed their egos, even if they cared nothing for them. As long as their egos were fed, people diverted to suck-ups like a moth to a flame, approximating wild spreading cancer.

Those were people with a low sense of worth, lacking significant public attention.

My aul man had a saying:

"Feed a man's ego, and you'll inherit their riches for a thousand years."

The difference was I was no suck-up. What was more, my hemicrania hadn't let up. Hence, I wanted my meds.

"I need Seroton."

"Prescription," retorted the chemist. I showed my prescription bottle.

"Please help... " I said, my brain burning.

"Come back when you have one," he said, boorishly.

The self-important chemist walked away, dismissing even my presence.

My head boiled in persistent hurt. All the while my rage had been rising. All the more reason the *fuck* should have been listening and catering to my every need. On the contrary, he had disappeared; moving onwards past the multitude of shelves bearing all sorts of prescription meds.

"Please," I said calmly, aware it was a two ways chance. But there was always plan B. One I'd hate to rely on, with the exception that my brain had, by now, made up its mind. Its addiction had to be filled in any way.

"Come back when you've got your prescription," barked the pharmacy, *Johnny Ray*.

I concluded that the apothecary was more interested in being in control, pompous, than to help meet my needs.

I had heard enough and with no holds barred, for Cody, all rules had to be broken. I barked back at him:

"I'll just have to get it myself."

He grabbed a phone and punched 9-9-9 for Garda's immediate response—"stay calm, stay focused and stay on the line"—when in the blink of an eye, I was on him and knocked him unconscious, which took longer than expected. The chap was *obese*. It was no wonder. With barely half the populace keeping fit, it was no wonder fatness ran rampant. And I'd be damned if the chap hadn't been on some current man-made ailment meds. Perhaps he had even *nicked* them from his own employer. I wouldn't put it past him. Eyes never told a fib, and he had those eyes, the ones of a worker who from time to time had taken advantage of their multinational. Then again with the bloody cost of pharmaceuticals, I couldn't feel sorry for his proprietor. The company had been making cash from people's dire sickness, sometimes expanding profit margins and forcing the unwell into their own demise, forever penniless. Greed had been at the core of every thinkable curative venture it seemed. "By the sweat of your brow" had come to mean nothing more than a system that enslaved the masses, like addicts, as we could not properly function devoid of our *fix*. Yes, today's meds were our dependency—our fuel.

I laid the chap's body on the carpeted floor, the act causing further trauma to my head as if my cortex was ablaze.

I hurried through medicine-fortified aisles, knocking down meds that were not Seroton, causing a wave of parachuting bottles that hit the floor reminiscent of ammo dropped in war zones in times of great war.

At last, my eyes settled on the drug that gave me the balance I needed to think clearly—Seroton.

I seized the container, popped it open and swallowed a ton of pills, contrary to doctor's orders.

I then left more than enough cash on top of the druggist's torso to cover the charge for my tablets.

I hopped out of the barricade that fenced off the inner sanctum and marched back past aisles of more drugs when my fingers lost their grip on the medicine bottle that fell to the floor and rolled forward.

A boot, polyurethane sole, black leather, knee-high, blocked the bottle's advance on the fake Chinese terracotta floor. The boot belonged to one of four building security guards that appeared from nowhere, built like machines; decent in pasty, long-sleeved, unisex security shirts and polyester double hook rubberized waistband trousers: two by the exit door, two behind me.

"On the fuckin' floor!" thundered the lead, leveling a nine-millimeter semiautomatic handgun.

"You better let me pass. I've got a bad dose," I said evenly.

"On the floor. Face down!" settled the arrogant bastard. They wanted a brawl, and they had it coming. I wasn't holding back.

I observed the pack. I gazed at my watch, every tick reminding me of time lost, then I leaped forward.

One fired. I swiftly grabbed the firearm and drove a blow to the man's jaw. He fell to the floor, comatose. The second man had been wounded by the first shot, and he was howling. The third man went cataleptic with a front snap boot to the sternum, sending him flying back to crash against shelves with great force. A reverse foot-thrust to the temple of the fourth chap's skull ended the fight immediately.

Four guards down for the count, and not a break of skin on my part.

I was born with a rare knack, and this was only a tiny window to my ability. Bear with me; you'll come to understand.

I repossessed the container of Seroton from the floor, pocketed it, and scarpered.

Vengeance in my soul grew with every obstacle. Cody's takers still had the upper hand and had me tamed, subduing my rage, like the suck-up they'd wanted me to be.

# 49

I stormed out of the drug store into the busy Dublin streets, climbed into my car and got out of there. I'd been used to razzers who'd been tempted with the idea of subduing the masses. But mostly I pitied them for trying my talent, as they always ended up in compromised conditions: as a rule, with broken limbs.

I pulled up in an empty parking lot outside a pub near Essex Quay. It was still daylight, and I wondered if Cody was still alive. I was exhausted and losing options quickly.

I slammed the wheel, clearly disappointed by my latest act. *Was I turning into a guttie? Was I becoming the chaps that had taken my son? Was I that callous to put four family men, who were maybe fathers and husbands hard at work to put cash on the table to feed their family, in provisional crutches? Was I now Irish the Bastard?*

*Shite.*

In contrast, I thought of Cody and his brittle heart. His knee braces.

Those men. Those four guards. If they had simply stepped aside, perhaps I'd have shown them mercy. I was after the tough guys who had taken my son hostage, and I was in no position to spend hours explaining why I had been looking for Seroton. I just needed it.

Hence, bringing the chaps to their willful and empirical demise was utterly by circumstance and not by choice. I'd been obliged to inflict pain on those that obstructed my advance in my greatest pursuit to save Cody.

I put it to the back of my mind, and relaxed, sighing deeply. But there was no such thing as rest when one was in search of an abducted child. And I was reminded of it when the mobile phone buzzed. I grabbed it and answered.

"Glad you're finally taking my advice."

I was confused for a moment, but then the voice continued.

"The medicine, it's helping."

How had he known? It aggravated me, although I had to hold it together, to show I was in control. But I wondered if he had someone following me. I had to know.

"Are you tailing me?" I said calmly.

"You're breathing better," said the mechanized voice.

"So, you're a doctor!" I said, then not confident if this was wise. An imprudent selection of words could end Cody's life.

"We're running out of time. In ten hours your son is dead. And that blood is on your hands," said the voice.

He had me by the balls. I wasn't sure what to say next, but it was worth a try. By chance, he'd take the bait.

"I'll endorse the record. But I want a face-to-face, or I won't—"

The worst possible development I feared, happened. The cellular phone in my hand went dead.

# 50

I felt dead. I had dared the Devil, and he had seized the moment. At this point, I regretted my feat. A truly uncalculated *tactical*—I thought at that instant—effort that'd get my only existing youngster dead and buried.

Had I been so grandly foolhardy to dare the psycho with the power to take Cody's life? How foolish had I been to test the fiend's forbearance?

I had to be calm. I had to make believe I had remained in control of my sanity for Cody's sake.

Once more I wondered if I had blown it. Surely, the dead tone on the abductor's mobile phone was significant?

I slammed my head on the controls, acknowledging I had been too aggressive in my unyielding approach. After all, he was the one with the upper hand. The demands were not mine to be made. Instead, I was to be the attentive listener and bow to fate in the hopes of seeing my child alive again. Truth be told, I had blown any further opportunity to recover Cody.

Cody.

I clutched my chest, with each breath harder to take. Anxiety was creasing my face when the silent cell on the passenger's seat rang again.

A second chance?

An opportunity to make it right. An opportunity to redeem myself.

Though, I reasoned, redeem myself of what, if all I had done was a modest aul man to Aidan and Cody, a faithful spouse to Hannah and a civil son to Jack Seamróg?

Nevertheless, I'd settle to be pardoned from my brash act. This was a fact. I was ready to bury the hatchet, as you might say.

"Hello," I muttered, feeling somewhat spineless, lacking grit.

"You're breathing hard again," said the mechanized voice, to which I said nothing. I was planning on playing good shepherd.

"I make the rules. You follow."

I boiled inside to tell the bloody wanker to kiss my ass, but I knew better now than to blow my chance of seeing Cody alive. I was aware that part of being a good victim was to allow the aggressor, at the right moment, to feel on top of things and to have ultimate power. Accordingly, I played along.

"I'm listening," I said with a bit of grace.

The computerized voice chuckled, which sounded more like a brief static clanging than a human expression. Yet I knew what the chortle meant: an articulation that was intended to enrage me further, except I knew better now. I was trained—as it were—to be Cody's takers' tamed puppy, something the tosser enjoyed grandly.

"You are bold. I will give you that face-to-face."

I had taken part in his game and had won, at least for the time being. So I said nothing. I was to play coward and listened silently.

"Half an hour. Corner of Cathedral and O'Connell. A green waste bin. You'll find a box. Follow the instructions." The voice paused.

"I'm listening," I said, ensuring that he knew I hadn't left. And I was aware he had been in control and that any miscalculation on my part would never happen again.

"Follow the instructions!" the voice underscored.

"You have my word," I assured.

"No deviation. Call the police or tell anyone, and your child will be put in the ground alive."

The voice paused for a second time.

I quickly glanced at my watch...

"You've got twenty-nine minutes now."

The phone went dead, something that I had strangely become accustomed to...

The automobile's engine had sprung to life ahead of the cell going dead.

I threw the gear in reverse when a throng of Garda two-bulb near Essex Quay surrounded my vehicle.

*Fuck.*

A siren sounded, and lights flickered. Gardaí, weapons drawn, aimed at the back of my stolen Maserati. Another mistake. The thought did cross my mind at the sight of Gardaí; I should have disposed of the vehicle in advance. Yet part of me had fallen in love with the Italian luxury car, a clear contrast from the banger I usually drove.

When I spotted Detective Laughlin climb out of his sedan, I realized the infraction of the stolen car should have been the least of my worries. Laughlin had been tracking me from the bloody shackle on my ankle. And just now, when I needed to be left alone, he had shown his bleedin face.

The kidnappers had been clear...

*Call the police or tell anyone, and your child will be put in the ground alive.*

The mechanized voice banged against my skull once more with a long-lasting thud that very nearly caused me to gag.

Given the current circumstances, I'd already brewed a scheme of my own to free myself from the guards. I'd lie, providing a false tip I'd receive that would send Laughlin and his task force on a fruitless errand, while I headed to location X to rescue my only breathing son. I was sure of my plan and I'd known the egotistical detective would take the bait as he'd be more interested in cracking the case for added prominence than anything else.

And forthrightly, I had only seconds to deliver my pitch, as time wasn't an ally. Detective Laughlin walked over to the driver's side of the car. He knocked twice on the window, which I rolled down at once.

I was ready to deliver my sermon, except Laughlin beat me to the punch.

"We found your son's body. You must come down to the morgue."

My heart plunged into my belly like a thousand bricks. My veins chilled to rime. Cody had been found. My only son dead. Dead. His cadaver laid in wait in a bloody mortuary while I rummaged around the city in vain to set him free.

Had I let my own kid down?

How had this happened?

Had the kidnappers been playing the fool's game all along?

I hadn't the slightest answer to my queries. The fact was my beloved Cody was dead. Gone. Bloodless. Bereft of life. No!

*Was Cody really dead?*

Surely, Laughlin was an expert, and he'd been accustomed to these procedures. He'd been skilled at identifying the dead after systematic examinations of their medical records. He maintained an outstanding track record, never missed a beat. He had ID'd Cody, and he'd been sure of it.

Cody was dead.

# 51

We arrived at the provisional city mortuary, at the O'Brien Institute, Malahide Road, Dublin 3, by the intersection of Griffith Avenue.

The trip to the O'Brien Institute, led by Detective Laughlin and members of the Gardaí in a convoy of XC70 special motor vehicles, had taken us a shocking five minutes, which meant I had approximately twenty minutes left to make the rendezvous with the kidnappers who had killed my son. I was intent to make the meeting. But first I had to ID Cody—an act I despaired about—and then, one way or another, find a way out of the place to meet the hostage-takers for a gathering of certain bloodshed.

I only had room in my mind to think of this malice while we drove to Dublin City Morgue. I had reasoned with the captors and followed their lead's instructions. I had played their bloody game, the role of a tamed puppy. I had played gutless to the point of feeling I had lost my honor, all for Cody's sake, for Cody to stay alive. Surely, the hijacker must have heard the subjugation in my voice. I hadn't called anyone. I hadn't called the Gardaí. I hadn't deviated from the plan. Assurance had been given by the hostage-takers that Cody had been alive and well.

Why then had the bastards taken me for a ball-bag?

I tried to think, to understand what could have perhaps gone wrong.

For sure—all of this—couldn't possibly be about a pub. *Had the Shamrock been so precious to them to provoke the murder of my family? Why had it—the Shamrock, a birthright from my ancestors passed on for many generations of Seamrógs—been so valuable to the kidnappers?*

Perhaps I had missed an angle. Perhaps I had not done my research properly. I hadn't asked Abel, my aul man's late trustee, the proper question. At the time, I had been more concerned about the inheritance of a bit of cash, to cure Cody of his disease and hopefully maybe some left-over to support us monetarily, than anything else. I hadn't thought about the Shamrock. *How the bloody hell was I to expect the unexpected?*

Surely no one else—existing business—had been forced to sign over their establishment? I was aware that landed property on Fleet Street was hard to come by and that most operations in the neighborhood had been pretty successful. Perhaps the kidnappers had relied on forcing my father to sell but murdered him in the process. And I was next until we were all dead, then the estate would be compelled to liquidate through a public estate auction at which point the gang could forcibly acquire the Shamrock.

But this process would still require that they cough up cash, which it seemed they weren't willing to do as they'd outright made a request of me to sign the tavern in whole to Fharma Holdings, one hundred percent as I recalled it. Free and clear with no other ownership, as it were.

Apparently, there was more to my misfortune than the eye could see. Nothing was straightforward. Nothing clear but utter confusion. I'd been in a maze of mayhem, and all my kin had been slaughtered in succession.

But I wasn't giving up. I'd soon have the opportunity to avenge the death of my folks in the most brutal fashion. I made up my mind that I'd hunt the bastards who brought death to my doorstep until the breath in me wilted.

At that moment, I thought of Cody. Tears sprung from my eyes. Surely, Cody couldn't be dead? I figured something must have gone really wrong. Perhaps the shot that was to keep his heart alive hadn't been administered in time. I was certain the kidnappers needed him breathing. That way they'd maintain the upper hand. Breathless, they'd know my purpose would waste away. Yet they'd also know I would seek revenge without end.

So why kill the kid?

It made no sense at all. I reasoned it must have been an accident, regardless; I was to deliver justice soon after offering Cody a proper Gaelic farewell.

Detective Laughlin, the mortuary's chief pathologist and I crossed the threshold into the chamber of the dead in the bowels of the institute.

The place was as bare as a vacant storeroom.

The four walls appeared more confined than the eyes conceived. A cramped cement block room. Perhaps it was the claustrophobic sensation I felt, which forced this alien perception of my examination. Perhaps it was the fear that rushed through my bones. My thoughts had been cloudy at best.

There was the smell of hoarfrost. My tongue was caked and dry, my body chilled to icicles as if no flesh and bare bones. I thought there might be the smell of rotten corpse, but there was nothing. The place was immaculate, not a drop of filth anywhere. It was as plain as a bare sheet of white snow.

The mortuary's chief pathologist's calm voice, as if respecting the dead, brought me back. He had been briefing Detective Laughlin and myself inside the icebox.

Large drawers lined the silvery wall. Each drawer had been built with a latch that when pulled, released the thick door, which then gave way to the inner recesses of the refrigerator, an interim resting place for the dearly departed. The idea that Cody was dead haunted me once more.

I wanted to know, with my own eyes as witness, if it was true, to be sure. But I also wanted this to end quickly, as a lingering progression would, without a doubt, send me to the depths of depression.

The chief pathologist's numbed facial expression crossed my weary eyes. He had been numbed from thirty years of going through the motions with countless families that had lost loved ones in sudden, unexplained, violent and unnatural ways. He had been charged with informing affected families on the condition of the dead under strict supervision of the coroner's office whose responsibility had been medicolegal investigations of certain deaths.

All the same, I was convinced he had once been more sympathetic and that the demands of this monotonous and delicate job had turned his compassion into hardened coldness.

"We found him this morning in an alley. His heart was removed at the time of death, I imagine," alleged the pathologist.

I looked away at the thought of Cody's body in a shabby alley. How could the kidnappers have been so merciless? I thought how I'd not return the favor when I found them, making them wish our paths never crossed.

"Post-mortem exam?" enquired Detective Laughlin.

"Possibly in two to three weeks. Perhaps more. We have a backlog, and we're short staffed."

I could not believe my ears, but I remained calm. Laughlin reflected for a moment.

"There's more," said the pathologist.

I gazed back at the chap, so did the detective.

"The inquest has been stalled."

"Why?" I queried.

"Seems there is no interest to pursue it—"

"Why? The child died a sudden and quite unnatural death," said Laughlin.

"Hell if I know. Perhaps same reason as postmortem. Short staffed and bullshite bureaucracy. All I know is there's been no rush on this. Everyone's playing busy," said the chief pathologist.

The city's system of governance was yet another issue. I wasn't sure if there was more to it or simply bloody red tape. I'd known Dublin City Coroner's Court had been slow in processing.

At present nothing mattered. Not an autopsy. Not an inquest. Not even judicial or divine justice. The only thing that mattered my settling of scores.

The detective nodded, thanking the pathologist who turned his attention to me.

"Mr. Seamróg. You may come back another time if you'd rather—"

"Which one?" I said evenly.

The chief pathologist pointed to one of the drawers.

"Three fifteen," he said, forcing a compassionate grin, which was not convincing.

"I'll be right outside should you need me, detective," he added, to which the detective nodded. Then he walked out.

Laughlin and I waited a moment. I guess he'd been waiting for me, actually. Offering me the opportunity to compose myself and be in charge of my emotions. I then took a step forward.

Detective Laughlin stopped me, a hand gently placed on my shoulder.

"Let me do it," he said.

# 52

Ten minutes was left to still make rendezvous with the kidnappers. Because Cody died in their custody, it was all the more important to make the meeting. There was still an opportunity to get to them before they'd vanish forever.

Accordingly, I never argued about Detective Laughlin leading the way. Every second counted.

Laughlin, his left thumb and index fingers rubbing his chin, marched to drawer three fifteen, then halted and gazed back at me with a gentle nod.

At that moment, the detective delicately pulled the latch, which unfastened the metal door gasket. A cloud of cold mist emerged, crowding Laughlin's mug.

The instant the fog cleared, Detective Laughlin extracted the stainless steel corpse tray, which easily rolled on small roller wheels, as a fog of ice continued to escape the depths of the freezer to the outer atmosphere of the cold chamber.

The clang of the tray being pulled, in a symphonic hum, raised high every one of my heartbeats.

When the fog of ice vacated yet again, a tiny frozen body lay on the corpse tray. My spirit sank deeper. My high heartbeat clearly audible as if my core would burst out of my chest. It became impossible to breathe, like being garroted.

Small spectacles of crystal frost shimmered from corner to corner on the dead body, like a frozen animal. The cadaver had been naked. Like at birth.

I unhurriedly gazed at the child's face. I gasped; it was Cody.

Following a proliferation of arcane fatalities and human error in accurately cataloging the deceased, Dublin city's Coroners Court, alongside Dublin city lawmakers, put into operation a system of identifying the dead with Biometric ID. Morgue patients had ID tags tied to their big toe which contained the unique data and was scanned with a biometric security device. I never bought the idea of the City's *"proliferation in arcane fatalities and human error."* It was business as usual. A big name, someplace, was profiting immeasurably from this affair, almost certainly a primary supplier of the bloody device. Benefiting from the dead, like the unborn, was big business, where the sky was the limit. At this point, I didn't care. It was the Gardaí's quandary, not mine. I was here for one reason and one only: to ID my son, Cody. An act I loathed, but it had to be done. I had to be sure. Cody's eyes were closed, as were his carbon-shaded lips, which had once born a pink of health. His body was ashen, stiff, and unscented. I approached Cody's cadaver. There, my son lay still as if frozen in time. A long and profound scar lined his sternum. The cavity had been stitched for better presentation. I assumed the work of a surgeon under the City Coroner's advice.

"I'm sorry for your loss."

I sensed the authenticity in his voice, but I knew better; he wasn't finished.

"But in my book, you are the number one suspect," said Detective Laughlin. I ignored the second half of his delivery. I was thinking how odd it had been that my tears had declined to well up, and after a brief moment of deliberation, I finally understood why.

"That is not my son," I said, with one hundred percent certainty. There were no imprints on this child's knees where knee braces would have pressed against the skin. Yet the features and all that is Cody was there in the flesh.

"Pardon me?" said Laughlin, turning to face me. His eyes locked with mine.

"That's not Cody."

I was firm now. It wasn't Cody. I was sure of it. I couldn't explain why. I just knew it wasn't my son.

"The physical profile from his health record, the weight, matches this body exactly... your son, definitely," said the detective.

"That's not Cody," I said evenly.

I was doing the staring now. My eyes piercing through his. He must have felt the sincerity in them. Yet he'd been the bastard detective always on high alert and seeking outlaws to fill his hall of fame and claim him further glory.

"How fitting," said the detective.

"I'm not following."

"A good denial, the best point in law," said Laughlin, tongue in cheek.

"Detective—"

"I'm not finished. You've got what you wanted. Haven't ye?"

"Detective—"

"Tell me," barked Laughlin, now crowding me and breathing in my face, "Off the record. No tape recorders. No cameras. Just you, me and lots of dead bodies. Was it you?"

"You don't get it. Do ye?"

"Tell me then."

"My son is alive—"

"Your son is fuckin' dead—"

"Enough!" I said, now crowding Laughlin and breathing in *his* face. "I'm running out of time."

I glanced at my watch. I had but five minutes to meet the kidnappers or bid my son farewell.

# 53

If I knew one thing for certain, it was to respect my gut feeling. And at this point, my gut had been plain-spoken:

Cody wasn't dead. My gut and I both settled on it. No way had my son been killed.

Cody gone meant the takers had no further leverage. Lacking leverage they'd lose my attention and lose my motivation to comply forever. My motive had always been the bait, one that had me trapped by the balls. If the kidnappers had demanded I jump off a structure, I'd ask how high. But my gut had always been on the nail, ninety percent of the time. Trusting it was never optional. It was—forever and a day—a must. I'd won the kickboxing title fight at the concluding hour having put my faith in it when I reflected for half a second how I'd take my opponent to the floor. Surely I could have made use of my godly gift, but I had found a way to turn it on and off and rely solely on my human strength, which I drew on to defeat my challenger. For those who hadn't been challengers in the ring, I'd know to switch on the strength of the gods for Spartan punishment. And the hostage-takers had it coming once I unearthed their place of refuge.

Accordingly, undeniably, I was thoroughly aware Cody was living. And somehow I inherited the daunting task of persuading the bloody detective.

"I've only got five minutes," I said to Laughlin, "or *he* will die."

Detective Laughlin ogled at me with cynical eyes.

"You're looking at him. Right fuckin' now," he said pointedly. "Admit to the murders, and you'll live trouble-free days behind bars."

Straight from the shoulder, I had it with him. I had to act at once and give reasons later. This was my newly concocted stratagem. Except in my mind, it began with me delivering this dialog:

"I'm sorry for what I'm about to do, Detective."

In half a second, Laughlin's eyelids rose to his brows; his eyes conscious of my newly brewed plan. Straight away, he pulled aside his lagging revealing a high-powered Sig Sauer shooter in his holster that his left hand swiftly possessed. Except I was quicker.

I jabbed at the detective's jaw. The nimble Garda officer was out cold like a string-less doll. Moving at lightning speed behind his frame, his shell falling back into my arms in a wilting stance.

I pulled him under his arms and positioned his flabby body alongside the frigid wall.

There was no time to waste. I headed for the door, making a hasty exit into the city mortuary lengthy hall as the entry to the *chamber of the dead* flung open.

"Stop!" barked the chief pathologist.

Like greased lightning, I thumped him on the side of his lungs. The pathologist was on the floor, gasping for air.

My caring nature always in play, I said, "Breathe. Breathe, easy. You'll be fine."

The chap breathed, but he was down for the count.

"You'll be back up in a bit," I assured him, anticipating my next move as I looked up.

A camera stared down straight at me. I realized the surveillance device had been dead set on me, and it was late to dismantle it.

I watched as the lens zoomed into focus. It was only seconds before a mob of Garda found their way down into this very hall. My contemplation was further confirmed once the ear-piercing building siren went off.

It was too late.

I had to ready myself for combat or be dead.

I dashed down the long passage, headed for the exit.

I reckoned it was only a matter of seconds before Gardaí stormed the corridor, and I was right, as my ears became aware of the trudge of boots on the cement floor in the darkened passageway space ahead.

I have twice mentioned, *Bear with me. You will come to understand.*

In each instance, I mentioned the notion of the strength I had inherited from the gods. And here, as in right now—in this vestibule that held me hostage, four kilometers from my place of rendezvous—I was to reveal in a three-dimensional-fighting-style, the meaning of divine muscle, putting to shame the strength of the likes of Samson of the *Book of Judges*.

I didn't need to transform into the all too clichéd superhero, clad in elastane garb, as the gift I possessed could be turned on and off, literally, like a light switch. And now it was on, as I was fixed on clearing my path out of this top-security complex without time for concessions. Gardaí had arrived and were intent on a shoot to kill with no prospect for further interrogation.

I was to be put to death. And the only party that could repeal this charge, Detective Laughlin, was down for the count. Had he been conscious, in my self-delusion I accepted as true the chap, even with his egotistical ways, would have ordered a cease-fire and lifted off the *shoot to kill* directive. I knew Laughlin had been more interested in cracking the case himself, for further self-deification, and hence needed me alive and in his sole custody.

A throng of Garda Regional Support Units swarmed the hall.

I halted; the time had come.

Like nature's warm-blooded hunting ritual, Gardaí enclosed me as if a pack of starving wolves, each positioning and timing just right before a mortal strike, hands by their semiautomatic guns in black leather holsters. Several were in tactical gear, complete bullet-resistant outfits, aiming their firearms, HK MP7 heavy duty armor-piercing submachine guns, purposely engineered to slay the souls of those deemed insane, or a menace to society. And now I'd been classified as one.

I shifted my stance and observed; the intensity in my expanded lime-shade veins blatant. I could taste the copper on my tongue. I was an armored tank, ready for *whatever*.

In a swift move, I was on the first man, and then the second as Gardaí fired at will, wounding each other. I delivered fast-paced hard shots.

I struck one Garda in the ribs, and he flew up in the air while I belted ten more. Then the landing chap I kicked once more in the ribs, like a rugby ball, to the darkened end of the vestibule; synchronously experiencing the highest intensity of adrenaline rush flooding through my veins from the high-risk deliberate muscular actions for the extended period.

An assailant bashed at my side. I jostled his shoulders, struck in the inner thighs, which brought down his frame then choked him numb. I then changed my stance from my primary battering position, and round-house smashed another guilty at the shank bone; frames crushing echoing in the vestibule. I followed through with a famous hook-blow to the max-illofacial death pyramid. The Garda was on the floor, comatose. I climbed over him while I straight knee-thrust two and spun to deliver a blow to another one's front. Hook-crescent-ax-back-sweeping strikes cleared the way all the while evading a volley of gunfire.

Those whose wrists I grabbed ended up in a bizarre spider-like web until the very last.

Just like that, I was gone.

# 54

When I made the exit into the outdoors, the Irish sun beamed on my face, thawing my bones from the ice of the frigid mortuary. I had been in the morgue too long. The squabble with Garda had been a rudimentary warm-up, never evolving into fully-fledged body calisthenics. Nevertheless, my heart was pleased with my quick departure.

I was sure of these facts: Cody lived, his takers had the upper hand, and I had but sixty seconds to make contact. Any deviation, I understood, meant never seeing my son alive—never. And knowing myself, I could not live with *never*. I had made a contract with the Devil that he'd take custody of my soul had the Man above botched me once more by claiming Cody's life. I'd shove a shotgun in my maw and squeeze the trigger. And I'd find myself at the doors of hell, readying myself to serve God's most favored and cast angel who'd rebel against Him, something the angel of darkness and me—for time without end—shared in common.

There was no time to waste. The instructions had been plainly spoken:

*Half an hour. Corner of Cathedral and O'Connell. A green waste bin. You'll find a box. Follow the instructions.*

Sixty seconds became thirty, and I had no place to go but through the green woods, full of shrubbery and tall stripped trees.

I cleared the iron barricade that fenced off the thoroughfare from the gardens and surfaced on Malahide Road at the same moment that a car, tires squealing, smashed into my side, but I was nimble. I spun over the vehicle's hood, crushing the windshield, and then over the top to land my two feet on the concrete of the busy road.

Speeding vehicles were heading straight at me, honking wildly.

I scampered past them, leaping forward and figuratively flying over them in some cases.

I had to keep track of time to ensure I'd make the kidnappers' deadline. I glanced at my wristwatch. Ten seconds, nine, eight...

When I looked up, a massive trailer truck, breaking the speed limit, screeched to a halt. Tires skidded. There was no time. The only chance I had was to take the hit. The truck slammed into my body sending me to break through glass, and crash on water, in an indoor pool.

I was thankful, but for a moment I saw lights, and I heard Aidan and Hannah telling me to open my eyes.

"Wake up."

I was in the indigo-hued pool, back against waving water, drifting, before I realized I had been out cold for a lengthy period.

I remembered the stillness of the pool water as if a lulling crib. I remembered my ma, Bella. Her stunning face. Her pearly whites smiling at mine. I remembered her tiny hands playing with my round babe toes. But most of all I remembered the smell, almost intoxicating. Bella had pinched her nose, "You peed in your nappy, babe. Ma's going to have to change you, little fella."

Bella pinched her nose once more. Saying those same words over and over again as if a broken record. I felt the piss slowly engulfing my body until my head, and then my nose was in it.

I jerked my head out of the pool water that reeked of a heavy chlorine stench. I hadn't been two years old in my bassinet or in the arms of Bella. I'd been in a bloody pool, numb for a bit.

My natural reaction was to cough out the acrid pool water, trying to rid myself of the chlorine taste that made it into my throat. Then my eyes opened slowly.

I saw the crowd, frozen in disbelief, in a state of shock.

I didn't care, as my first and only reaction was:

Cody.

Following the ordeal at the pool, I had already cleared Ballybough

Road. Less than three hundred meters to sprint. I gazed at my timepiece. There was no time left.

My heart lurched.

Bloody hell.

Cody will be killed.

# 55

Half an hour. *Corner of Cathedral and O'Connell. A green waste bin. You'll find a box. Follow the instructions.*

The abductor's voice played back in my head. I had made a hash of beating time, but I was determined to still make the rendezvous. Perhaps there was still a chance. They needed me. Without me, they couldn't get the Shamrock. Without me, Cody would be turned to some forsaken orphanage, and the tavern disposed of in a public auction, something I understood Cody's takers had not been willing to see happen. They wanted no complications. No lengthy probate. No courts. No bullshite. I figured they'd be pretty desperate to secure the Shamrock in exchange for Cody. Six hundred seconds late was no deal breaker—at least, I convinced myself of it.

I turned the corner of Cathal Brugha Street, running past a series of businesses and stores. Then I made a left on O'Connell, my heart pulsating with every thrust of my legs.

At the corner of Cathedral and O'Connell Streets, my sight finally settled on a green waste bin. I felt butterflies in my belly. They felt as real as my sweat dripping from my temple.

Were the kidnappers still game? Were they still willing to proceed with the exchange, whatever that meant?

My answer, which was more like a nerve-racking test of faith, rested within the waste bin. Perhaps they had not killed Cody. There was still an opportunity for me to make things right, for Cody and for me. We'd start over. Then a thought of Séamus crossed my mind. I don't know why. Perhaps it was because he had been family, even though for a limited time. I still cared deeply for the puppy. Gilchrist had been its carer while I hunted the demons that abducted my son, Séamus' best friend. I wondered if the terrier was all right. But then I filed that consideration for later, though just seeing Séamus' image in my mind brought me the courage I needed to proceed.

I charily lifted the lid off the waste bin, the butterflies feeling more pronounced than ever before. To my surprise, the kidnappers had been true to their word. I understood it to mean nothing more than what it was; their first set of instructions. So it meant nothing more than there was hope: a chance perhaps that Cody was alive.

There it was: a neatly prepared package sitting on top of some rubbish. I wondered if the kidnappers were watching. Surely, they must be surveying the area from afar: somewhere in a secluded pub, or maybe a deserted alley. I had to be cautious.

I scanned my surroundings, looking for what I wasn't sure. Perhaps I could make *them* out. Perhaps I could just see the chap with the blue trench coat with pulled up sleeves once more. He'd been a good lead, one I had foolishly let go astray. Somehow, I knew Detective Laughlin had regained consciousness. He knew of my whereabouts from the device on my ankle. Why hadn't he turned up? Why hadn't Garda flooded the area to take me into custody? I didn't know.

I grabbed the box and headed for the diner across the street. There, I would unseal the box, and vowed to follow their instructions to save Cody. I would sign the transfer papers for the Shamrock even if it killed me. So long as Cody was breathing, I would have died fulfilling my parental obligation.

As I pushed open the door to the old diner, a bell gave a loud jingle. Customers, chewing their meals, gazed back at my scraggy mug, down-and-out, before they turned back to their lunches, judging I was an insignificant person, a hobo, never recognizing my features, never suspecting I had been Cain Seamróg, *Irish*, the Fighting Irishman.

The place was jointed. Regulars enjoyed the company of buddies and family. I sat alone in an eye-blinding-lime-cushioned faux leather booth that was badly worn. I had been here many times before in my youth. The menu was appetizing.

I gazed at the package in my hands. A thought had crossed my mind. Why Cody? I mean really, why my son? He had been an unfortunate boy with a bad heart and ugly knee braces that limited his ability to enjoy life to the fullest. He hadn't done any wrong. In fact, all I remembered of him had been fond memories of good deeds. He'd been more mature for his age than most kids. He'd done things that showed his sensible and good nature to others. One such deed had been the day Aidan died. Hannah's spirit had been crushed as crushed ice. With no proper request from Hannah, he had taken matters into his own hands.

He had slipped quietly into the bathroom, hunched over the porcelain tub and cleaned it beautifully, unbeknownst to his mommy and me. He had struggled for two long hours scrubbing, spraying, and wiping. Then he had run a hot bath and laced it with mint and rosemary bubble bath. The bath had foamed and scented the entire room.

She truly loved a brand called *The Handmade Soap*—wholly natural and Irish. It was one of those petrochemical and paraben-free products that Hannah soaked in when she had a long and trying day. Then, it seemed every day was trying, but this day had been unlike any. Aidan had died.

So Cody had judged it proper to bless her with such an honorable feat, but the exertion rendered him very ill, and he'd been hospitalized for two successive days. One of the overly concerned nurses had made a call, and straight away, we were under investigation for child abuse, and neglect by the Child Protection Services Ireland (CPSI), which only disappeared once the CPSI determined there hadn't been any wrongdoing on our part. Cody had been interviewed by a slew of psychologists, social workers, psychiatrists, physiotherapists, and abuse counselors. We could never hurt Cody; we loved him infinitely. Each time CPSI would visit they'd ring the outside bell, whose clang had been disturbing to a resting Cody.

I could still hear the bell, until a clang from the old fish-and-chip shop's cook rang to announce a patron's order, and brought me back. There was no reasonable explanation for Cody's abduction, only that there were wicked people that roamed our streets who were more interested in inflicting pain on others than saving lives.

I gazed down once more. The bloody package was still in my custody. I could still hear my watch's tick. Something made me listen more carefully, as I watched the long hand from my timepiece. The tick and the progression of the long hand were off. I realized the ticking was coming from within the box.

Christ, a bomb.

The audible ticking had been dreadfully real and reminded me—if the kidnappers had wanted me dead—I had only but a few seconds before either seeing Cody again or being dead from a booby trap explosion.

"Afternoon, sir," said the waitress whose tag bore her real name, "Would you like to see a menu?"

Either I nodded or truthfully I had blocked her out of my mind, and she must have taken my silence for agreement.

Sorcha—no, that wasn't her real name—Emma was. But she looked like a Sorcha to me.

Sorcha returned to the counter, grabbed a menu and brought it back, extending it to me.

"Coffee?"

I shook my head no.

"Perhaps the regular? Fish-and-chips?" I shook once more, no.

"Get everyone out," I said evenly.

Sorcha gazed at me with electrifying eyes. She hadn't registered.

"This is a bomb."

The thought sunk in. She nodded at me, indicating she understood. She then turned to face the mass and gestured trying to grab their attention.

"Everyone," she shouted, "please."

Patrons were busy doing what they did best at a diner, chow down. Sorcha had to get to the point fast or else be dead.

"This man has a bomb!" she shrieked.

Everyone stared for a brief moment, then when reality set in, the place turned into a frenzy as patrons scampered, emptying the place.

It was my time to deal. Either open the box and sign whatever documents were possibly inside or meet my maker if it was a bomb.

I wiped the sweat from my brow and began to gently open the box.

There were multiple thin layers of plastic wraps. My shoulder blades began to ache, and tension mounted up and down my spine.

Beads of sweat broke all over me. My slippery fingers made it all the harder to lift the thin layers of casing.

I had finally reached the bottom wrapping. There was a box. And yet another. And more. I had counted ten by now. With each box, the size diminished, and the ticking got faster and louder, which meant I was reaching closer to the core of whatever Cody's kidnappers had intended for me to see.

Perhaps it was "proof of life" in the box, Cody's thumb or perhaps his left ear. I don't know why, but I'd seen my share of Hollywood films. They all ended with the abducted's body chopped into pieces and delivered to their nearest and dearest. Somehow I was able to push the evil thoughts from my memory and focus on the task at hand.

The package had shrunk to a small box no bigger than four by two inches in size. The tick was much louder and much faster.

Outside I could hear patrons cheesed off. They wanted back in. I heard Sorcha—you know, Emma, the waitress—calming her crowd. I even perceived the sound of a Garda siren. Someone—some *caffler*—had dialed emergency. Garda Síochána were en route. Yet again I wasn't sure if it had been Detective Laughlin trailing my ass or Garda responding to an emergency call. The siren seemed distant, but I understood within seconds they'd be on the premises, guns drawn and ready to kill.

I had to act at once, and take the bait.

Either way—by the abductors' count—I was a dead mate. I sighed. If I were to die now, this was to be the moment. Either I'd die, or Cody would live. I shut my eyes and opened the last shell of the box, choosing to let Cody live if this had been his fate.

There was a sudden beep, and the tick halted.

I opened my eyes. The content of the box wasn't a booby trap. It was something utterly unexpected: a rubber band, a loaded syringe no more than three inches long and a ticking clock fastened to a recorder even smaller than the syringe. The chronometer had died at 00:00:00.

My eyes closed for a short time. It's all over, and I'm not dead. I had been right—Cody's takers wanted me alive. But I quickly realized this was too easy when I read a tiny note that was glued to the play switch, which read: "Push Button."

I hesitated for a moment, but the approaching siren reminded me that time was running out. I pressed play.

"I hope you enjoyed viewing my work at the city mortuary," the mechanized voice said. Yes, that same bloody voice, the one I'd become accustomed to. "The syringe contains mixed psychoactive drugs. Inject in your left arm. You'll be out in ten seconds. Divert, and your son is dead. There is no time. Do it now."

And just like that, the tape ended.

I thought to myself. I'm being given a chance here. An opportunity to meet in the flesh. I was no longer to ask questions. I was to follow instructions and play the Devil's game. Garda were no less two minutes away. I had no time to think. It had to be done. And now was the time.

I secured the rubber on my bicep and found a vein. I tapped gently on it, which forced its sudden expansion. My blood flow had been regular and pumping. It was good for what I was about to do.

I inserted the needle, which broke the epidermis. Fluid pumped into my bloodstream.

Ten seconds and I was out cold, face first on the board.

# 56

I found myself on the edge of the Cliffs of Moher, looking into the Atlantic Sea. Warm clear blue sky. Clouds as pasty as cotton balls. Afar, vast verdant land dotted the horizon. It was all blissful, a truly heavenly sight, (though *heavenly* had been an expression I had refused to make use of following my ill fortune, which had brought death to my faith).

Nothing around. No animals. No people.

The ocean breeze gently swept my face. I was fatigued, frail. I had never felt so weak. It was almost illusory. Yet the splendor of this scenic view from Moher was invigorating. I felt at peace in my solitude, the pounding of waves settling down my senses.

From nowhere, I watched colonies of Northern Gannets fly up and wing away into the expanse of the Atlantic Sea.

I began to wonder how I'd got here. My mind was empty, nothing I could remember but the solace of the gentle wind from a breathing ocean. I had to try and focus, but I drew a blank at each attempt. I breathed in, breathed out, for thirty seconds. I wasn't sure where I learned this method, but it came naturally.

I focused once more, and a picture came to mind: a diner, the old fish-and-chip.

My memory was still hazy. I now remembered another factor, Emma.

I remembered her kindness. Though the name Sorcha was what I remembered first. I didn't know why. But it was clear, Sorcha. Yet another image materialized. The hideous lime-cushioned faux leather booth. The exact smell of it, the stench of old fabric. Then I remembered something else. The scream, but whose I couldn't make out.

Why was I here?

The light wind from the Atlantic Sea was steady and stroked my face while my mind dug deeper. Somehow it took a lot of energy for me to think. Each time I'd dig deeper, I'd feel worn out. I'd rest for a brief moment, and then I'd go for it yet again. I said to myself I'll try once more. If I had no success, I'd merely wander the area in search of answers. Then just when I thought to take it easy, an image became visible:

A syringe.

From there, things accelerated rather quickly.

A rubber band, a clock fastened to a recorder, a chronometer's digital screen marking 00:00:00, the words, "*Psychoactive drugs. Inject in your left arm. You'll be out in ten seconds. Divert, and your son is dead. There is no time. Do it now.*"

"Cody," I shouted, suddenly remembering. Then I heard a voice that nearly had me fall off the edge of the cliff.

"Daddy."

I hadn't savored the sweetness of this voice in a long time, but although happy, I was mystified.

I turned to face the voice, and there, running toward me, all in white, was my son.

"Aidan," I shouted as I broke into a run. Yes, I know. It wasn't Cody. It was Aidan, but I was still elated. Surely for a good reason: Aidan was dead. But as I ran toward him, I hardly made an advance, and now the distance between us was expanding the more he ran toward me.

"Open your eyes. Open your eyes, Irish," said Hannah.

I fell into a deep, black hole. I gasped. I couldn't breathe. I tried to force my vision to focus, but everything was blurred.

I could make out the lab and medical equipment. Then I saw an operating table in the center of the room. I wasn't sure how I had missed it. It was right in my line of vision. Something lay on the operating table. I couldn't quite make it out. I had to focus.

It was a body, hooked to lines linked up to a network of IV bags.

I was in no common medical facility. I deduced it from the non-medical equipment lying around. I must have been in some sort of seafood storage

173

barn, one on the coast, which explained my earlier peculiar delusion. I smelled salt water blended with the unpleasant tang of rusted metal. I had come back to real life—I'd woken.

I was strapped to an upright mechanically engineered and highly sophisticated version of a steel straitjacket, only better and stronger, my wrists, ankles, and knees chained. There was absolutely no way to escape.

I looked once more at the operating table, hoping for a miracle. There could be no mistake. Yes, this ailing child was Cody. I was certain this time—unlike the boy at the city mortuary, this child had the ugly knee braces that were so familiar to me.

"Cody," I said with a drained voice. His holter heart monitor had been removed from his chest, leaving redness of the skin in the place of electrodes.

His eyes were shut, but I could see the movement on his chest, he was breathing weakly.

A thought had crossed my mind. Was it to be this simple?

I had found Cody, and somehow all of this—his discovery—felt too straightforward. Yet, I quickly dismissed the reflection as grand contentment overshadowed my uncertainties. I hadn't set eyes on my beloved child in so long. Cody seemed to have even grown an inch, a maturity in his face that wasn't there before, perhaps due to undue stress. Nevertheless, vengeance was soon to be mine. I swear it, Cody. Vengeance shall be mine.

I watched his heart rate, which fluctuated like a poorly trading stock on the heart rate monitor.

# 57

Plastic sheets peeled apart. Tadhg, followed by three men, entered the area. Yes, it was Tadhg, the thug in the blue trench coat with pulled up sleeves. Except now he was all butcher cut hairstyle and rustic fisherman chunky sweater as if he'd been at sea. It was the same man from apartment 13-31B, the one who'd knocked me out cold, and to whom I too had returned the favor. The same man with the *Terminator* pose: *The abandoned flats. Nephin Road. Fifth floor. Ten minutes.* Now he had me. And I wondered how he'd punish me for the death of his mate—the one who died from a metal tube stabbing through his cranium.

My interest shifted to one of the other three men. He wore a pale medical overcoat on top of scrub top and trousers, and a surgical mask and cap; a surgeon?

Was he here for me? To torture me? To do whatever deemed *necessary* for me to turn over Jack's Shamrock to some dubious nominee directors, shareholders of Fharma Holdings?

I was sure I was right. Blood-spattered surgical instrument—retractors, rasps, trocars, drill bits—lay about on the counter. These had to be for torment. No one sane made use of a bone saw to slice off timber. Then again, perhaps he was a doctor who had come to attend to Cody. No. I reminded myself I was dealing with merciless criminals. They had already proven their callous nature by taking two lives: Jack and Hannah.

The other two thugs were clearly enforcers. Their posture, their garments, even their weapons gave them away. No smiles. Cheap suits. Mean faces. Trying hard to persuade the victim as to the pain they could inflict just with one stare. Real bastard *hardchaws*. Nevertheless, it was pathetic at best. I waited for the time I'd show them my own intimidation method. I'd not have to rely on my outer appearance. My act of wrath would sell it quickly. But with these shackles I couldn't proceed with my presentation, so to speak.

I struggled against my bonds. Impossible. Tadhg smirked, for a little too long. Wipe that bloody smirk, was all that I thought.

I wondered who these thugs were. I didn't recognize them. Who did they work for? Who was the boss? I didn't need to wait long. The long plastic sheets came apart once more.

A gent, height and build approximating mine, crossed the threshold. I didn't recognize him either, partly because he was wearing one of those eerie blank Venetian carnival masks. He was dressed in an expensive looking dark olive suit.

He stood there and stared at me. I kept quiet, trying to place him.

The masked man took one step forward; his henchmen moving beside him like a double act of attack dogs.

I watched coolly, although I could think of no one, previous to these series of events, who'd want to cause me harm. I had always lived a quiet life, and on no account had I caused anyone any harm.

Who was he? Why did he want me dead? Why was he after my aul man's drinking hole?

Then he spoke.

"At last. Irish. The Shamrock in the flesh. A bloody killing machine," said the mysterious man.

"Let me see your fuckin' face!"

"What a pleasurable guest you are," said the masked man as if he'd been speaking through a voice box machine.

"We end this here. Let my son go, and I swear never to come after ya."

I was aware I was pushing my luck, but I considered it was worth a try.

"The formidable Fighting Irishman," said the bloke.

"Your courage is remarkable."

"What are you after?" I said.

"The Shamrock. You turn it over to us. Your gasún lives. It's that simple. I'm a man of my word."

"It's just a fuckin' pub!" I barked, realizing I should have restrained my turbulence.

"Then you won't have a problem turning it over to us. Would ye?"

I spat on the ground, dismissing the con man's pronouncement.

The masked man turned to Tadhg, "Make him sign. Then you get your wish to kill Irish."

Tadhg nodded. His eyes full of revenge. My act had killed his mate, Liam. He was apt to return the favor. So was I for their unsettling my imperfect little life. Except I intended to stall him.

"Gardaí. They'll find me. The tracking device on my ankle—"

"See this beauty?" said the masked man, turning back to face me.

He flaunted a microscopic device in his hand.

"It'll send *them* searching round Dublin every half an hour. We've got effective tools."

Then the masked man departed without saying another word.

"You will endorse this record then your gasún is free to go. Then, I will beat you to a pulp," said Tadhg, the document in hand when the cellular in his pocket buzzed. He was annoyed by the call, but the thug took out his phone and answered, "Yes?"

Then he listened briefly.

"Right fuckin' now?"

He was further annoyed at the interruption, but the call appeared to be important.

"I'll be there in ten," said Tadhg.

He turned to one of the bulky henchmen.

"Something's come up. Make him sign. Then get rid of him."

Tadhg turned to face me, "You and I will one day get our chance to battle in hell."

"I look forward to it," I answered.

Tadhg smirked, and walked out, leaving behind the surgeon who was busy formulating some kind of concoction. This was my chance to think up something brainy at once.

I had attempted to break free from the shackles that held me captive. Out of the question. I had to be clever.

I glanced over at Cody. There was no improvement in his breathing. And it was evident he'd been respiring with more difficulty than before.

The henchman in charge approached. He was all business, although I could read the fear in his eyes. I knew then he'd known about Irish, the Fighting Irishman. Tragically for him, it was the commencement of his demise. Then again he had such strength in his arms. He was the size of three ripped chaps. I couldn't underestimate his muscle. And so for now, I had to play along.

"You play good, lackey, it ends very quickly. You don't, it'll be a bloody mess," said the enforcer.

# 58

First order of service ahead of being shot in the head, I considered they'd have me endorse the title deed of the Shamrock. I would have thought that any person could fabricate a bona fide deed utilizing ultra-modern machinery to replicate my signature, but apparently, it was imperative to the kidnappers to have my original penmanship on paper.

Perhaps advanced graphology analysis could be employed to substantiate the validity of the record and so prove a counterfeit. So, authentic, the legal document bore its weight in gold. I guessed in the event of any dispute they could then procure the fitting service of a certified graphologist to lend further authority to the bloody thing by having him issue forth an avowal to the fact that, under his expert study and analysis, the deed was, in fact, above-board to the best of his knowledge, skills, and abilities.

So, my *autograph*, as you might say, was a vital aspect of the scam. And it was surely rendered as less of a headache in the long run.

The henchman's hand pushed the document in front of me. Was he dim-witted? After all, I was held hostage by the bloody straitjacket. Had I mentioned the bloody thing was a German contraption? I'd seen the inscription on the jacket's left forearm's fastening: *HERGESTELLT IN STUTTGART, BADEN-WÜRTTEMBERG.*

I recognized Stuttgart and Baden-Württemberg. Therefore, German. I didn't speak German but realized it meant it wasn't Irish-made. But again, I don't know why my mind had drifted off so far to the trivial. Accordingly, I reeled my focus back to Cody who was losing life before my eyes, and then at the chap with the deed in his hand.

"I suppose I'll write my signature with my teeth?" I said evenly, persuading him with candid eyes I'd conduct myself appropriately according to their wishes if loosened from the straitjacket.

"I'll endorse it. But you must assure me that my son goes free. Then put two in my head," I said pointedly. "First you must let me free from these chains."

The hard man looked to the surgeon who, putting his faith in the weapon aimed at my skull, acquiesced while warning him to be on the alert.

I heard the cocking from a large custom-made version of the Sten Mark submachine gun from enforcer number two while hardchaw number one commenced untangling and unlocking the jacket, which seemed to take ages: seven bloody minutes to be precise. The gunman aimed the British-born firearm at my left sphenoid bone. From the edge of my sight, I saw the barrel staring coldly at my skull. I was well within its effective range of fire. Five hundred rounds a minute. One squeeze of its trigger and I'd be dead for certain.

In the end, the last brunt of shackles crashed to the floor.

They had made a grand mistake, as my hands were free, and I pitied them for succumbing to my pitch.

In the twinkling of an eye, I altered the gunman's shooter seven degrees west. When it fired, it missed me but hit the other thug, his brain literally exploding. Brain and skull bits spattered everywhere.

Before the first thug had taken in what had just come to pass, I had already got hold of his gun, and in a swift move knocked him out cold with the butt, a quick blow to his cranium.

The alarmed surgeon hadn't a chance to escape. Everything happened at high speed. A second of uncertainty, second-guess or distraction was enough to lose a fight: I'd learned the hard way in my early days of kick-boxing. This time, I'd been prepared. In actual fact, I'd been so quick ridding myself of the hard men that the surgeon had been stuck in a state of shock, awed at my agility, and he hadn't the opportunity to appropriately react. He made for the exit, but I was upon him and jabbed a syringe with psychoactive drugs—the same stuff I had formerly injected into my bloodstream—into the scruff of his neck.

The sinner collapsed to the floorboards, dribble pouring from his mouth.

It was time to reunite with my son.

I was so relieved. I wanted to be sure he was still alive before I freed him from the straps that held him hostage on the multifunctional stretcher trolley resembling a St. Vincent's psych ward batty. I dashed to the stretcher.

"Cody," I said impatiently.

His eyes opened at a snail's pace. They were half opened when my son recognized me.

"Daddy," a frail Cody cried weakly.

A tear wandered down the side of his temple. Mine came swiftly. I embraced him for a long stretch, holding him close. It was all over.

"Daddy."

"Cody," I kept repeating, hugging my child, and pouring kisses on his face when I perceived a rapid and unexpected thud.

*Damn.*

A loud and swift blur followed, and then the room fell sideways. The area went black.

# 59

Darkness loomed. No. Not the dull kind. Not the kind your sight stares at when the telly is switched off. But utter darkness as in pitch black. Devoid of one's sense of point in time, one's bearing. The kind of darkness that forces you to enquire whether you're dead or alive, in heaven or in hell. Yes, that sort of grand darkness. Not a jingle. Not a hum. Not a clatter. Not even an echo of my own inner expression. A hue of darkness I'd never born witness to.

Is this where one lies in wait for the Day of Judgment? Where the Man above resurrects the dead and casts judgment upon the souls of the sinners and the saints: whether one would spend eternity in the merry garden of bliss or the fiendish caves of misery? Or perhaps it was the tunnel that those near-death fanatics spoke so fondly about. One beyond our earthly existence, yet not heaven, as you might say, but the crossing to either seventh heaven or Abaddon.

I searched in vain for the light at the end of the tunnel, and I could see none. Nothing that corroborated the legitimacy of stories I'd heard in my formative years. None that told me I was comatose, waiting to be revived.

Where the bloody hell was I?

Now I heard voices. Yes, accented voices. Perhaps culchies on the south side of Dublin. Yes, the voices were *that* perceptible.

"You heard the story?" said one voice.

"Tell me," asked the other.

While the culchies chew the fat, I perceived the thud of weighty *objects* dumped in *water*.

The more groggy voice that told the story continued:

"The lad. Just a bleedin youngster. 'bout eight. He walks into the shop, you know. Hands the cash clerk a videotape."

"Like a VHS?"

"Yeah, VHS tape. Bulky shite. And the clerk's like '*Bloody hell's this?*'"

"So what did the bastard answer?"

"Hold it champ. Let me tell ya."

"All right. Go on then."

"Gasúr, all coked up, says play the tape. Clerk grabs the tape. Kind of looks at it, you know. Examines it. Like, what the bloody fuck? Then he lodges the fucker in the VCR's slot, and presses the play button."

"Then?"

"On the telly, the boy has a pistol trained on his aul man's bollocks. He squeezes the trigger and lets off. Kills the bastard. Reaches out from his aul man's chinos and pulls out a National Lottery ticket. *EuroMillions jackpot.* Top prize, a hundred fuckin' million euros."

"Bollocks!"

"Yeah, fuckin' incredible, mate. But that's not all."

"Really, huh? What's more?"

"Bloody chiseller is a nut case. He draws the matching bleedin gun. You know. The murder weapon from the videocassette and aims at the terrified clerk. He says, 'I *want to cash in that ticket, or I'll blow your fuckin' brains out.*' The chap gives him the finger, so he puts two in the chap's skull," concluded the groggy voice.

"But wait. I thought one could only cash about a hundred euros of winnings at a corner shop? What's more he's underage," said the mild-mannered voice.

"Case in point. The boyo is a fuckin' eejit," the groggy voice replied.

"Jaysus! Fuckin' ball-bag," said the mild-mannered voice. All the while I'd still been staring at my own darkness.

But their voices struck a chord. I must have been alive, but returning from a state of unconsciousness.

Then I recognized the sound of gentle waves. Now I understood I wasn't in a secluded room. But I still wasn't clear on where I was, and my eyes felt too heavy to unlock.

Regardless, I forced my eyes open. Rays of light rushed into my pupils, burning the center of my iris, obliterating my every attempt at peeking at my surrounds. Hence, I considered it ideal if I narrowed my eyes. So I did.

My ability to see, what little of it, was hazy. Except, I made out a fishing boat. Yes, I was sure of it. A traditional boat used for cod fishing. I could tell from the gasping Atlantic cod in the hollow compartment down below.

Next, I saw a name, L.G. CAVAN. Didn't mean anything: just a boat's name. So I moved on to see if I could make out anything of consequence. Fishing lines, outriggers, winches. Nothing that rang true to a criminal vessel.

Then a drop of blood from my ankle parachuted down below. No. Not on deck. Instead, in the dark ocean—the Irish Sea.

You see, I'd been suspended ten feet high up, upside-down, and my crown opposite the deep. It was then I took notice of the proprietors of the voices. Two goons, fishermen in scarlet, fishing dry suits with hoods, black turtlenecks and knee-high boots, were dumping a bulk of bloody fish pieces into the vast expanse of *Muir* Éireann.

I noticed my eyesight dimming, view of the ocean and decks below gradually vanishing. I wondered why. It was then I grasped what was taking place. I didn't need to be a chemist. I'd been drugged. For this reason, yet again, I passed out.

# 60

Bare as I was born, I had been suspended inverted by my ankles dangling from a gooseneck rope fastened to a hoist's hook. I had returned from the deep black hole where I had heard Hannah's voice once more. I knew she'd rejected my appeal before the Man above to be dead, on the grounds that I had to live for Cody's sake. I had to stay breathing, the only thing that could guarantee Cody's continued existence.

One of the culchies tilted his vision aloft at my chops. Our eyes met. I was in the worst shape of my life, but my talent had always been with me. For this reason, I'd known within half a second of our eyes meeting, the culchies were going for it.

"Drop him!" hollered the heavily accented and groggy goon. The other chap hit a lever and, like a bulky rock, my frame plunged into the bitter ocean, my crown hitting the water like a ton of stones. At once, I was again where I'd been, hostage of the all too memorable *darkness*. The impact was like a massive punch to the jaw.

Yes, I was an exceptional man. Except, I was no god, which all the more reminded me of my mortality. Hence, the recurring unconsciousness.

My weight pulled me down fast like a sinking ship. I resembled the dead sinking in the deep. A line of blood from my bruised ankle snaked through the deep sea.

185

The sea was still. Very still. In fact *too* still. But bloody chunks of chopped fish also sank around me into the deep marine.

I dropped deeper. And deeper still.

Then a *voice*. That same voice, as repeatedly in the short past, returned. At present more urgent and loud.

"Open your eyes."

I knew the voice too well, which bore the inference that the darkness I once more stared at hadn't been my laid-in-wait place of rest ahead of Judgment Day, but some impermanent ethereal trance. Hannah was dead. How could she speak to me at this moment unless I was dead? Except, I wasn't. Death surely didn't feel this way, a way that left me feeling incomplete, as if I hadn't achieved my purpose.

*Return. Return.*

Hence, it was then, half awake, that I saw a dark shape approach. It was large.

My primary hope was a whale. Yet my senses feared the worst. This creature could not be a whale.

Straight away, my arms moved. I was thoroughly alert, and the natural instinct was to reach high and swim up, but I didn't.

The beast was finally upon on me, circled around and faced me.

Bloody hell.

I had to reason, without delay. I was on its home turf. I could just surrender a limb or two. Make it easy, in the manner of speaking. Bleed to death from my wounds, and forfeit the battle. Or I could live. And there was but one way to live; slay the shark with my bare hands.

Only a man with the unwavering strength of the gods could slay the beast. But again, this was no fairy tale. This was no dream. Our run-in was as real as the fear I felt in my bones. We'd go toe-to-toe at this. A real fucking duel. However, to survive, I had to be high. Then slay the bastard on my descent from the high. This would prove to be no small feat. It was a bloody great white.

I had to catch my breath, except I was nearly thirty meters deep underwater and holding, a habit (holding my breath underwater) which I had practiced since the age of eight. I had gone for an unbelievable nine hundred seconds in one instance, which I could do at any time. Had the goons known this bit of information, they'd known they'd have been better off shooting me in the back of the head.

I'd be out cold en route to oblivion in no time. Burying me in the deep was their mistake, not mine. But first I had to fight off the bloody shark.

The fact was I had faced the fear of surviving the deep, but never a show-down with the king of the briny, four thousand pounds of fish. I considered setting off fatal blows to the hollows of its eyes.

Surely, the beast had been accustomed to delivering the pounding and not receiving it. In its carnal mind I was the prey, but in mine—to its unsuspecting egotistical mind—it was mine. Either I was to end up in his belly, or he in mine. That was the frame of mind of the insane. And if I had to triumph, I had to be at one with insanity.

One thing I knew best was to stay calm and seize control, all the while calculating my assault: a direct hit to the snout was never out of the question. I was not to be a run-through nibble. I knew it better kill me, or I'd beat it to death for trying. Quite candidly, when faced by a beast this size, one was usually fucked. That was a gamble I had to live with, but the thought of leaving Cody an orphan and property of some psych ward somewhere south of Dublin I couldn't live with. I realized out-swimming the monster was out of the question, but by the gods, I knew I could bludgeon the bastard. I just had to grasp, never let go and deliver an assault, the weight of a thousand men. I had to become invincible at least in my mind. That assured me either a satisfying death or a victorious escape. Either way, I was high on insanity and ready for a wild encounter. We were head to head, and I remained calm. The smell of blood provoked the beast as it circled back round. I swiftly followed.

Once more, we were head to head.

Strangely, I recognized Conor's hook stuck to the side of the shark's jaws. Yes. Bloody hell. It had been Conor's beast, the one I'd gone after on Conor's boat. The same deadly shark that'd precluded me from collecting my pay and satisfying the Butcher. And now that same beast was facing me, prepared to take a bite out of my flesh. I had to survive. And then while preoccupied with the thought of survival, Detective Laughlin's gadget, yes the bloody band on my ankle with the highly lethal voltage, began beeping red as in countdown.

My heart dropped to my belly. It was either death by bump-and-bite shark attack or electrocution.

Accordingly, I leaped to the fore, my claws set to gash the beast. My hand clamped on the hook.

The beast maneuvered; trying to eject me. I hung on.

More blood filled the deep from my bruised ankle.

The beast rotated eagerly, forcing me to lose my grip on the hook. Then the monster struck, except I was out of reach and back on the hook.

The bloody device on my ankle made matters worse, beeping without end, reminding me of certain death as it counted down. Blinking red, and faster.

I clubbed its gills and eye, blinding its senses with my clenched fist.

I was high on my intent to kill and cared none that the beast had been a threat of annihilation. It was either my ass or his. I cared nothing of violating its terrain. I was as Irish as it was and had as much a right to be in this place at this time as it had.

Another powerful jab to the gills, and a lethal blow to the eye caused an instant burst, fluid seeping into the briny water.

The beast jerked and retreated into darkness.

My arms reached high and began the rapid swim.

The bloody ankle band wouldn't shut up, beeping faster than ever and wanting my death. But now I can't hold my breath any longer. It had been longer than fifteen minutes. I wasn't that skilled. I had been in the deep more than twenty minutes without breathing. I thought it impossible, yet my mind—my survival instinct—had found a speck of breath to live on in my lungs. I didn't know how and I didn't care. Admittedly I worried about dying from decompression sickness, but I'd been reeling upwards, in the direction of oxygen, away from the bloody depths of the water.

Then, when I felt my arms thoroughly fatigued, when my heart was about to give out, I heard the goons' boat engine roar to life.

The killer device on my ankle now beeped so fast the countdown must be nearing zero. Worse, there was no digital display on the apparatus, hence, no way to make out how close one was to be dead.

Only swimming higher was the best guarantee of life.

I demanded more from my body. Except, I'd been on my last fight-or-flight response. It was all on me now, on the will of a demi-god to stay alive. Hence I pushed up till at last, like a submarine torpedo, my thrashing body shot up and out of the briny water; my dying, oxygen-addicted, lungs gasping for air. I was alive and high on my desire for vengeance.

I was at the side of the offenders' boat. The band on my ankle turned to sea-green then shut off. I maneuvered myself onto the vessel.

Like greased lightning, I was on the first goon and snapped his neck. Then I proceeded to the bridge and studied the maritime map. The compass showed we were approximately five miles offshore.

Without warning, bullets winged by.

I ducked aside, by mistake knocking the high-velocity gear. I had suffered a flesh wound.

Then a series of bullets pricked through metal partitions just above where I'd taken cover attending to my injury.

The boat picked up speed.

I stopped the bleeding on my bicep, wrapping a rag round it, and then I gazed up.

Fuck.

The bloody goon stood there before me. His firearm aimed at my face. For certain, this time I'd be dead. He was too far away, and I was too weak to launch one of my aggressive assaults.

"Die, you fuck," said the bogtrotter as he squeezed the trigger.

Click. A dud—an empty chamber. I smiled mordantly.

"You're fuckin' dead now." Yes, those were my words, "fuckin' dead".

The robust chap flung the shooter aside and lunged forward, grabbing me and jabbing at my ribs.

I clutched the attacker's ankle and twisted. The chap shrieked like a baboon. I grabbed his body with my superhuman strength and flung him outside the cabin; his frame smashing hard against the faux wood paneling. I followed behind. In my psycho mind, I'd become immortal, and I had yet to descend from my previous state of insanity. But the goon found another firearm, while I unearthed a box of explosives nearby. He opened fire in a slapdash fashion, intending to terminate me.

I dashed past the explosives and dove into the ocean just before bullets sliced through explosives and they detonated in a mighty inferno, destroying the boat.

Hours later, surviving a marathon-like swim in the mammoth Irish Sea, my exhausted body resurfaced out of the briny water, carried by rocking waves to the Gaelic shoreline.

# 61

Underwater, the drowning Taller boy in my vision, shook wildly, breathless, his hands in the same hot crimson-gold fire flame, except more intense than ever before. Surreally, the flames transferred onto my own flesh, burning me to the core so badly that I shrieked a high pitched cry from the depth of my guts as I woke, naked, in agony on the water's edge, crests of waves calmly riding into shore and slapping at my face.

Neptūnus, the Roman god of the sea, had been merciful, as he gave me another chance in life. I had lost my faith in God long ago and wouldn't credit the Man above for such a miraculous deliverance. So I decided Neptune had been my liberator, as he had commanded the slayer ocean to spit my flesh back onto land unharmed to carry out my wrath.

What this meant more than anything was that somehow the forces of nature wanted me alive, perhaps reminding me that though I had botched saving Cody, it was important that I keep breathing for Cody's sake. I knew I'd been given my last chance. And I swore it, on graves of those that had passed in vain, that I'd find Cody and punish the guilty. Hence, I thanked Neptune and the Celtic gods for delivering me from the belly of the deeps.

I was still alive to kill the offenders for their offenses, as Cody's final hours were as a matter of fact numbered.

I considered where I might be. I supposed not so far from Dublin. A few kilometers, perhaps.

I looked up at the lighthouse atop one of the coast's highest overhangs, far-off from the beach shoreline where I emerged. The sun obliterated my view. Judging from the sun's position, I figured it was around: 5:00pm.

I gathered my strength, all the while brewing a new decisive plan to get to the kidnappers as soon as possible. The plan was rock-solid. First I'd get to the lighthouse. I'd seek garments in the keeper's living quarters, maybe provisions that would give me enough energy to carry on with the remnants of my devilish and vengeful plan. I'd be certain to find fuel for the banger that was parked right outside the outbuilding.

Then I'd head for the city, ready for anything. I'd unearth the demi-god in me and no longer bear pity for those that brought destruction to Cody and had slain Hannah and Jack.

I settled on my strategy, and I was satisfied with its likely conclusion when, all at once, Garda sirens sounded.

Gardaí arrived at the beach, crowding the area like a mob of media-frenzy reporters covering a crime scene.

Armed police stormed the beach, barking orders at me: "On the ground. Get on the ground, now. On the fuckin' ground!"

In the distance Detective Laughlin stood there, gazing at me with a greasy smile, and then re-boarded his vehicle.

Gardaí pinned me down to the sand on my belly, brought my arms around my bare back and cuffed my wrists. Then they lifted me off the sandy beach, up the grassy incline, and forced me into the back of a squad car. And just like that, a fleet of Garda special motor vehicles rocketed off the Celtic coastline en route to one of Dublin's Garda stations.

Eventually, I found myself in an empty cell inside a Garda station. My wounded ankle and bicep had been patched up. I was pale, puny, and fevered, hunched over my knees in the fetal position, clothed in rags, a large, gray wool, emergency rescue blanket wrapped around me. I took pleasure in its warmth, which brought memories of my dead ma Bella. Her affectionate embrace felt like this, but perhaps it only happened two or three times because she died when I was still very young. Nevertheless, the memories of her warmth and tenderness returned. Except, I'd been immersed in the open ocean for an extended period. My mind was clouded, my body shivering, numbness in my fingers.

I'd been administered intravenous fluids, which took the edge off the hypothermia, yet my insides were still frozen.

Two officers approached my cell, the one holding a mug stepping closer. "Black coffee. White sugar."

The officer tendered a steaming mug and sugar through the prison cell bars. I never thanked him. I was desperate, no time to be mannerly. I needed to get better fast. I needed a focused mind. I snatched the mug and jar and emptied the carbohydrate into my brewed beverage, which caused the officers to trade looks. I didn't care. I had to get better for Cody. But in spite of this, the razzers were entitled to their own judgment.

"Wanker's losing it," said the slimmer of the two.

"Yeah. Took a bloody swim bare as bone in the deep and froze his bollocks," said the more athletic one, judging by the size of his biceps.

I gorged the hot coffee without stopping, steam emerging on my breath. I felt the instant heat in my core. I closed my right fist a few times. Its functionality had improved. I extended my legs, resting them on the steel frame chair. My fingertips commenced a series of pushups, raising my explosive strength. I then swopped to plyos which fortified my backbone and re-aligned my crux, all the while the two Garda officers watching unmoved, pitying me.

*Chap has gone completely nutty.*

They needed not say it. I translated the expressions on their faces.

My eyes blinked hale and hearty. It was time. I rose to my feet and approached the bars.

"I've got to take a leak."

They both had hysterics with the larger one shaking his head in disbelief.

"I'm not codding ya. Right now, please."

"Sure. And I want to shag Angelina Jolie," said the slimmer razzer.

The officers fell about when, like a shot, my hands gripped the large officer's wrists and yanked him, sandwiching the slim razzer between the fit officer and the long prison bars, banging the slimmer out cold, his ass opposite the large chap's bollocks, really awkward, as you might say.

"Can't help you with the charming Jolie, but you look grand together."

I handcuffed the officers to the bars and unfastened the gate from the key repossessed from one of the officer's belts.

Straight away, the distress signal sounded. My eyes blinked once more, maladroitly.

*Shite*, I thought when my vision darkened.

Dr. Lorcan had warned me. I was to experience intermittent blindness. Countless armed officers would be on their way down to the cells.

# 62

I had made it inside what I figured was the hall. Yes, blindly. Literally. I listened for the sound of heavy boots; my auditory senses heightened. They approached rapidly. In fact, officers had by now crowded the hall, hordes of Gardaí, perhaps a hundred, perhaps more.

I couldn't make out anything. Nonetheless, I could eavesdrop on breathing, heartbeats, and footsteps in the darkness. They were audible. Very audible to my ears.

If there was one thing I learned from Master Hachirou, it was:

"Irish, put off-putting thoughts out of your mind and force yourself, in your innermost self, into a state of unreserved tranquility."

This, as Master Hachirou moralized, was the place where the supernatural unfolded. And by the gods, I had experimented countless times in vain, even while attempting to evade bullies at my academy. Hence, the "supernatural" never unfolded, in a manner of speaking.

In my youthful years, when I confronted Hachirou, he had jogged my memory that the miracle—the "supernatural"—only cropped up in a grave moment of danger, as in life or death, when death knocked on one's door. That was when the gods of combat came to one's rescue, by unleashing the greatness in us.

Candidly, I wasn't sure what that meant or if it had been some gimmick

Hachirou had cunningly made up and preached all these years just to have lines of devoted disciples, in droves, enlist in his upper-level class just to listen to this bloody twaddle and cram his pocket with cash.

Repeatedly, Hachirou had assured me it was *real*. As real as the *naginata* he grasped in his hand before launching into a series of cutting motions. Equally, he had seen the *magic* himself unfurl through him in his teens, and told us that it had been in an instant of life or death. The gods of combat had shown favor and let loose his dragon, as you might say. I wasn't sure if it was accepted wisdom or otherwise. Nevertheless, all these years, I believed in him and in the mighty gods of "combat."

My eyes had been opened, as I attempted to peek at what I couldn't catch sight of, but a voice deep within counseled that I focus. I reckoned it was Hachirou's voice. Hence, I confided in his wisdom. I closed my eyes, I forced my brain into another dimension where I would set sights on my attackers without using my eyes at all, but through the lenses of my extra-sensory perception.

It was all but "magical" when the Gardaí leaped forward, their batons smashing against my face repeatedly with the intent to slaughter. I tasted blood. I punched countless times to little effect, yet, every blow of theirs seemed to count, their punishment forcing me to the ground. Except, I couldn't give up the ghost. I had to stay alive. I tried converging my thoughts enough to summon the spirits of the combat gods, as I had been in an absolute impasse like blinded Samson, the demi-god.

It followed that I perceived the cocking of weapons. Then a bloody shotgun let off, and inexplicably I avoided being shot. It was then I became conscious: Hachirou's "miracle" had unfolded.

I was finally the man clad with the gifts of the gods.

I rose to my feet, and it was then that the real punishment commenced.

I went straight to close range combat, establishing my assault on aural reverberation through enhanced touch and reflex, whereby I'd find my way in and around the attackers' heads and shatter their bones. I visualized bones crushing at the exact moment it happened. All happened at lightning speed. Targeting through touch and feel with spontaneous flow by means of precise vital points strikes, I didn't need sight, because my auditory senses had been enhanced a thousand fold. I could see my assailants before each strike through the shifts of steps, hot breath, and adrenaline afflicted myogenic muscular limbs.

Once I laid a hand on the attacker, the clash ended before it began as at once I incapacitated the victim with a choke. I advanced to find another's wrist which I locked then broke the elbow. I stabbed at another's larynx, struck at the bottom of someone's skull, a blow to the solar plexus following a block of my attack as a direct punch to the ears, then to the pressure points with spontaneous counters upon attacks that smashed primary joints: shin, septum, clavicle, radius bone, coccyx. I was sensitive to aggressors' energies, naturally invading their breathing space and retaliating once my fist made contact with the challengers' weakest points. I knew of the human body's six hundred *kyūsho* (vital points). Hachirou had been a grandmaster, as I dove right into my adversaries' weakest links in a kyūsho-jutsu combat and shattered their frames as they found themselves dropping to the floor unconscious and paralyzed. Like a comic strip stop-motion, each physical attack appeared to move from one victim to the next in increments of photograph-like frames, as if watching my own illusionary anime.

Assailants' organs collapsed and bones shattered as if seen through my extrasensory sight in three-dimensional frames.

And then my eyesight returned to pitch black, devoid of the anime impression. The vestibule lapsed into silence other than the blaring distress signal. Bodies of wounded Garda floored the room. The gods of combat had unleashed my innermost ability; in the process, I had unleashed the wrath of a demi-god.

As I moved along the vestibule, darkness moved as even now my sight was still blind. A voice I recognized stopped me in my tracks.

"I'll shoot you in the back if you leave me no choice," said a resolute Laughlin.

"You're going to shoot me blind-sided?" I challenged.

"I'm willing to take that chance. It's over. Turn yourself in," said the detective.

I heard the cocking of Laughlin's Sig Sauer. And then, steadily, I could see the end of the passageway where the siren speaker, just above the exit signpost, flashed. My vision had returned.

"Turn round, slowly," ordered Laughlin.

I obeyed the "grand ego" and faced him. His gun was aimed on my forehead.

"This close, I've never missed. Never!" said Laughlin.

"Kill me or piss off!"

# 63

Detective Laughlin fired, emptying his gun's chambers as he fired wildly with almost simultaneous reloads that took half a second as shell cases parachuted to the floor with each reload like a well-trained assassin. Each step he advanced, in the manner of a killing machine, never faltering, never stopping, no further inquiry or cross-examination. Laughlin meant to take life. He'd got fed up with my "fairy" tale, as it were. He must have snapped and settled on ending my existence to close his case. After all, his best record of resolving a murder case had been six hundred seconds. Mine had gallingly lapsed into quite a few days and counting. Nevertheless, I had intentions of my own, which, at present, was to stay alive for Cody.

I leaped, spun, slanted, and more with each squeeze of the trigger as silver bullets invaded my space, some with certainty wanting to graze me or pierce through my body. It took all the natural and martial arts skill in me to evade the inexhaustible discharges from Laughlin's shooter, except in the end I was but a mortal—lock, stock, and barrel—not a god. Hence, a bullet grazed my left shoulder. Straight away, I zoomed out of the hall; Laughlin chasing behind, firing a storm, countless shells dropping to the floor in a rapid succession.

Except for the rags on my back, I found myself, unshod, in the streets of

Dublin amid a crowd of St. Patrick's Festival Parade partygoers. The feast day was in full swing: traditional melodies at full blast, a mob of revelers in green clothes, heaps of leprechauns and other Wee Folk in a parade snaking through the streets of Dublin city center.

"Stop him," barked Laughlin, directing stand-in Gardaí on horses, serving the parade, to pursue me.

The chase ensued. Gardaí galloped, chasing behind, knocking spectators to the ground. The crowd booed, spitting profanities and more.

The hunt proved to be a true test of endurance. I leaped into a darkened alley. Horses pursued. Laughlin cut into a flanking street. In the alley, I stopped and turned to face an army of advancing Irish draft stallions, muscled and powerful. I knew if I kept running they'd soon be upon me. Hence, it was either them or me. For this reason, *it* had to be *them*.

Once the earliest charger was upon me, I summoned all my strength and soon as its skull had been within arm's length, I directly clobbered at its cervical vertebrae, sending the mare to the ground, out cold while I jumped for cover as all four Drafts behind lost their footing too, inside the narrow alley, crushing police officers in their plunge.

At once I exited the alleyway back into a crowded Dublin street where Detective Laughlin marked me.

I spotted a street vendor with loads of merchandise to sell for the festival. Detective Laughlin aimed his gun. While the vendor was watching the chaos further down the street, I snatched a lime-green hoodie, threw it on my back and disappeared into the throng of paraders.

Detective Laughlin roared in a fury. On the other hand, he maintained the upper hand, as he still had control of the contrivance on my bloody ankle.

Shortly afterward, I found my way to Gilchrist's place. I had found a public phone to ring his mobile after escaping Laughlin. At the news that he'd returned to Dublin, we fell into a heated debate. I feared for his safety, though he reminded me a thousand times that Séamus, who hadn't been the prime subject of our debate, was safe in Clontarf with Nana (his granny). When I wouldn't let up and made demands that he'd return to Granny for his own safety, Gilchrist emphasized he absolutely had to be in his flat in Dublin, and it was then I found out Gilchrist had some reassuring information to share. He convinced me to join him quickly. When I arrived, Gilchrist was quick to attend to my shoulder, patching it up as best as he could.

"It'll do," I said to my mate, moving my shoulder in a short dowel stretch to test its effectiveness, not bad. "So, what's the good news?"

Gilchrist pointed to my ankle.

"I've seen that gadget before. Remember Shamus?"

"Foreman Shamus?"

"Sure... serving a life sentence for whacking his aul lady."

"Sure. I remember."

"Yeah. Well, he had that bloody thing on his ankle. That's how they found him. But I've got some tools. Best we take care of it at once. Come on then."

I followed Gilchrist, my chum, into another room in his flat. All sorts of high-tech electronic equipment set the surroundings of the room like a nerd's lab, only better. In all the years, I had never experienced this side of Gilchrist. I was numbed.

"What the hell is this place?"

"My lab. This is the good news, mate. I can help get that bloody thing off your ankle."

"You're a drip... You could have told your oldest mate. I've known you since you were in your nappies."

Gilchrist grinned grandly.

"Just a hobby thing. Nothing grand. Single chap living on his own, you know. Nothin' else to do... And women have plenty pleasure with the *barman*. I'd rather keep it that way," said Gilchrist sitting in front of a desk piled with strange machinery.

"Your foot."

I sat on an aged ottoman while Gil propped my foot on his lap, working away at the contraption. It was the first time in a long stretch that I had calmed my nerves. And for a brief moment, I felt the pull to falling victim to my exhaustion, to take rest quiescent on Gil's hardened chesterfield. Except, Gilchrist's rich voice brought me back.

"We've got seconds before the Gardaí show up at my door."

Gilchrist examined the band suspiciously.

"What?"

"This is advanced tech shite. High-level military weaponry. You know, "007" gizmos," said Gilchrist, somewhat impressed. "Laughlin must have flexed his muscle to get green-lighted the use of—"

"Get the damn thing off."

"Hold tight. It will sting a bit."

"Put a figure on *a bit*," I asked which fell on deaf ears. Gilchrist had been deeply focused; submerged in his own world.

Gilchrist, the Shamrock's *deputy* boss and *barman*, my childhood chum, was hard at work attempting to save my life.

He connected a piece of equipment to the band and hit a switch. Straight away, electric current erupted from the band resembling lightning, which Gilchrist transferred to an electric device.

"The bitch has still got life in it. If the electric current had touched your skin, I'd be throwing shamrocks down your grave," said Gilchrist with a hearty laugh.

"Thanks for the early tribute."

"You're welcome, mate. Make no mistake this little bugger still works. No quick move. Now we remove the pin that holds the band together and *voila* you're a free man," concluded Gilchrist, but, as he pulled on the loose pin, unexpectedly, a gun blast echoed.

# 64

The barrage of bullets clang in my ears. The gunman seemed intent on obliterating Gilchrist's apparatus. It was sudden, loud and unexpected.

I still had to react quickly, because if there was gunfire targeted at the machinery, there was undoubtedly going to be more, and we, Gilchrist and I, weren't exempt.

My eyes set on Gilchrist. His hand was pressed against his chest. The sight of it forced the bloody *butterflies* to revisit my belly. I loathed that mood, as I'd ventured to consider that Gilchrist was badly shot.

My eyes were stuck on Gilchrist's hand, expecting the worst. His hand came down suddenly. My heart sank profoundly someplace I'd already hosted butterflies. He'd been shot through the chest. He fell sideways. It was then that my alertness returned.

"Slowly," said Tadhg. "Back away from him. And get on your knees. Don't be a hero or I'll end it all here with one through your brain."

Either way, I was a dead man. I had to display the strength of will and proper judgment.

In a definite shift, I grabbed a blade from one of the tool boxes and sliced it through Tadhg's shoulder.

Tadhg yapped and dropped the shooter, escaping through the rear window.

I intended on chasing behind, but Gilchrist's cough held me back. He hadn't been coughing blood. That was a relief, yet the idea of my lad being shot was never one that made one feel at ease. First order was to get help. Hence, I unhooked the phone, dialed 999 which was answered in half a second.

"Emergency service."

"Ambulance... I need an ambulance."

"Please hold while I transfer your call to the emergency medical dispatcher."

This sounded all too memorable, and quite candidly, I hadn't the time to stay on the call. I knew the call would be traced and *help* would arrive in time for Gilchrist. For that reason, I left the telephone unhooked. Besides, it had been Gilchrist's command. I had read his eyes. And the following further confirmed my best guess.

"Cody. Get to Cody," said Gilchrist with difficulty.

However, I had to be sure. Accordingly, I checked his pulse. He'd live, but he had to want it, to live. At times it was much easier to let go and give up the ghost, not fighting, not hanging on for dear life. At times it was grand, the feeling of evaporating from your mortal shell, breathe your last, as you might say. Gilchrist and Cody were my last relations. He had to stay alive. For Cody and for me.

"Stay alive. Stay alive."

Gilchrist was one tough bastard. He'd live. I was sure of it. He'd live.

"Get out of here," he barked, pulling from the strength in his lungs. And then the band on my ankle transformed from emerald to flashing red. Whatever Gilchrist hadn't completed (pin still in place) had triggered the bloody contraption back to life as in kill mode.

"Go," barked Gilchrist.

He was right. It was time to be off without abandoning my comrade. He had made me understand that Cody had to be saved. Hence, unshod, I dashed out hurriedly, escaping through the window, down the flight of steps on to a shabby alley that led to a busy Dublin street.

Ahead, Tadhg sprinted past a flood of cars. He'd been meters away, but with the adrenaline, in me, I could diminish the distance between us. And so, I chased behind.

Tadhg moved faster, leaping over cars' roofs, one after another. He was surprisingly athletically fit, moving in total-body workout motion like a traceur, except I'd been skilled at *parkour*.

Tadhg turned into an alley, pulled down a set of fire escape stairs and went up the set of steps like a spider. I followed behind.

Tadhg reached the roof and hopped onto the next structure. I followed and skipped; all the while my heart pulsating in rhythmic booms like the beat of a thousand drums.

Tadhg jumped off the building into a neighboring flat's window, shattering glass on impact, and disappeared. I followed and jumped. When I crashed into the flat's kitchen area, I heard a snap of breaking bones.

*Bloody hell.*

I had either broken a limb or my spine.

How then was I to chase after the escaping *divil*?

# 65

On notice I deduced the Irish gods had been with me, as the shattering snap hadn't been my limbs but a wooden kitchen unit. I checked my legs for signs of impairment. Nil. The gods had righteously spared me. Perhaps they'd pitied me. I didn't care, as I wanted my hands on Tadhg's gullet, to take his life.

Tadhg leaped past a tiny vestibule that led to the foyer, smashing the place as he ran. I chased behind. I'd still been a little disoriented from my fall and stumbled on a waste bin, and then resumed my pursuit into the hallway of the complex.

Tadhg, ahead, kicked the emergency access open, drew the blade from his injured shoulder, and swung it. I maneuvered away from the sharp object which stuck in an exposed wood structure. Then Tadhg flew down the flight of steps.

I chased.

Reminiscent of a tumbler, Tadhg snaked down the flight of steps. But he wasn't vastly more skilled than me, as I had taken the challenge straight on and followed. Yet, at each attempt I'd been given to grab the runner, I had missed. And at my most recent effort, Cody's kidnapper sent me flying backward with an unexpected and unstoppable high kick to my chest.

My frame slammed against the rail, nearly tumbling over it. I swiftly found my balance and once more I was on Tadhg's tail with even greater intent to bludgeon the bastard once I was upon him.

The band on my ankle flashed more rapidly. In successive flashes. The loose pin triggered its malfunction. The egress was right below. Tadhg hopped over the rail and landed on his two feet right below, never losing his sense of balance, and then he was out the door.

I directly dashed across; kicking the door open into a busy lane where a van crashed into Tadhg sending his corpse to smash into a large glass casement of a nearby bakery. The vehicle's brakes squealed to a halt.

I followed Tadhg into the confectionery. So did the panicked van's driver.

Pâtisserie workers hovered over Tadhg. I knelt beside him and checked his beat. I couldn't lose him. He was my card in. I gazed at the driver. She was all butterflies, shaky. I understood *that* feeling, except there was no time for proper manners.

"I need your car," I said evenly.

The woman never faltered. She straight away handed me her keys.

I lifted Tadhg and flung him over my shoulder, and proceeded to the van.

"Are you mad?" asked one of the bake shop workers.

"This man needs medical attention. I intend to rush him to the hospital."

"But the ambulance is on its way—"

"Step aside. I'm climbing in."

"Where are you taking him?"

"It isn't your business," I replied, shoving one of the gawkers aside, tossing Tadhg in the back side of the vehicle, shutting the door, and gassing the accelerator while still on 'Park.' The crowd separated and then the van took off at full tilt.

Moments later, tires to the van burned the concrete as the automobile came to an abrupt stop outside St. James's Hospital, Dublin 8.

I climbed off and disappeared into the building; only to resurface with a wheelchair. I'd grabbed a doctor's coat.

I grabbed Tadhg's body and placed him in the wheelchair and found my way into the reception area of the hospital.

The entrance and corridors were chaotic. A receptionist attended to a thousand phone lines at a time. Medical staff dashed back and forth in their attempts to keep the dying alive.

I went about unnoticed, wheeling Tadhg to an empty operating theater; shutting the door behind me and closing all the window blinds.

Inside, I transferred Tadhg onto a previously blood-spattered operating table. Tore his shirt apart, exposing his upper body. I checked his beat once more. I had to be sure and work without delay. I couldn't get a pulse. I listened for his heartbeat: silence. Someway I knew he was still alive, among us, sort of, so I had to reel him back from the dead.

I started chest compression to draw on oxygen reserve in his blood and lungs. I left him, in search of a defibrillator, which I found in a glass cabinet my elbow smashed into. Cody and I had been aficionados of the medical drama series, *The Clinic*. Owing to it, Cody had coerced me into touring Dublin's hospitals where we learned a thing or two on how to operate the device. I'd been glad of Cody's coercion, as it had contributed to my gaining a new talent, as if life had known of this test of faith. I was grateful for this pre-existing knowledge to operate the device that could discharge electrical force to the heart. I went for it.

I switched on the defibrillator and jammed the electrode pads on Tadhg's chest. His body immediately went into shock, jerking.

I followed through, forcing oxygen using a silicone resuscitator, and his body went lifeless once more.

"I know you can hear me."

I commenced a brutal pounding hard on Tadhg's torso.

"Don't fuckin' die... you bastard."

My hands returned to the pads, ensuring they'd been set to zap hard and heavy, I adjusted the device to its highest setting. I then pressed the pads hard in the thorax area in prone positions for the pads usefulness. Tadhg convulsed from soaring energy that traveled through his blood vessels. I supposed if he'd been at the gates of hell awaiting purgatory, at present, he'd surely be given his return-to-Earth slip. I was right. Tadhg coughed.

There was no time for formalities. I flung the pads back in place when Tadhg put the boot in my chest, sending my frame to crash into the wall. My eyes blinked open. Tadhg, the undead, was upon me before I realized I was down. He jabbed at my face without letting up; blood erupting.

Tadhg grabbed my skull and smashed it hard against the tiled wall. I slumped toward the floor. Tadhg hovered over me. He stared down at me one last time, his eyes red with rage. Then he raised his boot and jammed it down at my body. I clutched the bottom of the boot and promptly wrenched, rupturing his muscle and femur. His bone's fracture was as audible as the beep on the band on my ankle which was rapidly approaching highly lethal voltage mode. Gilchrist's attempt at removing the bloody thing had caused its malfunction. If I did nothing to rid myself of the band, I'd be dead within seconds.

# 66

Tadhg shrieked from the agonizing pain in his ankle, except I wasn't done returning my favor of inflicting my own vengeance, as I unleashed a sequence of blows with immense destructive force to Tadhg's vital points. I broke every bone in his body. Tadhg screamed. I ripped the loose pin from the band on my ankle and jammed the lethal gadget in his face, finishing him off with a boot that sent his frame flying across the room, smashing against the glass porthole while a thousand volts and more burst out of Tadhg's features.

"Some battle in hell?" I said mordantly.

It was only then that I became conscious I had killed the one person who knew of Cody's location. I cursed myself for being more than usually vengeful. Dead, he was of no further use to me.

I hoped he might be carrying something on him that proved to be a significant clue. I wasn't certain. Chaps like Tadhg were too chary to be too obvious. I was aware of it. Nevertheless, I searched him. What I found was a small map of the city. I pocketed it when I realized my bare feet had become sore. Hence, I checked Tadhg's boots, 10.5. I was a 9.5. *It'll do*, I thought as I strapped the boots on. Then something came to mind.

I rushed out of the room, locking it properly to allow no further entry without a suitable key. (I was still dressed in medical attire and had cleaned the bloody mess off my face from the gladiatorial brawl.)

In the corridors of the hospital, I stopped a nurse and asked her if she'd witnessed any new emergency arrival, specifically a gunshot wound to the upper body. The lady concurred and pointed in the direction of an operating theater further down the corridor. I thanked her politely and headed in that direction.

I entered the operating room with medical tools I had found in the hall, playing the part fittingly.

There, Gilchrist's body laid on the operating table. Surgeons efficiently attending to him: shifting him, checking his vitals, poking syringes, and cutting through flesh.

Gilchrist was plugged into many IV lines. I felt sick watching doctors working on Gil.

Being the expert that he was, the lead surgeon went at my *auld segotia* with all the composure of a chap with four decades of surgical practice.

When I entered the room, I observed quietly from the back end of the chamber while doctors busily operated. But I was noticed.

"Don't just stand there, scholar," said the surgeon. "We can use an extra hand."

I wanted to be sure that Gilchrist would make it. I couldn't let another pass on before my eyes. I'd never forgive myself. And so I slowly approached when the surgeon dropped a hemostat in my palm.

"Dig in. I need you to clamp the small bleeding vessels."

My eyes gazed at Gilchrist's insides. I was staring at my childhood friend's organs.

"Will he live?" I said calmly.

"Patient's approaching hypovolemic shock. Lost a lot of blood," said the surgeon gazing back at me. Our eyes met. I wasn't sure if he'd known I was a phony. Hence, I froze.

"Houseman, aren't ye?"

I nodded. It was best to continue the lie, but this time my barf rose to my gorge. I had to retch.

"Toilet's over there. Use it before you vomit all over my patient," said the surgeon, directly returning to work on his patient.

Somehow I'd known Gil would make it. Henceforth, I rushed to the lavatory and retched into the jacks. I found the sink and hovered over it while splashing water on my face.

Then I began to breathe easy while staring at myself in the mirror. *This can't be real. This can't be*, were natural thoughts that crossed my mind.

"Cody," I said, smashing the mirror with a clenched fist. When my vision went three-dimensional, I saw once more what I had dreaded all these recent days: underwater, Taller was drowning, hands in flames. And then I blacked out.

# 67

I woke in a run-down and forsaken alley near Abbey Street. I could smell piss. I took in graffiti. Must have been the local neo-Nazi skinheads who believed all non-Irish had to be condemned and slaughtered. Then my eyes settled on Seroton tablets on my hooded sweatshirt and a Bushmills whiskey flask in my hand, except I wasn't on my own because I heard an unfamiliar *voice* when I returned to awareness.

"Are you going to glug that last bit of drink, mate?" asked the street junkie, reeking of malt in his unpleasantly hot breath. Unknowingly to me, I lay on the pavement in the chap's corner lodging flanked with grocery trolleys and foul bedspreads.

"How long have I been here?" I asked of the junkie.

"One full moon, mate... You were in the horrors... wailing 'bout your gasún. Best you let me drain that bit of whiskey for my own pleasure... and you find your chiseller," said the lollygagger who eyed me as if I was as nutty as he was.

I handed the bloke the whiskey, all the while wondering how I had got here. The slouch grabbed the bottle and moved away from me. He'd been slumbering next to me.

Then my mind ventured off to happier days. Two years earlier. Sitting around a table in Jack's dining area in the course of a beautiful Easter night. Cody was about five, Hannah, Jack, and Aidan, around ten. We were happy. Perhaps my happiest days. It was St. Patrick's Day. Lime hues and ribbons conquered the feel of the room. I remembered Aidan's words distinctly; *I've entered tomorrow's fight.* I remembered the table lapsing into an unsettling silence, my smile fading. I remembered my words: *we've had this discussion. You're not ready. Who else knows about this?*

I remembered Jack and Hannah trading a guilt-ridden expression. I remembered catching on, while Hannah tried to reassure me that Aidan had been ready for the fight; me arguing against it, and Jack's pointed words; *I say he's ready. He's got the Vikings' blood of our ancestors flowing through his veins.* I remembered telling Aidan it was out of question...

I remembered a boy—snowy white kimono, black belt—grabbing Aidan by his collar and in a startling motion spun, flipping Aidan up in the air and over his back onto the cerulean mat. I remembered Aidan's spine shattering; his body relaxing, dead on the floor mat. I remembered Jack and Hannah rising from their pews on oak wood bleachers alongside a young Cody witnessing his brother's death. I remembered entering the arena, seeing my son's figure on the mat, and sinking to my knees.

I remembered scowling at my son, Cody and then gazing back at the road ahead. Cody's words; *I want to be a fighter.* Hannah acknowledging in our kitchenette while she cut potatoes and eggplant; *he reminds me of you...*

For these reasons, I acknowledged I had been in hell and hadn't left, as Cody's life was still in the hands of the wicked. A tear nearly emerged from the edge of my eye but settled there.

"Sonny boy," said the vagrant, staring into my eyes. "Greed is a disease that has no cure but is quenched through evil acts. You must seek the *divil* and fight him at his own sport."

By some means, the bum had said something, though I wasn't sure what it meant. Maybe I had to summon my strength for one last time, as the abductors had counted on me abandoning hope to advance their wicked plan.

I thanked him and began my walk away from the alley into Abbey Street while pocketing my Seroton container.

I was not ready to part ways with my painkillers. It became a natural dependence. But there was still one thing I had to do.

# 68

After summoning my strength, I walked a kilometer or two to a Dublin cemetery. I knelt facing four Celtic tombs. The inscriptions on the stones were of my kith and kin: "Bella Angus Seamróg," "Cain 'Aidan' Seamróg, Jr.," "Jack Aidan Seamróg."

"Hannah Seamróg, a Beloved Wife, and Devoted Mother."

I touched the stones reverently, kissed them gently. I dropped shamrock clovers, gathered from the nearby field, on them while tears, at long last, found their way down my jagged jawline, resembling a slow-moving stream. I rose and stood still and tranquil for a brief moment. And then, when I felt the wind of my ancestors' ghosts passing and subsequently blessing me, I walked off at once. There was no turning back. At this point in time, I became the *divil*, as you might say.

If I were to find Cody, I'd have to locate the kidnappers.

To accomplish the task, I had to commence where they'd failed.

On my way to *that* location, I walked past a martial arts club. I paused briefly; looking through the structure's glass window. I watched a group of juveniles, bounded by professional fight club trainers, engage in a competitive match. I stared for a long stretch, thinking of my own brood: Aidan and Cody. Then I reached into my pocket and pulled out Tadhg's city map. It was time to move. I broke into a run in the direction of the Diner.

Moments later, I was seated in the same booth as before my own kidnapping, staring at Tadhg's city map. There was only one marked location, the diner. Next to the mark, were the words, "Pick Up." Yes, the diner had been the place the kidnappers had failed to erase their trail, so it would be the place I knew to start my search.

It was as busy as ever. Waiters had yet to attend to me. I waited patiently while thinking of ways I'd locate the captors. I got distracted by the sound of the piped telly. I looked up. Some news about Ireland's Taoiseach, the prime minister, delivering this year's Fred Curtis Crystal Shamrock bowl to POTUS—President of the United States, on St. Patrick's Day, an ancient tradition. Candidly, I didn't care. While politicians scored points, Detective Laughlin chased his own tail, people lived their happy lives, I was busy chasing ghosts and attempting to track Cody's kidnappers. I had not a second to rest. That was the life I swore to live till I found my boy.

As I had a second look at the map in my hands, Sorcha approached my booth, yes, the server from before who had witnessed me pass out from injecting mixed psychoactive drugs in my vein. She wanted to take my order, except my hoodie sheltered my face. I wanted her to recognize me, so I removed my hood. Sorcha did remember me and took two steps back. I had to restore her confidence quickly.

"I don't have a booby trap," I said calmly.

One way or another, she knew that. She wasn't daft. She was quick like most waiters are. They have to be alert; quick on their feet. Most can be intelligence agents because of their innate ability to foretell one's need. Perhaps read minds. She was that kind of person. Sorcha relaxed and stepped forward.

"Coffee?" she asked.

I gazed back at the map. Sorcha still stood there eyeing me intently.

"I'm not looking for trouble. Just a coffee and I'll leave."

Sorcha hesitated. I read her emotion. She swallowed, threw a glance at the nearby telephone. I eyed her further. She glanced at the phone once more. I wasn't sure why but Sorcha was uneasy once more. I didn't want Gardaí here. Perhaps she had been thinking of making the call.

"I'm leaving now," I said.

"Something I did?" she asked.

"No. It's best if I leave now," I said.

"I'm sorry," said Sorcha as she turned to walk away.

*Sorry for what?* But I quickly dismissed that thought. Perhaps it was just a meaningless expression. Hence, I clutched the map in my hand and rose to my feet to leave. But the words hung in my mind. I had to know. I turned to Sorcha.

"Sorry for what?"

"Excuse me?" said Sorcha.

"You said, 'I'm sorry,'" I reminded her. "Sorry for what?"

She turned back to face me. She hesitated at first. But then again when she witnessed the hurt in my eyes, she felt the obligation to voice these following words:

"I'm sorry the man took you before the Gardaí arrived."

I was flabbergasted. Sorcha had seen the men who had abducted me while I fell into unconsciousness. *Was there more?* I had to know.

"Do ye—"

Sorcha straight away cut me off, stepped closer within breathing space and whispered, "If it's worth anything to you, the man who took you, I followed him by car. I'll write down the address."

# 69

A head of writing down my abductor's address, Sorcha described to me in detail how I'd come to be snatched from the diner. Right outside the Diner, a Vauxhall Vectra had come to a screeching halt. An unidentified man jumped out of the car and entered the diner. The man then exited in a hurry with me, unconscious, and dumped me inside the vehicle that subsequently took off speedily.

"Everyone else was kind of shaken. But I've always been a curious little girl. Like Sherlock. So I jumped into my car and followed while everyone had been too busy paying attention to the convoy of arriving Garda. It all happened fast. But I was on their tail all the way to the garage," said Sorcha. "Here's the address. I hope you find what you're looking for."

I either kissed Sorcha or embraced her warmly, I don't remember, as I was out of the establishment hurriedly with more hope than I had had since I'd started searching for my chiseller. Twenty minutes later I was standing outside the garage. My eyes were covered in sunglasses and my head in a Leinster rugby striped beanie hat, one I'd picked up off the street. It was Cody's favored team.

I cross-checked the address against the shriveled piece of paper from Sorcha. It checked out like a charm.

Cliath Motors Repairs & Service Ltd had been centrally sited off R114,

Firhouse Road. A small and private shop, small enough not to look like being a place where clandestine deeds occurred. Then again this was my prejudicial thinking. Nothing was proven for sure, just my mind wandering and attempting to understand why the proprietor of this place had been involved in my abduction.

When I stepped into the shop, I first searched for a SIMI sign—that the place was a member of the Society of the Irish Motor Industry. There was a large signboard above the lifter on the cement block: all makes serviced, certified oil change, brake service, pre- and post-NCT servicing. At a rapid glance, nothing out of the ordinary. I knew the place was a legitimate operation.

I saw a mechanic laboring under an automobile on a second lift. There was no time to waste as I hovered over the wrecked vehicle being worked on. Half his body, the bottom part of belly to feet, was exposed as he worked strenuously under the engine. I kicked his left buttock, gently.

"I won't kill you if you tell me where to find my son. If you don't, I haven't got a choice."

The man pulled out from under the engine. A black, dark-skinned, Irishman. Bald shaven with a long dark beard, Spartan style. Almost Taliban-like, which for a moment made me consider for half a second whether Al-Qaeda had kidnapped Cody. But I quickly thought no more of it, as the guy was overly western. The fella was dressed in a U-neck black skin-tight cotton singlet, striped track-suit pants, and trainer's bottoms. He bore a grand tattoo of a nude whore on his right bicep and an imposingly mean mug.

"Who the hell are ye?" the mechanic said.

"Who are *ye*?" I said.

"I'm Cliath. Unless you're off your nut, you better tell me who you are or else—"

"Else what?" I countered, removing my shades and rugby hat, fire in my eyes.

"Shite!" Cliath reacted, observably stunned.

"I've had a pretty gammy day. So, you better speak," I said. Cliath saw the ruthless expression I bore. Though he was a tough guy, I figured he must have known about me and my abilities. At once he shed the menacing hard mug and poured out relevant facts.

"A chap came to my shop, paid me fifty euros to transport you here. He had a photograph of ya. That's how I knew what you'd look like when I picked you up from the old diner. I brought you here. Then his men took you."

"That's all?"

"Sure. I swear it," Cliath said.

"Did he have a name?"

"Who?"

"The bleedin fella. Did he have a name?"

"No names, just fifty euros."

"Fifty euros?"

"Fifty."

"Just like that? Fifty euros and no name."

"Sure."

"How did he find ye?"

"Like you found me."

"And he vanished just like that?"

"Just like that, mate," said Cliath, but I was on his throat so fast he was unable to move, while I squeezed, slowly throttling him.

"A name. I want a name."

"There was no name. I swear it. There was no name." The chap choked. I wanted a name. Therefore, I squeezed further almost crushing his windpipe.

"You will suffocate. I want a name," I barked and squeezed till the breath in his lungs began to purge. Except he wouldn't budge. Henceforward, my hand shoved his frame by the exhaust-pipe bender.

"I don't have to remind you this contraption provides ultimate clearance for hard-to-bend pipes. I won't hesitate to sacrifice one of your limbs. Give me a name."

"Marc... "

"What?"

"The name was Marcus... Marcus Lynch."

I had finally got a substantial lead—a name: Marcus Lynch, though I had never heard of him. Perhaps he was an associate of my father. I wasn't so certain. I knew all of Jack's connections. Marcus didn't ring any bells. Maybe he'd been a new acquaintance, although in good conscience I had my reservations. My father disliked new business relations. He only dealt with known merchants of the Shamrock. Marcus was in my mind, in fact, a glimmer.

"Positive?" I queried once more.

"That's what *his* men called him," said Cliath, dropping to the concrete as I released my grip. By the time his gagging cough had subsided, I was gone.

# 70

I sat before a brightly glaring workstation monitor behind a desk at an internet café. Night fell hurriedly, which reminded me I had been harried at my task. My eyes scanned down an online phone directory. I punched the 'Enter' button.

An extensive list of Lynches displayed on the screen. I clicked on the print icon. The nearby printer awakened from idle and promptly went to work spitting out pages of Lynch phone listings.

I grabbed the listings when my head started to ache again. I tipped the Seroton container onto my palm. Nothing left. Not one tablet that could lift the ache. My cranium felt as though it would explode; I pressed my palms against my temple attempting to crush the pain to no avail. The pain was too much. I left the café and spotted a Dalbhach Pharmacy down the street. I headed for the drugstore, sprinting forward while shoving walkers out of the way.

Even as I made it inside the pharmacy, I rubbed my skull trying to rid myself of the throbbing.

I watched the counter. A female chemist in a fitted white lab coat walked away from the counter. I hurried past aisles but tripped over some stock on the floor. The noise of my fall made a dull thud, which caught the chemist's interest.

"Is someone there?" the alarmed lady said.

I kept quiet, except I was in great pain. My hands grasped my head. The pain was dreadful. I let out a quiet moan, but in the calm shop, even that was audible.

"Is anyone there?" the chemist asked. She came nearer and entered the aisle. I leaped behind the counter.

I searched through racks of bottled medicine, my right hand did the searching while the other eased the soreness entrapped in my cranium. I breathed heavy; hunting, from first to last, a series of packaged drugs. One palm no longer had any power over the ache.

I fell to my knees. Now both hands on my skull, I massaged my temples, rubbing, pressing. Nothing helped. I looked up. A camera turned at a snail's pace. I dropped down as much as necessary to escape from the camera's vision. The pain drilled yet again without prior notice. I moaned, looked to see if anyone approached. No one was in sight, not even the chemist. I wasn't certain where she had disappeared to, but it was of no concern for now. As long as she was clear from my path, I'd be clear of hers.

I rose and found a different rack, rummaged through it.

Nothing.

"I'm calling the police. If you're still here, you should go!" boomed the spooked apothecary, her footsteps hurrying away in a grand echo. I fell to my knees once more, pressed my skull, and at the same time my eyes came to rest on the container on the floor, Seroton.

Like an addict, I ripped the top of the container open and ingested a dozen tablets. It was time to run off. I pocketed the bottle and stormed out.

Night fell on the city as I made my exit onto the streets of Dublin. I thought of Cody. Another day had wasted away while my son was still in custody of the kidnappers. I couldn't reason clearly, as my brain demanded rest. And by chance, I found myself near Essex Quay where I'd left Barrister Donagh's Maserati. I smashed the driver's window. I climbed in.

Inside, I leaned back against the seat headrest. Closed my eyes. Breathed.

I searched the glove compartment and found a watch and a hunting knife.

I tore down under the dashboard with the knife and wrenched electrical wires. Linked wires. The engine came to life. When I secured the seatbelt on, all doors—without human intervention—locked, a voice surfaced through the amp.

"I warned ya. Now you get to die. A death much worse than you will ever imagine. In sixty seconds the car will explode. The world we live in is a lot larger than yours or mine. You have no idea. You should have rid yourself of the vehicle when you had the chance. Tonight you die, and your gasún dies."

I recognized the *voice*; it was Barrister Donagh.

His voice cut off at which time a ticking echoed.

I synchronized the watch. Fifty-four seconds. I pressed the seatbelt release button. Naught. The bloody thing was bolted.

I grabbed the knife and began cutting into the seatbelt. The ticking progressed. I glanced at the watch dial.

*Bloody hell.*

Ten seconds, nine, eight...

# 71

I ripped the damaged seatbelt with the might of the gods, freed myself from the strap and slid through the broken window.

I emerged; leaped away into a dark alley when the watch's big hand ticked down. The Maserati exploded with a mighty bang, flames reaching high into the sky. I'd known of cars getting programmed from a distance or perhaps even from a remote location. This was a message that somehow Donagh had been linked to Cody's kidnappers and they wanted me dead. I wasn't waiting around to find out, as my elbow smashed the driver's side glass of yet another new sports vehicle. Within seconds, I had disabled the alarm.

I hurriedly climbed indoor and hot-wired the coupé. The Global Positioning System (GPS) robotically switched on.

"Welcome aboard, Miss Isibéal. Please enter your destination."

I shook my head, alarmed. *I really must upgrade.*

Then I smashed at the GPS to shut it off which effort I judged successful, and then I jammed my foot on the accelerator. The sports vehicle rocketed into darkness.

Moments later, I was inside an Eircom phone booth near Cliath Motors Repairs & Service Ltd, handset pressed against my ear. The list of Lynch names were all crossed. The phone rang without end.

I hung up when I caught sight of Peter, the beggar boy, on a bicycle.

"Hey," I called out. "Hey."

I dashed across the street, heading toward Peter. I wondered why a young lad was wandering through Dublin's hours of darkness without a proper parental chaperone. I could hear the loud music blaring from Peter's *iPhone* Skull Candy earplugs.

"Hey. I know you. You owe me cash, and you look like shite," said the little vagabond.

"Didn't your parents teach you manners?"

"Just havin' the craic, mate," said the smart-mouth. Nevertheless, he was right. I looked like shite.

"A boy your age roaming the town at this hour of the night is dangerous."

Peter pulled away his shirt. A large Magnum pistol bigger than his hand was shoved into his jeans.

"You're just a kid—"

"I live in the orphanage right 'round the corner. I've been working these streets since age seven. You want something done it'll cost ya."

I had to smile.

"I don't have all day, Mister."

I realized I had to deal with him as a peer. He was a child of the night.

"I need you to deliver a note."

I handed him a folded piece of paper.

"You need to lay some cash right here, mate," said the smart ass, repetitively pointing to the palm of his hand.

"How much?"

"Fifty euros."

I counted a couple of coins into Peter's palm.

"You're shitting me?"

"That's all I've got," I said evenly.

"You're pathetic." Peter returned my money and climbed back on his bicycle, took off.

"Wait. Wait."

"What?" Peter barked. "I need money, mate."

"I know. Believe me, I don't mean to be discourteous. But that's all I've got."

"Then you best do it yourself—"

"I had a son," I said.

Peter stopped once more.

"He was your age. He died tragically. These men... on that paper I gave you... they kidnapped my seven-year-old. He's got a bad heart. If I don't find him tonight, he's going to die. I just want him back. I'm not a rich man. But I love my kid... "

Peter turned to face me.

"Fine," answered Peter, settling his bicycle by a lamp post.

"That's the garage?"

"Yes."

"Just hand the note, and your job is done."

"All right then. That's child's play," said Peter, disappearing into the auto shop.

Inside the garage, Peter entered while I watched from a distance. He watched Cliath under a car, working away.

"Hey," said Peter, cool and calm.

Cliath moved from under the vehicle and stood up.

"Fuck you doing here, lad?"

"Some fucker said you'd pay me fifty large if I deliver this to ya."

Peter handed the folded note.

"Beat it," said Cliath while opening the message.

"What about my money, gobshite?"

"Piss off!" said Cliath. Peter showed off his *piece*.

Cliath reached behind his back and displayed an even larger .357 Magnum. Peter didn't stare twice; and scampered. Cliath opened the note.

"Pick up job. Come alone. Marcus Lynch."

Cliath pulled out his mobile, dialed a private number, and switched the call to be played through the mobile's speaker. The phone rang five times. Then there was a sudden beep. The answering machine picked up.

"You have reached L.G. Cavan. Please leave a message at the sound of the beep, and someone will return your call."

A second beep echoed.

"I'm on my way," said Cliath then shut off the connection. He glanced at his watch, pocketed the note, grabbed a fleece jacket, climbed in his Vauxhall and drove out of the garage.

I hurried to my vehicle parked nearby and saw Cliath's vehicle leave. He was heading toward the M50 Motorway.

I followed four cars' length behind.

# 72

It was a long drive out of the city into the countryside, so I had a second to think about Laughlin. Why hadn't he apprehended me by now? Surely he had all the chance. Yet, he gave me a free pass at every occasion. I found it odd, but I knew the bastard to be smart. I resolved quickly that I must have been *his* bait. I was fine with it, as long as, in the end, when the dust settled, he could resolve his case and I could resolve my own and prove my innocence. Hence, I was satisfied with playing Laughlin's bait.

Ahead, Cliath entered a long stretch through Ireland's most eye-catching dark hedges, a picturesque panorama of Ireland's beech trees thickly tangled above the narrow passing lane. Inside my car, the broken GPS came back to life and malfunctioned, tracking every turn in a distorted machinelike voice.

"Turning left on Upper Cliff Road."

I banged on the bloody GPS unit to silence it with no success.

"Proceeding on Upper Cliff Road."

I clubbed at the digital screen with my fist. Naught. I glanced ahead; Cliath's vehicle had come to a halt. He climbed out of his vehicle before his sedan was robotically pulled in place and disappeared into a sci-fi-style underground garage, concealed beneath a patch of flourishing grass like a *James Bond* film. *Just where the bloody am I?*

"You have arrived at… " announced the GPS.

"Signal lost. Goodbye."

The GPS automatically shut off.

I scanned the area: a beautiful, secluded mansion in the middle of nowhere, secreted in the picturesque countryside of the wealthy Irish, by the sea.

Posh automobiles lined beautiful sea-green shrubbery past the entrance gate. A large fountain faced the entrance to the manor. Water recycled each time it dropped back down to earth. Soft lights emitted from lamp-posts. Green ivies snaked up the sturdy building, a home that breathed wealth, splendor, and nobility.

My eyes caught sight of a structure—an old barn house—undergoing some renovation. By its proximity to the sea, I realized this must have been the place where I was kept when I last saw Cody. I then noticed "L.G. CAVAN" on the side of the barn, illuminated under a dim light, a label I had seen on the culchies' boat. Yes, the one who'd wanted my death. Another clue that I was at the right place.

Rather than heading for the barn, my guts advised that I follow Cliath. I did, and then snapped his neck and swiftly disposed of the body in the nearby bushes.

I was prepared to meet Cody's hostage taker. The self-styled Marcus.

I moved into the mansion through unlocked doors, crossing the threshold into a dimly lit hallway. Walls were bejeweled with high-priced canvases, and bud vases on stands propped alongside the wall. The corridor stretched forever. There were more canvases. More expensive jars.

Suits of armor-clad with Irish Viking swords dotted the walls, followed by oil paintings of nobles: contemporary personalities, sovereigns of the Church, queens, kings, sultans, prime ministers, princes of the modern-day world, and officers of the Republic of Ireland. The paintings were magnificent replicas of real-life photographs.

I was near the end of the vestibule.

Melody, soft laughter and conversation emerged from the grand ballroom three doors down. I was restless as I hurried. A thug, masked, in a black tux, stood erect by the entrance door. I promptly hid behind a door and waited, my anxiety growing with every second that passed. While the man wasn't looking in my direction, with his mobile to his ear, I moved to another area. Then the thug faced the lobby, chatting into his mobile.

The tough guy turned away from the hallway but only realized my hands were on his face as his neck snapped cleanly.

I pulled the heavy chap by his ankles to the next room and shut the door softly. I glanced at the entrance he had been guarding. A thought crossed my mind.

*Cody.*

Then I was set as I entered the grand ballroom, my fists clenched, to face a masquerade ball. Large chandeliers amid the most exquisite light ornaments dangled from the ceiling. Servants in masks passed champagne in fancy flutes. A podium rose erect before the mass with the most graceful drape laced over it. Comestibles sprawled long tables, the finest cheese, meats, seafood, and fowl. A live orchestra of time-honored Irish choir in masks played musical instruments.

The prosperous Venetian carnival-like masked company hushed and glanced at the sight of me, the lone guest devoid of disguise. The music stopped. All guests turned to face me. Guests were clothed with the priciest garments: Dolce & Gabbana, Burberry, Louis Vuitton, and Hermes.

The crowd parted as I marched unhurriedly in the direction of a masked man, incontestably the host, with a distinct air that set him apart from the multitude, wearing a Gucci tuxedo with a matching suede Count-Dracula–like cape, unmistakably a gentleman with taste and appearance of great wealth. The place hushed as guests ogled at me making my way in the direction of the high-profile masked man who called off his protection with his right hand lifted in the air.

I halted, ensuring that his guard dogs obeyed, as I was ready for anything and my fury would prove, likewise, unforgiving.

The masked man turned and withdrew into a hallway.

I followed.

There was a lift at the end of the corridor. The masked man, presumably Marcus, entered the lift and faced me—all business. The doors closed. I ran to the lift. I stood erect before it. There was a button signposting downward. I pressed it countless times as if doing so would force the bloody lift back up quickly to service me. In due course, the lift came back. I entered and searched for controls. There were only two knobs: 1 for the first level, and strangely -1 for an adverse first level. Almost certainly some subterranean vault. I pressed negative one. The winch immediately went to work, descending into the belly of the lower ground level. At once, the doors unlocked. The shrouded man stood in a large doorway.

Our eyes met.

It was as if he was calling me to follow. He entered a private room. I followed. The masked man settled behind a large writing desk as I entered and slowly approached, stopping before the desk. The silence between us was veiled with intensity.

"I have been expecting you," said the masked man.

"Where's my son?"

"Please sit down."

I took a seat facing the masked man.

"You were always the strongest one," said the shrouded man.

"Where is my son?" I had rage in my eyes.

"I assure you. Killing me will never buy your freedom. The world we live in is a lot bigger than yours or mine. You have no idea."

"I want my son... Cody."

"We'll get to that in a minute."

I was in no further mood for the bloody riddles and rose. From my erect posture, Marcus was wholly aware I meant business.

"I don't care about ya. I don't care about your business. Give me my son, and it'll end quickly—"

Marcus removed his mask, causing me immense terror as I fell back into my seat, struggling for breath.

# 73

Marcus was an exact replica of me. A perfect clone, as it were. "Spine-chilling, isn't it? As in staring at yourself in the mirror, only better. More fluid. More bona fide. In the fuckin' flesh."

"Christ!"

"You want explanations, don't ye?"

I was too stunned to act in response; nevertheless, I wanted answers. Marcus never waited.

"The dreams? Visions? You have them. Don't ye? The taller boy drowning. Hands in flames. Yes. Yes. I know. I have them too. Our eternal bond."

"Who are you?"

I was in shock, unable to make meaning of anything.

"Your identical twin. Shunned at the age of five for the unlawful death of our beloved mother."

"I don't have a brother."

"Oh yes, you do, brother," Marcus said. "And he shall *put a ring on his hand*."

I was taken aback.

"Those words..."

"Yes, in your dreams and perhaps from our father. Because of his guilt, he grew fond of the Book of Luke. Fifteen. Twenty-two. 'The father said to his servants, Bring out the best robe and put it on him, and *put a ring on his hand* and sandals on his feet.' The parable of the lost son," Marcus said. "I am the lost son. Your blood brother."

"You're Marcus Lynch."

"Yes, I am. But I'm also Cain Aidan Seamróg. Discarded like cattle at a young age. I was, after all, the wicked son. Troubled and cursed. Hence, our Father, swayed by his most faithful mate Abel, handed me off to an organ consortium to have his own son put down like bleedin livestock. The kind of people that make you disappear, as if you never existed. But the conglomerate, unable to harvest my organs, thought best to keep me alive. And I endured. I planned. Rising to the highest ranks of the organization. Believe me. The father you knew is not the one I remember. Nefarious and heartless, that is our father. But I was as much his child as you were. His fuckin' blood and he forsake me—"

"It can't be—"

"Father went to great length to ensure your memory of me never survived. I know of the heavy drugs in your childhood."

Irish's eyebrows were raised.

"Don't look so troubled, Irish," said Marcus, "I am Cain, and so are you. Father named you after mother. That is to say your middle name, Angus. I'm Aidan. Ever wondered why you named your dead son Aidan? Because I've been alive in your subconscious... We are one in the flesh—"

"Did you kill my mother?"

"He should have taken my life or forgiven me when mother died. I was a sick child. Mentally unfit. A loose gun. A shot in the head. A dead mother. A father's affection lost. But in you, he saw mother. Leaving you mother's most prized possession, the Shamrock, the emblem of our ancestry. Our family treasure—"

"You killed my father over a fuckin' pub—"

"No. Over preservation of our ancestry. Over business principles. The Shamrock is better off in my care, in trust!"

"You killed my wife—"

"It was an accident. My men made a mistake."

"Release my son to me, now!"

"Will you agree to sign the deed?"

"It will be over my dead body, *brother*."

"You're ungrateful."

"Enough!"

I leaped over the armchair, thrust Marcus against the writing desk, my large hands crushing Marcus' neck.

Marcus, limbs relaxed, never fought back. He lifted his left index in a cautionary stance and pressed a knob that pulled apart long curtains covering a sizable glass panel.

"There. In pink health."

There was a recovery room with white walls on the other side of the heavy see-through glass, filled with medical paraphernalia.

I glanced through the glass from where I stood. It was then that my heart lifted, a mood I hadn't felt in a long while.

A sleeping Cody, breathing at ease, recuperating from what appeared to be a surgical procedure. It was unmistakable, given the many IV lines and the organ care system.

"The boy at the morgue. He had a physically fit heart. Your child needed a heart. It was the perfect match. As I've said, we're not all *evil...*"

I was at a loss for words. Marcus had saved Cody through a most wicked deed.

"We saved his life," he continued.

I was numb, yet part of me happy, even though I felt deep guilt resembling a razor-sharp blade slicing through my flesh.

"He is well, isn't he? The boy is my kin. My blood."

My fingers on Marcus' throat loosened.

My eyes stared at Cody through the glass window. For the first time, Cody was peaceful. I had never experienced this sense of serenity on his face.

# 74

Never before now had it occurred to me so profoundly that the world we inhabit nurtured distinct progeny—good and evil. Right here, right now, I was in hell, an anarchic world where deception ran rampant. One where evil wore beautiful custom-made Sicilian suits and looked as innocuous as the models on the covers of fashion magazines. Marcus was that and more, a chap with the build of a Celtic god who lived in hell on earth. My mind turned the hands of time, and I found myself back in time.

I considered how many times I walked crowded streets of Dublin. How many of them I had crossed. How many hands I had shaken. How many I had spoken to. How many I had entrusted with Cody. How many lived ordinary lives in a veil of demonic secrecy. How many roamed the city? Waiting for that moment when they could turn one of us into one of them, one like Marcus—a wayward soul. *Just how many were out there?* I had thought before my lips spoke:

"Organ trafficking."

"Your son is cured. A brand new heart. Beats like a charm. The Shamrock. That'll buy your child's freedom. On the other hand, your life, I can't negotiate. You have caused us much loss and nearly exposed the consortium. They want you dead," said a stern face Marcus.

I was upon Marcus before he could blink an eye, and pounded on his face with ferocity. With the strength of a hundred men, I crushed his neck.

"I want to live. Do you hear me? Shamrock's not for sale, and neither is my boy," I shrieked.

Marcus choked, refusing to fight back. Perhaps we both knew it was time he gave up the ghost when the door to his secret room burst wide open.

"Let him go!" ordered Detective Laughlin, aiming right at the back of my skull. "Let him go."

I released my grip at which time Marcus grabbed a revolver at the base of the elegant mahogany desk with a high kick to my chest sending me airborne backward and smashing against the large glass.

"Put it down," decreed Laughlin.

Detective Laughlin repeated, "Put the gun down!"

"I'm warning you..." Marcus said.

*People will tell you just about anything to scare the shite out of ya.*

Most of the time it was horse manure. A chap once threatened to kill my aul man when I was fourteen. I had gone off to Bosca Farm sixty-eight kilometers from Dublin. My father sent me to get some hops. He'd use it to make malt beer for special customers back at the Shamrock. Gilchrist agreed to tag along. We hadn't any experience in selecting the proper hops.

Farmer McMurphy duped us into bagging our pails with fusty hops. We had no idea if they were fresh. We'd traveled so far, for so long. When we made it home, my aul man fell in a fury when he saw the bloody hops in the back of the truck. He and McMurphy had it out on McMurphy's cornfield. Farmer McMurphy's unmatched beating stunned me. I mean the chap was sensibly twice my father's size. As my aul man stormed off, McMurphy yelled out, you've *just signed your death sentence* and fired two rounds from his twelve gages massive double-barreled shotgun.

My father acknowledged later that McMurphy had intentionally missed. He was a skilled shooter.

*See,* he said. *People will tell you just about anything to scare the shite out of you.* Marcus' warning returned and meant nothing more than a broken line to fill the empty air. They meant nothing—a practical way to catch my attention. I was never moved.

Had Detective Laughlin not been there I'd ripped Marcus' head from his neck. I imagined his murder would render me unable to prove my innocence. I was willing to settle for that. One way or another Laughlin had found me. He must have been on my tail for some time. I abhorred his guts, except my alter ego was relieved he showed up there at the right place and time.

# 75

Detective Laughlin aimed the shooter with such precision there was no way he could miss. Shooting through the thoracic cavity would wreak havoc on the heart and incapacitate the felon. All these years at Garda Síochána College. That's what these chaps trained for, days like this one when they got to choose if you live or die. Except the choice was always tough to make. They're taught to ask for surrender. That made the decision easier to bear, and more people got to live, just behind bars. Shooting at dummies at target practice was much easier. Killing a chap was much harder, though Laughlin had his share of homicides. He had been in the force for two decades—a highly decorated officer.

Drug busts, prostitution, booze trafficking gone wrong, always ended in an explosive shootout. Hence men had to die. Added to the list was human organ trafficking. Now was another face-off, except it was my blood brother, an international tycoon in a luxurious setting operating under the radar in a veil of deception, not a common thug.

I saw Laughlin's eyes. He loathed taking lives. He'd rather put Marcus in jail. At least his conscience would be in the clear. It seemed ghosts of the past haunted his thoughts.

"Put the fuckin' gun down!" said Detective Laughlin.

Marcus locked eyes with mine, his expression firm and candid.

233

"I'm sorry, brother," he said before turning the revolver on himself and firing a clean shot through his heart. I felt the lead alloy bullet pierce through my chest at the precise moment. The bond we once shared was severed the moment that the bullet traveled through Marcus' heart.

The man who had *taken* my son was my own flesh and blood. In some way, I didn't want his life to end in such a tragic way. Perhaps I was slightly responsible, although I wasn't too sure of why. All the same, the thought that I'd visit him in jail crossed my mind a few times before he pulled the trigger and ended his life. I must have asked myself this question till the deliberation dissipated—did Marcus deserve to be dead?

Marcus' lifeless body hit the floorboards.

*Call it natural reflex. Call it what you want.* I dashed over to Marcus. I knew he was dead. I checked his pulse despite the consequences. Perhaps it was a way to show my compassion to one of the same blood. Certainly he was not a monster, but nevertheless, he had made some poor choices. Above all, I had to be sure Marcus was dead. Hence I shut his eyes and laid his head to rest on the terracotta floor.

"Get your son and get out of here," said Detective Laughlin. He meant it, so I nodded, though still unsettled. I removed my father's ancestral ring from Marcus' finger. Yes, the old gold band with a Shamrock clover engraving. I settled it on my ring finger where it belonged—a sign that an old tradition shall endure.

I looked at Laughlin. He waved me away. I understood he, at long last, acknowledged my innocence. No words were exchanged. A simple nod was good enough for both of us. I'd been running for the last ninety-six hours. Now was the time to move on. Detective Laughlin was throwing me a rope, a second chance for a new life. One with Cody in it. Perhaps it was a way to redeem himself for taking so many lives during his career, some who he possibly believed might have been innocent. Perhaps for all whom he had killed in the line of duty. This time I saw his eyes. I was his redeemer.

Yet, I knew, based on my recent offenses that Laughlin and his squad would come after me at some point, for the damage I had caused to the city and to Gardaí.

Nevertheless, right now, Laughlin had handed me a temporary freedom pass. Hence, I tossed the container of Seroton from my pocket into the waste bin and disappeared, never looking back.

Six months later

# 76

We found ourselves where we started. Atop Ireland's uppermost overhang upon the coastal field, the Cliffs of Moher.

Mud-covered and bloodied bare-chested bearded chaps in Irish kilts hunted me, rugby ball clutched against my chest. I dashed through the mud like lightning.

The sport had been amplified. Chaps plunged, cutting through space like vaulting jaguars hunting their prey. Vital fluid squirted from wounds. Yet the love of the game was greater now than ever before, an intensified addiction out of this world. Men were lunging at each other for a piece of the ball in my hand. The brotherhood we all shared off the field was unbreakable. On the field, we were gladiators, Gods of combat. Destroy and conquer—the object of the sport. Goliath was fast approaching. His massive frame sending chaps flying into midair and down onto the mud. I gazed ahead.

"Daddy," called a remarkably healthy Cody who had long since ditched his knee braces. He dashed across the field shirtless and in an Irish kilt with his arms held out. It was time to pass on the baton. Cody was ready.

# 77

R uthlessness was the lifeblood of the game. It made us fall in love with the sport, pure adrenaline pumping through our veins.

The chaps chased behind, hungry to break bones. Wolves wouldn't have out-chased them. In the vein of the hunted escaping its hunter, I leaped over chaps wanting the ball in my hand.

"Kill Irish," they yelled. "Kill that slippery bastard!"

*Dead Mate Rugby* was lethal. We understood the repercussions.

*Live or let die* dotted Goliath's muddy bare back and served as our motto. *Better live, Irish*, I thought many times. Hell, I can't die. I'm too strong. I'm no superhuman, yet my soul embodies a gift, unlike most men. Perhaps the personification of an Irish god. Perhaps not. But I'm unique in my own way.

"Cody," I called as I flew over a falling bulldozer of a man and threw the ball to Cody, Séamus dashing along before Goliath tackled me and pinned me down on the muddy ground, inches from the Cliffs of Moher.

My eyes stared down at the foot of the cliff. Why did people dive to their deaths on this very spot? It was something I'd never understand. Why not shoot yourself in the head? I suppose that would take the plea-sure out of the rush as you fly down the rocky cliff to a kiss of death at the foot, where massive waves bashed. An attraction pulled me, like a magnet, luring me in.

*Bloody hell.*

No, I wasn't skipping into oblivion. I had Cody—alive and in the pink. As far back as I can remember he'd never been so healthy.

Cody caught the ball in a motion that showed off his free legs and vigorous heart, proving he was truly my kin. Yes, the forward flip with the oval object clutched under his arm while spinning in midair felt out of this world. The re-energized gang loved it and gave chase. My eyes were away from the cliff. I followed his tiny frame along the grimy field where his torn runners left passing imprints.

"Did you see that, Daddy?" he bellowed proudly.

*Run. Run, Cody,* I thought. Feel the heart pumping? Feel the breeze in your legs? That's the sensation of a champion in the making, Gasún. *Run. Run, my boy.*

He must have heard me. Now a martial arts student in training, he must have read my mind as he dashed across the field with unbelievable speed. Surely this was no learning for the lad, but an expression of pure talent. Gladiators dove and tackled missing him by inches, landing on the filthy mud where they would have pinned him down.

He's got my bones. He's got my *gift.* Undeniably the others saw the same. The gift was unfolding before our eyes.

How likely was it that a boy born with a rare cardiomyopathy and brittle legs was beating men at their own mortal match?

Hell, he was my boy, a proper Seamróg.

See, the Man above had found favor in me. Perhaps this was my time to bequeath faith a second chance. Cody was not short of a miracle. Point in fact, he *was* the miracle.

Cody shouldered away a small player. The chap flew into space and landed flat on his face, appreciating every moment of it.

I gazed at my son cross the finish line. We had done it again. Hence, I kissed Goliath reverently on his temple.

"Today, you lose again," I said in high spirit. Goliath always enjoyed our little routine. That meant he played well, though he would have liked a win.

I rose, then looked to the players. *Oh, how they fancy the bloody endings.* Their absolute darling. They worshiped the ending from the start of the bloodshed.

"May your bones heal ye," I chanted blithely.

"May your wives feed ye," the gang followed.

The best chant would come to say, "In six full moons, let us break bones again!"

The gang of rough and bloodied rugby gladiators cheered hysterically, "Yeaaaaaah!"

They embraced each other.

"Ready?" I asked Cody.

Cody nodded. We departed, saying our usual goodbyes. I felt in my heart the game was a great prep for Cody's next stop, a martial arts combat.

We arrived at the Martial Arts Club Center off Pearse Street soon after lunch. We had a bite on the way from the local chipper. Cody loved eating in the car. Fish-and-chips—his favorite. He ate just enough that he'd hold it in his belly at this next ordeal. What I remembered next was me seated on the bleachers, watching a competing Cody emotionally fighting a somewhat skilled lad roughly his age.

Cody kicked, jabbed and took the lad to the mat with great ferocity. The boy got back up, grabbed Cody by his lapel and in a blink of an eye, flipped Cody up in the air and over his back onto the mat.

My heart stopped. I stood tensely next to barking Séamus. The arena fell into a great hush. I felt helpless. I attempted to swallow but I couldn't. Somehow I thought staying still I'd be able to control myself, had the worse happened to Cody. I loathed this moment. Hell, I could barely see Cody. The boy hovered over him.

*Was Cody all right?*

I'd been through hell before. I wasn't going back. *Cody, get up. Get up, boy. Get up, Cody.*

# 78

Cody struggles, fighting his opponent, on the floor mat. My heart raced. It wasn't déjà vu. Aidan was a dominant fighter. Cody was learning. He had great composure. *Hold your form, Cody.*

When the bell sounded, I felt my nerves stay relaxed. That feeling returned to haunt me. I blacked out for a moment taking me back to when Aidan landed on the mat. I heard the spine snap once more. Aidan was winning the fight when a single distraction took his eye off the prize and claimed forever the only life he'd wanted. I've tried hard to rid myself of that memory, the horrible sound that marked the end of his life, the sound that's possessed my soul since Aidan's death. Like an enduring buzz in my ear, it just keeps buzzing. When will I ever find peace? Lose a child, and you'll come to understand. It's like trying to wash the blood from a murder off your conscience. It just never goes away. It's a permanent psychosomatic imprint on your soul. Even repenting would never wash it away. You're doomed forever. Even in hell, you're destined to remember. *Oh, how I miss you, Aidan. Your memory will forever hold a place in my heart.*

Séamus' bark brought me back. *Hold it together, Irish.*

Cody's alive. The thought conveyed such grand relief.

The arbitrator separated the two lads. He grabbed the lads by their wrists, stood in the center of the arena and raised the experienced lad's hand. I sensed my heartbeat return to normal. Perhaps this subsequent thought should have never crossed my mind. But it did. At least he didn't land on the mat and snap his spine. As wrong as that came about, that was comforting enough. Every now and then a loss is a win. Surely now and to me, it was just that.

Séamus jumped into Cody's arms. It looked like they've been companions for ages the way Séamus excitedly leaped into his master's arms and licked Cody's face. A bond between a dog and a man is genuine friendship. No high expectations, just true companionship.

"How bad, Daddy?" asked Cody.

"Mommy and Aidan would be proud. You were grand! Great form. He's a champion. Never been defeated. There will be a next time," I replied holding back tears. "You are now Irish. Master Hachirou would be proud."

"I love you, Daddy," said Cody.

"I love you very much," I said.

We embraced for what seemed not long enough, a few short seconds. I could have stayed in that embrace forever. The Man above didn't take my Cody away. I was thankful. When we broke apart, I ruffled Cody's hair. It was a moment I imagined I'd never live to see with my own eyes. My boy, with the funny legs and the weak heart, was competing for junior pro martial arts. A father's dream was never quite simple when it boiled down to it. To be alive to witness the success of his brood. Never to bury his own child ahead of his own death. At that very moment, I must have thanked the heavens a thousand times. Perhaps it was all a test of faith, a faith that had been dwindling for years ahead of Aidan's death. Whatever it was, I was grateful my son was alive. Pure miracle!

We started off toward the exit when my mobile phone vibrated. I jumped, not realizing the darn thing was in my rear pocket. Cody glanced at me.

"Who is it?" asked Cody.

I didn't answer. The phone was pressed against my ear.

I was all ears.

"Yes?" I answered.

"Daddy?" said Cody.

"Now?" I asked.

"Daddy? Is it time?" anxiously asked Cody.

I must not have heard Cody. I anticipated the call. A call I knew would come soon.

"All right, we'll be there in three hours," I said.

"What's the matter, Daddy?" asked Cody.

"It is time," I said.

"Conor?" asked Cody.

"Yes," I answered. Cody smiled. Séamus barked. We rushed out of there in a flash for another three-hour drive heading for the Celtic Sea.

# 79

At sea, there was a light rain. Conor and I had plenty of trips on the Celtic Sea. The ocean is rich in history lost to the world. Each time I looked into the depth of the sea I saw images of many lives replay before my very eyes like a documentary playing at the local theater. I must have seen Viking vessels more than I'd wished. So much blood in these waters. Yes, these waters had seen many fallen fellas. Yet, few have lived to tell their tales. Tales of love, peace, war, death, forever lost to the Celtic Sea.

Conor's boat was larger than it had ever been. We were in the middle of the ocean, in no man's land. Calm waves brushed softly against the bottom of the boat. The stillness of the sea was a premonition of what was to happen next. Like a boxer ahead of a match in his locker room meditating ahead of knocking out his challenger in the ring. We were meditating. Except I was ready. Ready to confront the beast.

The water pounding the bottom of the boat maintained a musical rhythm that synchronized with our action and promoted our enthusiasm. I had dragged a giant fishing pot out. Conor, Cody, and Gilchrist, in a wheelchair, dumped chunks of meats into the ocean.

We were after *the beast*, Conor annoyingly reminded us.

I kept quiet about my head-to-head encounter with the sea monster.

Besides, he wouldn't have believed me. I can hear the aul codger saying, "You must be talking out of your ass! That brute would've split your bones in half. And left none for proper burial... " He would have gone on about his own encounter with a basking shark as an adolescent. I wasn't having it. No time for fairy tales. We were on a mission: to catch the damn fish that nearly caused my early exit.

Cody brought another fishing pot. More blood filled the ocean. More bloody meats sank deeper into *An Mhuir Cheilteach*. When Séamus barked, my heart raced. It felt like déjà vu. I sensed the rush return to possess me, the exact one I felt when facing off the killer shark in the deep dark sea. I watched over my shoulder. The fishing line tightened. The powered fishing rod had been awaiting its proper use, fastened to the boat like a flagpole.

"It's here," I said.

I dashed to the line and felt its resistance in my hand. Yes, that bastard was ready for a third round. Only, I didn't do third rounds. My challengers were known to be out cold within seconds of round one. This creature had the guts to challenge me past two. I was cheesed off, my ego challenged. The last man standing was either going to me or me... No, it's no mistake, I said it correctly *me or me*, as in my *ass* or my *ass*.

"Sailor," yelled Gilchrist.

"Aye-aye, Cap'n," said Cody when he slammed a large knob that awakened the power-driven rod. The line pulled from the ocean. Gilchrist played Captain and Cody, the young sailor. Before my son's death, we'd watched *Pirates of the Caribbean* eighteen times over the course of three nights. I cherished that memory forever. A memory destined to claim a special spot in my brain other than the many happier faces of my Hannah.

"I've got the wheel," Conor said.

The aul man's a bloody fanatic. He'd die on his boat if it boiled down to it.

"It's on the hook," I said.

"We've got the bastard!" Conor said.

We embraced each other victoriously when the line jolted back and forth and the motor locked. Not a moment to wait. I jumped into the ocean. The adrenaline kicked in before I could react. There it was. Caught and battling for its freedom. For the first time in my life, I dared not approach. I stared when a hand tapped my shoulder—Cody. *Bloody hell*. What was he thinking? No fear in his eyes. Heck, forget the young sailor. Not even the Captain jumped. But my little. Cody. I mean the bloody lad acted swiftly, more like *Master and Commander*. Cody aimed, ready to fire the modified high-powered pump-action underwater shotgun Gilchrist built, capable of delivering incapacitating high-voltage electro-shock rounds, to subdue the beast.

I thought today I'd forgive the fucker. Perhaps we'd go at it in a third round another day. Hence, we let the bastard go free. That felt grand. Some kind of relief, I guess.

*Sure, why not!* I thought.

# 80

Four place settings on the table.

I brought in a steaming pot of lamb stew and placed it on the table, where I sat across from Conor.

Cody sat opposite Gilchrist in his wheelchair. I glanced at everyone with the happiest and broadest smile, truly genuine. I then looked at Cody and nodded. They bowed their heads, *including me*.

"Dear Lord, bless this meal. Bless those who have less than ourselves. And let the spirits of the dead rest in peace. In the name of the Father, and the Son, and the Holy Spirit," said Cody, performing the sign of the cross.

Altogether, we said, "Amen."

I felt a renewed sense of purpose. My son was here with me. That was a testimony in itself. Perhaps I'd give God a second chance. Perhaps it was the other way round, and he was giving me that second chance. I don't know. All I remembered was the look in Cody's eyes. Pride and true happiness. For once I had saved a life. I hadn't let him down.

"That's a good lad," I said when we had wrapped up with *Amen*.

We were all *men* at the table, including Cody. He had finally joined our ranks. No, there was no formal rite of passage or any bullshite that transitioned a little lad into manhood. This was little Cody. He earned it outright. Not much can be said to give a reason for this. It was just so. Now he was among men. He was a *man*, a proper chap.

Gilchrist got edgy as usual. He had the biggest stomach of all four of us.

"Lads, I'm starving. I could eat the Lamb o' Jaysus through the rungs of a chair," he admitted, at which turn of phrase we all shared a hearty bit of craic.

I ruffled his hair. That one gesture validated how we cared for each other. Gilchrist was the brother I never had, one that would have never caused my family harm. He always chatted about how he looked up to me and all. The truth is, most times I looked up to him. A second source of inspiration. *Strange, isn't it?* He never realized. Most of the time I took the punches and protected him. And I admired his life—simple and genuine.

"Pass the knots," said Conor.

He reached out for the basket with a mountain of freshly baked Celtic Knots. Oh, that aul Conor—how he loved that white dough. Could care less for that new trend, the multigrain. Just plain aul white. That's how he liked it.

"Let's eat," I said, gobbling shots of Bushmills.

Time to chow down. My boy looked up into my eyes and smiled softly. Oh boy, that smile. How special. I could die. You never know how special someone is until they're taken. Had he died, Life would have meant nothing. I had made that decision early after Hannah's death and Cody's abduction. Had I not found him, I'd take my life. Except the question was always, would that ensure that I'd see them again? I wasn't so certain. But I was willing to make amends with the Man above.

My thoughts were cut short when the phone rang.

*Who the bloody hell was ringing at supper?*

Jack, my aul man, had been generous in his Will. Hence, Butcher had been satisfied on past dues to bring the mortgage account current, enough anyway that he'd shut his gob for a while.

"Hello?" I said when I grabbed the phone and put it to my ear.

I'd turned tipsy from the celebratory shots of Bushmills on an empty belly. Nonetheless, I answered promptly, "Who, might I ask, has the pleasure of disturbing me evening feast?"

I lowered the handset, winked at Cody while sharing a chuckle with the lads cackling at the dining table.

"Go on," I said into the receiver, grinning at the mates.

My eyes blinked when I heard the pointed mechanized voice.

"You have forty-eight hours to deliver the Shamrock, or we will be forced to repossess the heart. And we will find you, and we will kill you, Irish."

My core dropped to my belly when the phone went dead.

Was my brother Marcus Lynch really dead?

# GLOSSARY

*Aul* old.
*Aul wan* a man who behaves an old woman.
*Auld segotia* a good friend.
*Bad dose* serious sickness.
*Ball of shite* a piece of junk.
*Ball-bag* a total idiot.
*Banger* a timeworn vehicle.
*Beor* a good-looking female.
*Black pool* Dublin, originating from the Irish *dubh* (black) and *linn* (pool).
*Black Stuff* dry stout; Guinness.
*Bleedin* an Irish word that gives emphasis to anything (expression).
*Bollocks* used as an expression of irritation; frustration.
*Bolshie* belligerent and stubborn.
*Bowsie(s)* a street corner and up-to-no-good minor.
*Boyo(s)* a boy or a juvenile.
*Bucketing down* pouring rain.
*Bullshite* bullshit.
*Caffler* idiot.
*Chap* a fellow; a man or boy.
*Cheesed off* pissed.

*Chinwag* a talk.
*Chiseller* a child.
*Codding you* to make a fool of somebody; to trick someone.
*Craic* good fun.
*Crock of shite* a piece of junk (car).
*Culchie(s)* appellation for country folks.
*Danny boy* about twenty pounds (cash).
*Dead Mate Rugby* the fictional ruthless street rugby sport.
*Divil* a devil (depiction of a person's character).
*Dodgy bloke* a rabble-rouser.
*Drip* an irritating individual.
*Eejit* idiot (most times meant playfully).
*Feilistrín gorm* Ireland's blue-eyed-grass.
*Flanker(s)* a rugby player.
*Gackawacka* a foolish; idiotic character.
*Ganky* an unfriendly lady.
*Gardaí* Ireland's police force.
*Gasún* a child.
*Gasúr* a child.
*Gobshite* an idiot.
*Guttie(s)* a criminal.
*Hardchaw(s)* a tough hooligan.
*Havin' a craic* having a good bit of fun.
*Hooker(s)* a rugby player.
*Horseshite* horseshit.
*Houseman* a student doctor.
*I could eat the Lamb o' Jaysus* starved.
*Jacks* toilet.
*Jackeen* country folks' disrespectful appellation for Dubliners.
*Jaysus* Jesus.
*Jibber* a wimp; one terrified of trying new things.
*Johnny Ray* the person in charge.
*Johnny-jump-up* a mixed drink with a pint of Guinness.
*L'art du déplacement* parkour.
*Lad* a fellow; a man or boy.
*Loosehead(s)* a rugby player.
*Márbh* dead.
*Mate* a good friend.
*Mhuir Cheilteach* the Celtic Sea.

*Muir Éireann* the Irish Sea.
*Orthetrum coerulescens* a dragonfly.
*Praities* potatoes.
*Quit acting the maggot* stop acting foolish.
*Razzer(s)* a police officer.
*Shite* shit.
*Sléibhte Chill Mhantáin* the Wicklow Mountains.
*Snotty-bock* one with a runny nose.
*Specky four-eyes* a person who wears eyeglasses.
*Sprog* a child or kid; a baby.
*Tighthead(s)* a rugby player.
*Tosser* idiot; annoying.
*Two-bulb* a Gardaí vehicle.
*Vitamin G* a pint of Guinness.

# Translations

These translations are provided for explanatory purposes.

**Irish to English**

*Dia spede!* God spede!
*Fan.* Stay.
*Lean bán.* Baby.
*Lig dom é a dhéanamh.* Let me do it.
*Sir, dea-lá.* Sir, good day.
*Slán leat.* Goodbye.
*Slán, Athair.* Goodbye, Father.

"Blessed is the man who endures...; for when
he has been approved, he will receive the crown of life which
the Lord has promised to those who love Him."
**James 1:12**

*This work is further dedicated to victims that are plagued with human trafficking the world over. May the Lord help you find peace and love as you move on to a greater life beyond that of your past.*

# Acknowledgments

Again, my sincere thanks to every person who rallied round and steered this book in the right direction from idea to eBook, paperback, and hardcover. To Nakia Ngwala, my partner and publisher, a huge thanks; to Gerry Coughlan for providing insightful feedback on the most fitting use of Dublin's slang and the Irish language, and further for his gracious gifts of Dublin slang and terms from his precious library; to Carolina Fiandri and Andrea Orlic for their fantastic cover designs, and to Jerry Dorris and Carolina Fiandri for their elegant interior design; and to all my friends. Many thanks also to Tracey Becker, Ella, Liv Radue, and Bella. Thanks, too, to my wonderful readers who make certain that my book is kept alive and well.

*About the Author*

**Mayi Ngwala** is an award-nominated author. He lives in the United States with his wife and their two sons.

Accused of heinous crimes, Irish scrambles through Dublin's under-belly to prove his innocence.